Jackie Epstein is a former Hollywood columnist, tennis columnist, publicist for television and motion pictures, public speaker, and community activist.

The widow of Journalist Robert Epstein, Jackie authored the award-winning memoir *Never Tell Mommy,* children's story *Mr. Moon Learns How to Sleep,* booklet of poems co-written with husband *How to Keep Romance Alive,* and memoir *My Love Affair with Hollywood.*

Ninety-two-year-old Jackie has four children and six grandchildren and resides in Carlsbad, California, near her beloved ocean.

Walking a Duck in L.A. is dedicated to Aunt Pearl, who faced life head-on and inspired me to question what I did not understand.

To Grandma Lena, who never enjoyed life, yet unknowingly gave me the foundation of love and care that enabled me to endure whatever hurdles life offered.

To Eddie, a black school janitor who saved my life and introduced me to my love of music by teaching me how to play the harmonica.

And, of course, to my late husband Robert Epstein, who gave me the love and support that allowed me to fulfill my dreams.

Last but not least, to Los Angeles of yesteryear, the city I loved, where dreams became reality and people of all colors were family.

Jackie Epstein

WALKING A DUCK IN L.A.

Austin Macauley Publishers™
LONDON · CAMBRIDGE · NEW YORK · SHARJAH

Copyright © Jackie Epstein 2023

All rights reserved. No part of this publication may be reproduced, distributed, or transmitted in any form or by any means, including photocopying, recording, or other electronic or mechanical methods, without the prior written permission of the publisher, except in the case of brief quotations embodied in critical reviews and certain other non-commercial uses permitted by copyright law. For permission requests, write to the publisher.

Any person who commits any unauthorized act in relation to this publication may be liable to criminal prosecution and civil claims for damages.

This is a work of fiction. Names, characters, businesses, places, events, locales, and incidents are either the products of the author's imagination or used in a fictitious manner. Any resemblance to actual persons, living or dead, or actual events is purely coincidental.

Ordering Information
Quantity sales: Special discounts are available on quantity purchases by corporations, associations, and others. For details, contact the publisher at the address below.

Publisher's Cataloging-in-Publication data
Epstein, Jackie
Walking a Duck in L.A.

ISBN 9798886933994 (Paperback)
ISBN 9798886934007 (Hardback)
ISBN 9798886934021 (ePub e-book)
ISBN 9798886934014 (Audiobook)

Library of Congress Control Number: 2023903651

www.austinmacauley.com/us

First Published 2023
Austin Macauley Publishers LLC
40 Wall Street, 33rd Floor, Suite 3302
New York, NY 10005
USA

mail-usa@austinmacauley.com
+1 (646) 5125767

I am thankful to everyone acknowledged in *Never Tell Mommy*.

Today, 23 years later, I thank Charlene Fox, who gave me the push to begin writing again, and Corinne Sawyer, Barbara Villasenor, Dr. David Land, James Fish, Alan Mindell, and all personnel at Austin Macauley Publishers for helping bring *Walking a Duck in L.A.* to reality, and making a dream come true.

Chapter One
October, 1985

My mother died a year ago, and thank Gawd, I had nothing to do with it!

Five years ago, my parents divorced, and Dad remarried. And now, he has called, asking if my husband, Charlie, and I will come over for dinner. Dad has invited our four kids, too.

I'm surprised to find myself accepting the invitation because I've tried to avoid Dad as much as possible since he walked out on Mom as she was planning their 50th wedding anniversary. And, to add insult to injury, Dad had left Mom for Ruth, my mother's best friend.

When Charlie heard about the commitment, he wasn't very happy. "Why, Jolene?" he asked. "Why do we have to go?"

"I don't know how I got us into it, Charlie," I told him. "And to be honest, I don't know how to get us out of it, either." Then I rationalized, "Hey! Mom is gone. The kids still think of Dad as their grandfather. Maybe it'll be okay."

Grudgingly, he accepted my decision.

Despite the awkwardness and frustration, I felt about the situation. I couldn't help but smile at the absurdity of what I was about to say. "And, if you can believe it, Charlie, I even used to like Ruth—when she was Mom's friend."

My husband's boisterous laughter filled the room, and my soprano quickly joined his deep baritone. As we fell into each other's arms laughing over life's quirky twists of fate, I felt such enormous love and gratitude toward him. "I love you so much, Charlie," I told him. "Thank you for understanding."

I knew how hard it would be for him. He'd never liked my father. And now, ever since Dad left Mom, Charlie could hardly bear to be in a room with him. But he would do it for me because Charlie is a person who thinks about others instead of himself.

But most importantly, Charlie is a one-woman man. Almost a dinosaur, I'd often thought. There aren't many loving, faithful, exciting partners in life. And he's so much fun, a great father, dependable, and my best friend. I sometimes wondered how I'd gotten so lucky. Then I had to admit that it wasn't just luck that brought Charlie into my life. I knew what I was looking for as I dated many young men before meeting Charlie. I wanted a man who was the opposite of my father and everything my father wasn't.

After our laughter had led us to desire that night, I held onto Charlie during our lovemaking, wanting never to let go.

So, here we sit, Charlie and I, in Ruth's apartment. None of the kids showed except our daughter Eden. "Prior commitments," they had told Dad.

"Probably too uncomfortable," I comment to Charlie.

So, it is just the five of us, plus Ruth's oldest daughter and her seven-year-old granddaughter.

Ruth and her daughter are in the kitchen preparing coffee and dessert. Charlie and I sit and converse in the dining area, which adjoins the living room where Dad and the child sit on the couch, looking through his stamp albums. The apartment is small, airless, almost stifling. There isn't any fresh air because the one sliding glass door that could offer the cool breeze coming in off the not-too-distant Pacific Ocean is closed. Ruth had told us to ensure that the door remained securely closed so that 'her things' wouldn't get dusty.

"Her things!" I think. "How dare she! Her things." Everywhere I look around the crowded room, I see items that had belonged to Mom. Personal effects Dad had taken from Mom's apartment after she died.

Being an only child, I was the sole beneficiary. Numbed by her death, I hadn't wanted or needed her legacy, meager as it was, and I kept only a few pieces of jewelry to give to my girls and a few sweatsuits she loved. Then I'd asked Dad if he wanted or needed anything before I gave the rest to the Salvation Army.

"I might be able to use a few things," he'd said.

Within hours, he'd shown up, accompanied by a heavy-set man driving a rented truck. They'd taken almost everything, the two of them, taking it for Ruth. Almost all. Mom's furniture, her dishes, a favorite china teaset. Even crocheted coverlets for the arms of the wing chairs my mother had prized for so many years.

The band around my forehead tightens. Throbbing behind my left eye began. "Damn!" I said out loud. "Another migraine is coming on. It's this apartment. The air is so stagnant." Between Dad chewing on his cigar butt and Ruth's neurosis about dust, it's no wonder I felt so lousy.

Charlie leaned across the table, asking what was wrong.

"Nothing! Nothing! It's just hard, seeing Mom's things, being here, remembering…"

I remember that night so well.

Charlie had taken Mom's hysterical phone call.

When we'd gotten to her apartment, she'd collapsed into our arms, sobbing as she told us what had happened.

"I was discussing the menu for the party when your dad got up from his chair and said, 'I can't do this, Liz.' Then he'd gone into the bedroom and started packing. I followed him to ask what he meant? At first, he said nothing. Then he said he was leaving. Just, 'he was leaving,' nothing else. I said, 'What do you mean; you're leaving? Where are you going? We're going to be celebrating our 50th anniversary, for God's sake!' He kept repeating, 'I've got to go. I've got to go. I'm leaving!'"

"Jolene, he hasn't gone away since…since he's been out of work, so I thought he was joking around…you know Dad."

Charlie and I nodded. Yes, we knew Dad.

Mom continued, "Then he said, 'No, Liz! I mean it. I'm leaving, for good!'"

She began sobbing so hard it took time for her to continue. "Then he picked up his bag and started to leave the room. That's when I realized he meant it. I tried to stop him. Begged him to stay. I kept asking him where he was going? Why? Why was he leaving? Why was he doing this to me? And that's when he finally told me." Her face contorted with pain and hatred as she said, "The bastard!"

"What? What'd he say, Mom?" I asked her, becoming impatient. "Tell us, already. What on earth happened?"

"He said," she had difficulty getting the words out. "He said, 'I've got to leave, Liz, because I'm in love with Ruth.'"

"Ruth!" Mom screamed out. "My best friend, Ruth! The stinking bitch! The two-timing whore!"

Her screams became whimpers. "He left me for my best friend, Jolene. Can you imagine that? Didn't even make excuses. Didn't even apologize. Just, 'It happened, Liz. We're in love. Ruth wants to get married.' And he walked out, just like that."

Later, I learned that Mom had shrieked at him, "Sleep with her, for God's sake! Screw her! You don't have to marry her."

But Dad did have to marry Ruth because she had morals. Said she'd been a virgin when she'd married. She'd only been with one man her whole life and hadn't slept with another man since the death of her husband ten years before. She insisted that she had to be married to sleep with a man. And certainly, Ruth wasn't about to sleep with her best friend's husband, who just happened to be my mother.

That was how my parents got a divorce in their 49th year of marriage. After everything they'd been through, no one could understand this. No one. Certainly not me. Not until months after the divorce and Dad's new marriage.

He'd called, asking me to meet him for lunch so he could explain his actions, hoping I'd understand.

"I still love your mom, Jolene. I'll always love her," he told me when we met. And then he added, "I just couldn't live with her anymore."

And the strangest thing about it was that I was surprised by my reaction. I not only understood what Dad was saying but almost had respect for him saying it. My startling response resulted from the fact that it was the first time in my life that I could remember Dad being completely honest with himself and me.

I knew how far apart my parents had become before he left. Mom was disenchanted with him not working since he was fired from Sears almost two years before. Selling refrigerators had been demeaning enough for him. But being fired from that job. Well, that had been the last straw for him. It left him with no self-respect. Even Dad's fantasies were taken away. He was left with nothing and didn't get dressed after that or shave. He sat around all day in the same chair in his bathrobe, chomping on dead cigar butts, puttering around with his stamp collection.

Always very private, I was surprised when Mom confided in me about their sex life at that time.

"We haven't done it since he was fired," she had told me. "He claims he's become impotent!" With sarcasm and shades of anger, she told me, "I don't believe he can't do it, Jolene. I think he just doesn't want to do it with me anymore."

No one ever knew when Dad was telling the truth or lying. So, without sex, my parents didn't have much going on in their marriage. There had never been much going on besides a lot of sex, laughter, pain, and lots of crying, but still… Mom loved Dad with all her heart. I knew that. He was the only man Mom ever loved or would love. And they loved to dance. That was the only thing Mom and Dad did every weekend—they danced at the Culver City Senior Center. Ruth, Mom's best friend, also danced there.

To pay the bills, Mom had gone back to work again. She'd found a part-time job selling clothing in a cheap second-hand store. Though disenchanted, Mom still adored Dad. She'd just become more realistic. She was not happy with the old pattern in their lives again, with her working and his having an excuse not to work. When she was younger, she'd been willing to overlook, do anything, and had done everything to make him happy. But now that she was older, she wanted a few luxuries for herself—like self-indulgent time. He'd robbed her of that again, too. Her reaction to that buried resentment was to withhold the idolatry she'd always given him these many, many years. His reaction—he left her for Ruth.

I knew all the whys and wherefores about Dad walking out and his new life. But I don't think his honesty and new happiness was worth the grief it brought Mom. That night was the beginning of the end for Mom. She paid a horrible price for Dad's pleasure. Horrible! Within a year after Dad left her, Mom developed terminal cancer.

Looking around Ruth's apartment at Mom's familiar pieces, I felt even more uncomfortable and am sorry I said we'd come. Yet, when I accepted Dad's invitation for this evening, he'd been so grateful, so relieved, hoping to reunify the family.

"Well, he should be grateful," I thought. "He should be."

It hasn't been easy tonight, trying to be social with Ruth, watching Dad get the old idolatry Mom used to give him. It was almost sickening to watch Ruth compliment him, act coquettish to feed his ego. But I guess it worked. Dad has learned how to type and works at a youth center now. He's also become a volunteer at the Senior Center, directing plays. It's strange how much Dad's fire has returned, even as Mom's flame was snuffed out.

As they sit on the couch, Dad says something to the child. She giggles.

I glance up.

My father runs his hand on the back of the little girl's neck. Unaware I'm watching, Dad's hand slides down and caresses the child's shoulder. Showing discomfort, the child starts to move away. He whispers something into her ear. She changes her mind, giggles again, and allows him to pull her closer, almost in an embrace.

Shocked, I stare. "Oh, my God! He's still doing it," my mind screams at me. I have to stop him, have to warn the little girl. I lean forward to shout, "No! No! Stop! Stop touching that child!"

But no sound comes from my lips. Nothing. Nothing. A lump in my throat has formed. Again, I try to shout out a warning—still, no sound. There is only the taste of bile rising from the pit of my stomach, pitching toward the hardened lump constricting my throat. Leaping up from my chair, I become light-headed and lean heavily on the table. Charlie reaches out to offer assistance. I shrug off his arm and run from the room, to his surprise.

Slamming the bathroom door behind me, I drop to my knees in front of the commode. Sobbing, my body wrenches, convulsing, trying to reject all the bile it holds. Thrusting, heaving movements that have accompanied me most of my life continue. Heaving, heaving, heaving, yet, nothing is leaving my mouth or body. Nothing! I cannot throw up. Since I was a child, I have rarely been able to vomit, even during the nausea of my pregnancies or the pain of migraines. Only once, when I've gotten food poisoning in Mexico, have I been able to reject anything except foul-tasting bile.

The poison inside of me remains, lodged in my body, intact. I continue to dry heave until at last, exhausted, I rise from the floor and finally respond to Charlie's concerned questions as he pounds at the door, wanting to know if I'm all right. Telling him I'll be out in a minute, I splash water on my face and rinse my mouth. As I wipe my face, I stare at myself in the mirror.

"Gawd! How awful you look," I think. "How awful."

Pale beneath my tan, my full mouth, usually covered with colorless gloss, turns slightly down at the corners. My small, surgery-altered nose is red from crying, and my once finely chiseled face has begun to show aging from being in the California sun all my life. There are tiny wrinkles near the eyes and drooping skin under my high cheekbones. However, my eyes still command attention. Slanted eyes, changing from gold to green. Eyes that show the world how I feel. Those now puffy eyes look back at me, showing great pain and fear.

Opening the door, I tell Charlie we must leave.

Later, as we drive home, I try to explain what happened.

"I had no idea, no idea…" I stop, roll down the window, gulp some air. "I thought I'd handled everything. It was the past—the past, Charlie. But, my Gawd. When I saw my father with that child on the couch. It was too much. I'm 54 years old, and it felt like it was yesterday. Like it was happening all over again—to me. It's still there, Charlie. The pain! The guilt! Everything is still there. I can't believe it…"

What I saw, or thought I was about to see on that couch, seemed so horrific that I shuddered.

"I had no idea it was still there and hurt so much, Charlie. I had no idea…"

My husband's large hand engulfed mine—the warmth seeping into my chilled, shaking body. Usually, when I feel his hand, I feel secure protected. Yet tonight, my world continued to seem shaky, gray, clouded.

"What am I going to do, Charlie?" I ask, "What?"

"What do you want to do, honey?"

"I don't know. I thought I'd resolved everything. But I was wrong. I guess I need help, Charlie. Is there something or somewhere I can go?"

"If there is, we'll find it, Jolene. Don't worry. We'll find it."

Chapter Two
January 1986 Therapy

Rushing down the San Fernando Valley office building hallway, I stop in front of a door marked 310. Glancing at my watch, I think, "Late! Always late. Time! My perpetual enemy." Removing my sunglasses, I place them on top of my head, creating a headband for my long, straight, bottle-streaked blonde hair. Taking a deep breath, I open the door and enter the room. Apologizing for being late, I sit in the one empty chair and glance around.

Seven females sit silently in that room lit only by daylight. They vary in age, but I'm the oldest. They also vary in dress and ethnic backgrounds. Yet, in body language, there is a similarity in all except one, Ramona, the Valley Incest Therapy's facilitator, who sits tall in her chair. The other women recline casually in the chairs or couches on which they sit, trying to appear at ease. Yet all look as if they might unravel and bolt if confronted with something unexpected.

"Would you introduce yourself, please?" Ramona nods toward me.

Uncomfortable, I twist and untwist a handkerchief I hold as I say, "My name is Jolene."

"Tell us a little about yourself, Jolene," Ramona urges.

Becoming more uneasy, I shift in my seat then begin softly, "I...I've been married to a great guy for 30 years. Umm, we have four wonderful children. Umm... We have a grandchild on the way, and... Umm, I, I'm a writer-realtor."

I glance at Ramona, wanting to stop. She nods to continue.

"Tough life! And on top of that, you're a knock-out," one of the women says sarcastically.

Feeling defensive, I want to tell her I've never felt attractive, inside or out, but I remain quiet.

"So," the woman continues in that same tone of voice, "If everything is so hunky-dory, how come you're here?"

My face tightens, anger flares up internally. I look down, continue to twist the hanky, still don't answer. I, too, am wondering why I'm here. I didn't want to come, be in this group. It was hard enough talking to Ramona one-on-one those few times. I shouldn't have let her talk me into this, this group thing.

Ramona takes over. "On the surface, Jolene's life does seem rosy, almost perfect, doesn't it? But there are issues to be resolved because Jolene's father made sexual advances to her from the time she was three and called her his 'Little Mommy'." She adds, "Isn't that charming?"

Still, there is little reaction from the women. A murmur here, change of position there. Nothing more.

Who are these women? I wonder. Don't they have feelings? Why should I share my darkest feelings with these robot-like strangers? I don't like being here. Don't like it at all. An urge to run almost overcomes me. I stifle it.

Continuing, Ramona becomes serious again. "In addition to taking sexual advantage of his young daughter, Jolene's father tells her never to tell her mother about what they were doing because it would kill her."

That statement evokes a reaction from a few of the women.

"Kill her?"

"Why?" one asks?

"How could it kill her?" another one queries?

"Her mother, or Mommy as they called her, would die," Ramona tells them, "because her father said it would kill her to know he loved his 'Little Mommy' more than his 'Big Mommy'."

"Oh, my Gawd!"

"Bastard!"

"Now I've heard everything!"

I'm beginning to feel more comfortable. At least some of these women aren't robots, I think. At least a few are in touch with their feelings.

"Well, you haven't heard the best of it yet," interrupts Ramona. "Jolene spends her childhood being her father's love toy, being constantly afraid a slipped word or accidental gesture might cause her mother's death. And she was kept in that situation until she was a teenager, long after she desperately wanted out."

"Filthy rotten bastard. He should be deballed, tarred, feathered, and hung from a tree," one woman spits out the words with disgust.

"No! No! No! You don't understand!"

The words surprise everyone in the room except me because I'm the one who is uttering them. "No! My father isn't a bad person. He loved me. He just loved me in the wrong way."

Without exception, every woman in that room looked at me with pity. Ramona held her hand out and said, "It's a good thing you're here, Jolene. You have a lot to learn. Welcome!"

Wary, I extend my hand, not trusting Ramona's last word. "Welcome" is something I have never felt since I was born…

Chapter Three
1931

Many things are happening in the growing city of Los Angeles this year:

Snow falls.

It is so unusual that schools and workplaces shut down. So frightening snow was to some Angelinos that they stayed indoors until the 'white stuff' was no longer visible. But it is so exciting to others that they play in it until it melts and disappears. Within a few hours, it is over. The snow is gone. There is nothing left except white memories, treasured and exaggerated for years.

The Academy Awards are held.

Cimmaron starring Irene Dunne and Richard Dix wins Best Motion Picture. Actors Marie Dressler and Lionel Barrymore win Oscars as best performers.

Clifton's Cafeteria opens.

Decorations include palm trees, waterfalls, and wishing wells. The first of its kind, Cliftons is an immediate success. Their motto is: "All customers are to be treated kindly and with respect." Sharing their prosperity for 90 days, they feed over 10,000 people who pay minimally or cannot pay, filling empty stomachs and retaining the individuals' pride.

Engineers designed sturdy steel prongs and installed them along the railings of Suicide Bridge in Pasadena. They were supposed to deter people from flinging themselves to death in the Arroyo Seco Gulch far below the bridge, in the affluent community just north of downtown Los Angeles.

Yet, 79 people managed to leap to their death off Suicide Bridge this year. You may wonder why.

People are leaping to their death because the year is 1931, the Great Depression.

There is no work, no food, no dignity, no hope for many. For some, it seemed easier to die than to start over. Easier to leap off Suicide Bridge.

This year so much is happening in L.A., where almost 1,250,000 people live.

Snow!
Awards!
Free meals!
Deaths!
The Depression!

And a celebration of the birth of a child on 6 April 1931.

After 18 hours of labor, a doctor performs a Cesarean section at exactly 8:35 P.M., and a newborn enters the world on this particular Saturday night. This baby is the first infant born in the brand new maternity ward at Cedars of Lebanon Hospital, located on Franklin Avenue in Hollywood, California.

The infant is healthy, weighing 8.5 pounds and measuring 21" in length. The only questionable attribute is a hesitant cry, rectified immediately by a sound whap on its ample behind.

Within moments, hospital loudspeakers announce its arrival. Cheers are heard. Balloons and streamers appear. Tasty refreshments are provided. Nurses, doctors, hospital staff, visitors, and patients begin to celebrate.

But the baby's mother, Liz Hartman, isn't celebrating.

She lies unconscious on the operating table as doctors and nurses stitch and clean her up.

A hospital cap covers her head. Escaping curls lie dampened on her forehead. There are signs of gray meandering through the ringlets like invaders. Crows' feet at the corners of her long-lashed closed eyes mar an otherwise uncreased, sallow face with rounded cheeks. The new mother, Liz Hartman, looks far older than her mere 22 years.

Liz's family, the Sorkins, stand grouped in a corridor looking in at the lone baby, housed in a nursery designed to hold many. They look and listen for sounds from the sleeping infant as they hold food-filled paper plates and sip punch from paper cups. All but one member peer into the nursery, tapping the glass barrier, uttering strange adult sounds, trying to make contact with their new relative.

The one who stares with clouded, sightless eyes, not toward the nursery but at his plate of food, is Abraham Sorkin, Liz's father.

Stocky with thin white hair, Abraham holds a plate near his chin with one hand and picks at the food with his fingers. His shaggy, gray-flecked mustache sidetracks some of the food before reaching his lips.

Sarah, his wife, stands next to him.

Time-worn with weighted shoulders, she is dressed in black, both dress and shawl. Her appearance is that of mourning rather than celebration. Sighing, she looks into the window and says, "Ach! Another burden! Another burden!"

"Get a new record, Ma! That one's scratched!"

Marcus, red-cheeked, with a mischievous grin, and built like a middle-weight wrestler, is Liz's younger brother. He confronts his mother by making scratch-like movements toward her face.

She flinches and responds in an eternally-pained voice, "You're scratched, Marcus. Tetched in the head like your father." Silent tears slip down well-worn grooves in her sunken cheeks.

"Not now. Not today, please!" says Reuben, a larger, male version of Sarah. Reuben, Liz's older brother, the eternal peace-maker, pats his mother's shoulder while hiding his amusement at his brother's antics.

Marcus lifts a leg and emits a ripping fart.

"Marcussssssssssssssssss!"

"Whew!"

"Not in the hospital!"

"If not here, where?"

Laughing, Marcus slaps his leg and emits another.

For a moment, both Abraham and Sarah show agreement in their disgust. Then Abraham reddens in anger. Sarah begins to pray.

`Emma, Marcus's wife, pulls at Abraham's arm. Small, pretty, and dark-haired, she gushes, "Forget Marcus, Abe. Liz had a beautiful baby. Beautiful, but bald!"

Only Sarah doesn't join in the raucous laughter.

"Beautiful! Of course, beautiful," shouts Abraham.

He holds out his plate. Emma takes it and guides him toward the window. "All Sorkin babies are beautiful!" the old man bellows.

As he presses his face against the glass, with his nose squashed and hands splayed, he cocks his head and sniffs, trying to smell the new baby. Hear it. See it. Capture the new grandchild his eyes cannot see.

"Beautiful! Yes!"

Then all crowd around him, even Sarah, to peer into the nursery, nod, and agree.

"Beautiful, Dad."

"Sure is, Abe."

"Yes, beautiful!"

"Not bad."

"Are we too late? Did we miss it?"

The Sorkin family pulls back from the window as a man and woman rush toward them.

"Sorry! Got here soon as we could."

"Ooh, look, Artie! There's the baby!"

The missing father's oldest brother, Arthur Hartman, dressed in a tailored silk suit, black hair slicked back like the suave screen actor Tyrone Power, offers cigars and congratulations as he greets them in his confidant way.

Former Hollywood starlet with her Carole Lombard face, his gorgeous wife, Lottie, delivers pecks on everyone's cheeks, taking care not to get her make-up smudged. One hand holds onto her hat, the other presses a strand of pearls and fur stole to her chest, protecting them from the Sorkin food plates.

As Lottie stands next to Abraham, she stares at the baby, the look on her face a mixture of awe and envy.

Abraham sniffs, "Ah! Smells like Lottie!" He reaches out brushes his hand against her bosom.

She recoils.

"Sorry. Didn't know you were so close!"

"Of course. How are you, Abraham?"

"Fine! Fine!" Lottie moves further away from him then turns to Emma. "How long was Liz in labor?"

"Eighteen hours. Then they cut her," Emma tells Lottie. "Poor Liz. Thank goodness, mine just popped out. Boy! If I had to go through what she did, I'd never have had a kid."

"I would. I'd do anything to have a baby." Lottie stares into her husband's face.

Arthur looks away and nods to Marcus, "Where's Dan?"

"Thought he was with you."

"Nope!"

"Does anyone know where he is?"

No one responds.

Arthur jokes, trying to cover for his brother, "Dan never misses a party. He'll be here soon, I'm sure."

Marcus shrugs, "Sure!"

Later that night, three exhausted young women lie in hospital beds, resting or sleeping, or are propped on pillows as they nurse or cuddle newborns. Two beds remain empty.

Liz lies in a sixth bed nearest the door, eyes closed. She has regained some color. Her flushed cheeks look almost rouged, full lips glisten. A mass of unsheathed curls cascades on the pillow.

A nurse approaches her bed, a tiny wrapped bundle in her arms. Reaching down, she touches Liz on the shoulder. Liz's eyes open, but she doesn't move. Placing the baby next to Liz, the nurse coaxes, "Come on, little mother. It's feeding time!"

"No!"

"But Mrs. Hartman…"

"No!" Liz closes her eyes and moves away from the baby. Sighing, the nurse lifts the newborn and walks from the room.

Moments later, a young man with flaming red hair disembarks from a streetcar at Vermont and Fountain, a few blocks from the hospital. In one hand, he holds violets. In the other, a Fedora hat.

Daniel Hartman presses away creases in the pants of his old but expensive loose-fitting suit. Removing a cigar from a pocket, he clamps it between his thin lips, the upper framed by a pencil-thin mustache. His aristocratic nose projects from a pale-skinned face dominated by deep-set blue eyes.

Dan squints at the traffic and plants the Fedora at an angle on his head, feeling jealousy. He'd forgotten. It's Saturday night, a night to play. He should be in one of those cars, he thinks, going to the Palladium, spinning across the polished dance floor like the old days, moving to the music of a Big Band, night clubbing at Ciros, the Mocambo, enjoying a movie.

"Damnation!" he exclaims. "How the hell did I get into this mess?"

Flushing, he strolls toward the hospital. Thoughts rush through his mind as he ponders his dilemma.

He's been unhappy before, he knows. But never like this. This is different. This awful feeling isn't like the frustration and anger of his boyhood. Then he hated the color of his hair, the Catholic boys who beat him up daily because he was a Jew.

"Christ killer!" they used to call him.

Nor was it his boyhood frustration of living in Canada and not in America.

"Because of quotas," his sister Pola would say. "America can only take in so many Jews a year, Dan. But someday we'll get there, sweetheart, I promise you. Someday!"

His sister Pola was the brightness in his life when he was young. Pola sparkled. She took care of all of them, his mother, him, and Barney, the youngest. She was a gem, Pola was. Life sure short-changed her, not just him. But their dad had died, so young Dan couldn't even remember him. The other brothers and sisters left as soon as they could. No wonder.

Their mother, ole Rivka, was constantly whining, whining, and complaining. He couldn't remember ever seeing a smile on her face or hearing her laugh. All she did was moan and groan, moan and groan. He couldn't wait to get away from miserable ole Rivka, away from Canada.

Well, he'd gotten to America, but Pola never did. She was still in Canada with ever-complaining Rivka. He'd gotten to America because his brother, Arthur, had sent for him. Sent the money to come by train so that he could work for him.

Dan got away from Canada, the Jew-haters, and Rivka. He'd made it. He was here, in America. Life was better here. He'd even gotten used to his red hair. But Catholics! He'd never feel comfortable with them. Never! Besides Catholics, Dan hated living with Liz's miserable parents.

"Gawd!" he exclaimed. "The Sorkins! Living proof life could be miserable!" Compared to them, Rivka was a saint.

He hated his job, too. Selling shoes, kiss-assing customers, his stupid boss. Now that he isn't working for his brother anymore, he isn't earning big bucks. Hardly any money! That's the worst of it, and he thinks, no fun money. And now a baby! What a lousy time to have a baby. Stopping, he looks up at the hospital looming ahead. Fear floods his face. "I'm not ready for this!" Turning abruptly, he walks briskly toward the corner where another streetcar approaches, thoughts racing through his head.

Remembering a conversation he'd had when he told Arthur about Liz's condition, he slows down.

"It's the last thing we need right now, Arthur!" Dan had confided to his brother. "I told her to get rid of the baby. Told her I'd find the money somehow. But she was afraid of dying or something and refused. And Liz was the one who made me promise there wouldn't be any kids. Women! You never know what they're thinking."

"Do you know how lucky you are, Dan?" Arthur had embraced him. "How lucky you are to have a son? To have someone to carry on your name? I'd give everything I own to have a son, Dan, everything!"

"A son!" Dan stops. Turning slowly, he looks at the towering hospital ahead. A number of the windows are lit. In the darkness, they look almost like stars, he thinks.

"A son!" he shouts, causing a young nurse rushing past him to smile. Spirits lifted, he whistles as he walks rapidly toward the hospital.

A few moments later, Dan stands in the doorway of Liz's room. Calling out softly, he asks, "Liz? You sleeping?"

Her eyes open. Seeing him, tears well up and spill down her cheeks onto the pillow.

Taking a few steps into the room, he looks around expectantly. "Hi! Hi!" he exclaims with excitement. "Where's our son?"

Her eyes show disappointment as she tells him, "I'm sorry, Dan, really I am. You don't have a son. You have a daughter."

Fedora on his head, violets still in his hand, Dan turns and walks out of the room without a word.

Three days go by.

Dan has not returned.

The baby has not been named.

Family and hospital staff keep asking, "What does Liz plan to call the child?"

She refuses to discuss the subject. The family becomes insistent.

Liz tells them she doesn't care what they call it. Maybe when Dan comes, she'll name it, they think, but he doesn't show up. The baby should have a name.

"I don't care! I don't care!" Liz screams at them. "Name it whatever you want."

The family convenes. They remember that Dan and Liz had made a list, and Jolene was on it.

So, the baby is named Jolene Arletta Hartman, following the Jewish tradition of naming newborns after deceased relatives; Dan's father, Jacob, and Abraham's father, Achem.

The hospital gives Liz a complete layette in honor of the first baby born in the new maternity wing. She shows no pleasure or reaction over the layette, the given names, or the infant, and the hospital staff is appalled. They can't understand her behavior, but the Sorkin family understands. They knew Liz never wanted a child.

"Jolene," Liz will tell anyone in the future who will listen, "wasn't planned, you know. She's the product of a manufacturer's mistake! A lousy broken rubber, that's what! A lousy broken rubber!"

And as far as Liz is concerned, Jolene is just another of life's long line of miseries.

Liz's earliest recollections were of her mother crying, praying, lamenting life's agonies, complaining about life's miseries, or questioning God.

"Why are we so cursed, so burdened, God? Why must we bear children, suffer so?" Sarah would ask, then look toward the heavens, waiting for an explanation. She would resume her chores when none came, unaware of the tears coursing down her face. Her tirades included living in America, a country she never understood and hated, while lamenting at being a wife, a mother, a woman.

Listening to Sarah, Liz thought motherhood was the second-worst thing that could happen to anyone. The first was being a girl.

Liz hated being a girl.

There wasn't a day that Liz didn't want to be a boy. She couldn't relate to girls. They were stupid, always giggling, playing with dolls. Her happiest moments were rough-housing with the boys. She could outplay, outrun or beat up any boy who disputed her. And she could toss more baskets than any boy on the block. Fists, never words, were her weapons of defense.

Though most of her buddies were boys, Liz befriended Barbara Gerston. Barbara was different from other girls. She was profound, ethereal, sickly, and delicate, and someone Liz felt needed protection. Liz trusted her. The only other person Liz trusted was her brother, Marcus. Having Barbara as her friend and Marcus and his buddies treating her like one of the gang, life wasn't too bad outside the house.

But inside, there were always her mother's monologues.

"Boys! To be a boy is to be blessed! They go where they want, do what they want, get educated, become somebody."

"I can become somebody too!"

"Hah!"

"I can too!"

"Impossible!"

"Why?"

"Because you're a girl!"

"So?"

"So, smart mouth! First a girl, then a woman. Then you'll see. Women are cursed!" Sarah would look at her daughter with pity.

"Oh, Ma!"

"You'll see. From the day you're born, you're cursed. You must marry, have children! There is no choice. Girls are cursed from the day they are born!" And she'd spit in her hand as if to cleanse it, "Poo! Poo! Ach! Such a burden. Such a curse."

Sometimes Liz was embarrassed by her mother, who always dressed in black, had no friends, went out of the house only to market or pray at the synagogue.

"*Meshuganah*. Crazy in the head!" neighbors said. Liz heard them knew they were wrong. Her mother was miserable, yes. Crazy, no!

However, Liz had to admit her mother did have a strange sense of humor. The only thing that made Sarah laugh was getting a bargain.

Like the time when Liz was five or six and a man had come to their neighborhood, knocking on each door, offering to take out children's tonsils for five dollars each. Sarah told him to go away. She'd said there were three children in the house, and she didn't have 15 dollars. He bargained with her, saying he'd do all three for $12.50. Sarah shut the door in his face. He knocked again, calling out that he'd do all three for ten dollars. Sarah opened the door.

And that's how Liz and her brothers, Reuben and Marcus, ended up having their tonsils removed on the dining room table that day. Sarah was so delighted with her bargain that she bought ice cream for them to celebrate.

Whenever her mother spooned ice cream into bowls for special occasions after that, Liz remembered how she'd smile or laugh briefly, recalling the incident and say, "Ach, remember the tonsil man? Remember?"

In Liz's mind, the unusual sound of her mother's laughter always mingled with the delicious, cold, slippery experience of vanilla ice cream.

Crazy, no! Unusual, yes!

So Liz refused to believe what Sarah said about girls being cursed. She didn't believe her mother until three days before her 14th birthday. That was the day blood ran down her legs.

Terrified, she was sure she was bleeding to death. Stuffing dirty rags into her pants, she crawled into bed and waited to die. Crying, hurting, and miserable, she said nothing to anyone, just laid there, waiting for her final moment.

There was pain in her pounding head, her back, her belly. Her nipples on her already overly ample breasts were sore. Her mother was right; she was cursed. Like Sarah, Liz began questioning God, crying out to the empty room, "God! God! Why did you make me a girl? Why am I dying? What did I do wrong? Why am I so cursed?" Like Sarah, Liz received no answer. And she stayed in bed, waiting, waiting, knowing she would not awaken in the morning.

Yet, she did wake up, still hurting and still bleeding, but not as much. Assuming this was her last day on earth, she questioned God and still received no answers.

After checking Liz's forehead for fever on the third day, Sarah shoved three tablespoonfuls of cod liver oil down her throat. Liz almost didn't make it to the bathroom.

On the fourth day, Liz sipped chicken soup and began to think she might survive. Still, she now knew she was cursed.

Miraculously, on the fifth day, the bleeding stopped. God had forgiven her.

Thirty days later, the bleeding returned. Fortunately, she was with her friend Barbara, who explained what was happening and why. That is when Liz fully understood her mother's words that girls were cursed. She didn't want this monthly curse. Didn't want to have babies. She couldn't stop the bleeding, but she was determined to take charge of her life. She and Barbara made a pact. Binding their pinkies together, they took a solemn oath.

"We will never, absolutely never, marry or have children. We will get an education and become somebody!"

Then they would fall on the bed, laughing so hard, it brought on one of Barbara's coughing episodes. Sometimes, those strange attacks were so severe that tiny pellets of blood would appear on her handkerchief.

They were so innocent, trusting, and thinking they could have a hand in their destiny, could actually 'become somebody.'

The girls' daydreams and plans continued until they were 16. Then life took a series of ugly twists.

A few months after Liz's 16th birthday, Abraham fell down a flight of stairs and injured his head. No one knew if he'd lost his footing or had too much to drink. What happened was never explained. But it didn't matter what caused the fall. What did matter was how it changed everyone's lives.

The accident damaged his optical nerves. Within six months, Abraham was blind. This former fun-loving, partying man became entirely dependent upon others. He had to be cared for. And it was Sarah, the woman Abraham had avoided these many years, who now had to take on that responsibility. Sarah, the wife who hated him, now had to serve his every need and be in his presence, day and night, be his eyes.

Silent anger engulfed the Sorkin household.

Who was to work, pay the bills? Liz reached out to her brothers: Reuben, attending college, said he'd do what he could. Marcus, busy with a new family, also said he'd help out. Neither did very much.

Abraham and Sarah turned to Liz.

"Quit school," they told her. "Education isn't for a girl anyway."

Sarah's forewarnings had become a reality.

Liz left school and found a job as a waitress. The pay wasn't much, but the promised tips seemed good.

Barbara left school that year, too, as her cough had worsened, and she became bedridden.

But the girls' dreams and friendship remained intact.

"Someday, we'll be someone special; a librarian, an actress, a nurse, the first female basketball star. Somebody!"

Daily Liz stopped by Barbara's house after work. They continued to plan their future and share their dreams. Great pleasure came when Liz could make Barbara laugh, see her smile. And great pain came as she watched her dearest friend weaken, become frailer with each cough. Daily they saw each other until the day Liz came to visit, and Barbara wasn't there.

"We had to take her to a sanitarium, Liz," Barbara's mother choked out the words. "Unexpectedly!"

Liz couldn't go to the sanitarium to visit her dearest friend because she was too contagious, But they wrote daily. Letters were exchanged until the day no letter came.

At the funeral, Barbara's mother took Liz aside. "They told us she was reading a letter from you, Liz dear. And that she just smiled and closed her eyes. 'Just closed her eyes.' That's what they said."

Laughter, dreams, and hope disappeared from Liz's life that day. They disappeared as quickly as visual images had vanished from Abraham's eyes.

Six days have passed since Jolene's birth.

Time to go home. Dan hasn't been heard from yet. Marcus is elected to pick up Liz and the baby. When he arrives at the hospital, he is told Liz can't leave. Her appendix has burst, and her body is full of poison. "Peritonitis!" they call it.

Twice that day, Liz almost dies.

She is lucky to have been in the hospital. It saved her life. But the doctors couldn't save her female organs. So Liz got her wish. She would never be able to have another child.

"We almost lost her," the doctor tells the family as they gather in the waiting room. "But she's a strong young woman. She should make it. She's been asking for her husband. Which of you is...?"

Silence greets the doctor.

"Well... Let us know when he gets here."

Liz floats in and out of consciousness for days, calling for Dan.

"I don't understand," the doctor tells the family. "Her vital signs are good. She should be getting better. It's almost as though she doesn't want to live! How can that be? She has a new baby."

Marcus knows why. Punching walls on his way out of the hospital, he vows to find Dan and bring him to Liz—or kill him if he doesn't come!

Marcus finds Dan the following evening in a cheap boarding house. In the designated room, Marcus pounds on the door. Sausage-like veins bulge on his neck and face as he hammers the door repeatedly.

"Open up this door, you low-life!" he bellows. "I know you're in there. You sniveling, two-timing, whoring bastard! Open up this Gawd-damned door, or I'll break it down!"

Inside the room, Dan and Sadie Samson, a waitress who works at the same café as Liz, cower in the bed. They stare in fear at the shuddering door in front of them.

"Liz is dying, you poor excuse of a husband!" Marcus's angry words fill the room. "If you don't get to the hospital damn quick, so help me; you'll need a cement collar when I get through with you."

Marcus's heavy tread can be heard receding as Dan reaches for his pants. Trying to stop him, Sadie wraps herself around him and begs him not to leave. Shrugging her off, he continues dressing.

Later, Dan stands outside the intensive care unit at the hospital, berating a doctor, "What in hell have you done to her? When I left, she was fine."

Ignoring the accusation, the doctor inquires, "Are you Mr. Hartman?"

Dan nods.

"Glad you're here, Mr. Hartman. Medically we've done all we can for your wife. It seems she doesn't want to live. I hope you can change her mind."

The doctor walks away without waiting for a reply, leaving Dan standing, face ashen.

Pressing himself against the window of the locked entrance to the intensive care unit, Dan mouths, "Don't die, Liz, please." Repeating the phrase repeatedly, he keeps whispering, "Don't die, Liz, please don't..."

Liz doesn't die.

But it is months before she can go home. When she is released, Dan wheels his bald wife to Arthur's car, which he has borrowed. On her head is his Fedora.

Liz is bald because the very drugs which had saved her life had also removed every hair on her body.

Chapter Four
1932

There is great joy in the City of Angels this year. Los Angeles is hosting the Olympic Games. The Games are such a monumental event that the Coliseum, located in Exposition Park, has been enlarged. Now, it can seat 105,000 people. The city experiences monetary gains too. Thousands of fans enjoy and cheer Olympic Games throughout the city.

In the Sorkin household, Sarah is unaware of the jubilance of the city. Sarah is only conscious of her increasing burdens.

Liz has been in and out of the hospital, and Sarah cares for her when she's home. She also has to cook and clean for her blind husband and son-in-law, whom she detests. Plus, she is the full-time babysitter for her ever-growing, sloe-eyed granddaughter, Jolene. Even though Sarah receives pleasure from the young child, it doesn't balance the hardships of her other responsibilities or lessen her tears.

"Ach! To have the innocence of this child!" she moans, holding Jolene close as she rocks her on the front porch. "To not know life's pain," Sarah cries out, pressing the pudgy youngster closer to her withered breasts. And the trusting grandchild snuggles into the comfort, feeling secure, knowing that her every need will be resolved by her loving and caring grandmother, Bubbe Sarah.

Such a pair! The delighted, contented child. The black-shrouded grandmother. They sit, rocking back and forth, back and forth in the shadows, rocking, rocking, rocking. Sarah sometimes sings words learned from Yiddish lullabies almost forgotten. She sings, half hums, trying to lull her granddaughter to sleep. Sometimes, the lullabies evoke memories of childhood, painful and never forgotten.

Sarah was an only child and was high school educated. To be educated was unusual for a Jewish girl in a Russian village. The elders had shaken their heads and told her father, "Bad omen!" they predicted. "It's a curse for a girl to be so learned!"

"What difference?" he told them. "Boy? Girl? What difference? With knowledge, she can help in the store until she marries."

But her father had been wrong. The elder's prediction had come true. Knowledge in a girl proved to be a liability. To be plain was awful enough. But to be unattractive and intelligent? That scared what few available suitors there were. And at 26, Sarah remained unmarried.

Concerned, her father sent word to other villages, "A handsome dowry awaits a bridegroom!"

Word reached 22-year-old Abraham Sorkin. A tailor, Abraham had avoided the Russian draft by supporting his widowed mother and three sisters. Since his mother was now dead, and his sisters had married, he was vulnerable to the draft again. Marriage seemed like a way out.

Sarah's father approved of Abraham. A marriage contract was arranged, and a wedding date was set. Strangers, Sarah and Abraham met at the altar.

They were perfectly mismatched.

A virgin, Sarah was taken by force on her wedding night. In short order, Abraham proved to be a heavy drinker and a womanizer.

Distraught, Sarah went to her mother for comfort. She received the same advice that her mother's mother had given her. "Be thankful you have a husband, Sarah. Do your duty and pray, daughter! It makes the burden easier."

Within months, Sarah was pregnant. A son, Reuben, was born. Abraham was proud, a son! Sarah's father was delighted, a grandson! A year later, Sarah was pregnant again. Her father was jubilant.

Abraham was not happy with the idea of more responsibility. "I'm taking the family to America," he told Sarah's parents. "There is more opportunity there!"

To America! To another world across the sea?

Sarah begged Abraham to reconsider. She pleaded with her parents to intervene.

"Wives do not dispute their husband's wishes," her tearful mother told her, grasping her tightly to her bosom.

"You are lucky to have such a good provider," her grieving father sadly agreed.

For Sarah, the journey to America became a living nightmare. The sea was rough, accommodations were terrible. Seasickness was a constant companion. Within weeks, she had a miscarriage. Her nightmare continued. They reached a strange new country, then traveled to an even stranger place called the City of Angels (Los Angeles).

Abraham bought a tailoring shop on Normandy Avenue near Western in Hollywood, then moved his family into the two small rooms above. There were no Jews in the neighborhood, no one from the old country. The nearest Temple was downtown, miles away. Sarah felt abandoned, helpless, lonely, and terrified.

Wrenched from the comfort and security of her parent's love, Sarah cried and prayed to God to save her. Daily, she begged Abraham to return to her beloved Russia. Her pleas went unheeded.

For Abraham, Los Angeles and America were paradises. In short order, he could speak, read and write the language of his adopted country. There were proud days when Abraham became an American citizen, a Mason, then a Shriner. From the day he landed on America's shores, he shunned Judaism and everything that had to do with his past. Abraham was an American! He worked hard, loved a good joke, dancing, whiskey, and women. He especially loved women, except for Sarah. She depressed him, always crying and praying. He avoided her as much as possible. The only time he forced himself upon her was when he had too much to drink. During those loveless sexual encounters, Sarah conceived seven more times. The results were: three miscarriages, two stillborns, two live births—Marcus and then Elizabeth.

Sarah became fanatically religious, never became an American citizen, and refused to read or write English. Her spoken words retained ever-present hints of the old country. Poor Sarah. She never set foot on Russian soil nor saw her parents again, and she hated Abraham, Los Angeles, and America to the day she died.

Jolene's stirring brings Sarah from her reverie. As she lifts the now heavy child out of the rocker, she groans, "Such a good *kindelah*!" (child)

Jolene has grown so much this first year. She never crawled, just sat, stood, and took her first steps a few days ago. Now, she is discovering her voice. "Bubba! Bubba," she calls out repeatedly. Thrilled by the sounds, Jolene repeats herself incessantly. This repetition occurs with every new word she learns. It pleases Sarah but drives Liz crazy when she's home.

"For Gawd's sake!" Liz would yell. "Can't you shut her up?" listening to her child's excited repetitions until she can stand it no longer. Liz is healthier now, with not too many complications. Her hair has grown back. Not so thick, perhaps. A lot more gray, almost salt and pepper. Even though it's awkward because Sadie is still there, she still works at the café. They speak only when necessary. If Liz had her way, she'd quit. But Dan still can't find steady work. She has no choice. It's more than awkward because Dan still disappears for days at a time. Excuses come forth; job hunting in another city, cousins in Vancouver. Often she doesn't know where he's been and wonders if he's still involved with Sadie. But she doesn't ask and closes her eyes and heart to the truth because she doesn't want to know. But everyone else knows. Sadie is still in Dan's life.

Liz refuses to discuss the subject if someone brings it up. "What you don't know won't hurt you," she'll retort if people start on her.

"How can you put up with this stuff, Liz? How long you gonna to take it?" Marcus sometimes asks in frustration.

"It's hard on Dan, Marcus," Liz tells him. "Living with the folks. With me sick a lot. The kid. It's hard!"

Hard on Dan? Maybe.

But no one realizes how hard it is for Sarah.

No one has any idea how much Sarah's misery has increased, how many more tears flow unheeded.

Chapter Five
1933

On March 10, 1933, things began to shake in the Sorkin household. Everything else in Los Angeles trembles, too.

Liz grabs Jolene. Sarah pulls Abraham from the house. Hysterical, they join screaming neighbors running down the street. This scene is happening throughout the city. Hundreds of thousands of Angelinos run out of collapsing buildings. They try to avoid shattering glass, falling trees, careening cars, buckling sidewalks, and streets. Most do. Some don't. Cracks, holes appear, dark chasms where victims fall and disappear forever. There is no tally. No one knows how many die.

The 'Big One,' as it comes to be known, has been the topic of conversation for months:

"Chickens, stop laying eggs three days before a temblor."

"It frees women of female complaints."

"Cleanses the area of carnal sin."

"Moon's pull."

"Caused by excessive oil drilling."

"It's the hot, muggy weather."

"It's a curse placed on us by Chinese medicine men."

And on and on.

For a while, each of the 150 aftershocks brings back the fear, the feeling of panic. In time people forget, remake their lives, busy themselves. Frayed nerves begin to heal.

In the Sorkin home, it is the same.

At first, aftershocks provoke fright. In time, embarrassed chuckles. All join in the exchanges, all except Sarah. She no longer cringes when the aftershocks come. She doesn't even cry or pray, and no one pays any attention. Everyone is busy getting on with their lives. Not one person in the Sorkin household has any idea that the 6.3 earthquake is the last burden Sarah is willing to bear. And she continues her chores in silence.

Still, none ask her why she is silent.

As Liz strolls toward the house after work on an evening in mid-November, a neighbor calls out. In her arms, she holds Jolene, who weeps non-stop. The neighbor thrusts the sobbing child into Liz's arms. "Here! Take her! Take her! I haven't been able to stop the crying. Your mother won't answer the door."

Confused, Liz asks, "But why…? How…?"

"Your father is with a friend, and your mother asked me to watch the baby for a few minutes, said she had something to do. Then she went back to the house. It's been more than two hours now. It's enough already! Enough!"

Before the neighbor can finish her sentence, Liz races up the stairs. "Ma! Ma!" she shouts. "Ma!" There is no answer. "Ma!" she shrieks. "Where are you?" Opening the door, she smells gas and pulls back. Shoving Jolene into a stroller, she tells her to stay there. Liz covers her lower face with her skirt and enters the house. Almost gagging from the fumes, she runs from room to room searching, screaming for her mother. The odor seems to be coming from the kitchen. As Liz races toward the closed kitchen door, she is almost overcome by the fumes. Terrified at what she might find, she pauses in front of the closed door, then shoves. Nothing happens. She pushes harder. The door resists, then gives a little. Frantic, Liz hits, beats, and presses at the door, forcing back the rolled-up towels on the floor that block it. Inch by inch, the door gives. Not wanting to see, but knowing she has to, she gives one final thrust. The towels give way.

Liz stares and stares, crying out at what she sees. "Oh, Ma!" she sobs. "What have you done?"

Sarah's tiny head rests upon an open oven door in the kitchen, her thin arms dangling in death.

Liz's disbelief turns to awe as her gaze stares at her mother's face because it is the first time in her life that she has ever seen Sarah look so happy and peaceful.

Without Sarah, plans must be made for Abraham.

The business is sold. Liz hears of a woman who cares for the blind. She lives on the east side of town in Boyle Heights. Arrangements are made.

Dan borrows Arthur's car to drive him there.

Driving to Boyle Heights is a new adventure for Jolene. Going someplace is always an adventure. But still, she is unhappy and repeatedly asks, "Where's Bubbe? Where's Bubbe?" until Liz yells, "Shut up!"

Cowered, Jolene concentrates on the new sights. It is exciting when they reach a bridge dividing downtown from the Heights. Under the bridge is a train yard, which causes her to shriek with pleasure. But her enjoyment turns to misery as they cross over the bridge because a sickening odor engulfs them as it wafts through open car windows.

Everyone reacts.

"Ugh!"

"Those damn meatpacking plants!"

"Whew!"

Jolene nuzzles into Grampa Abe in the backseat, trying to block out the overwhelming smell. Unable to avoid it, she cries, "I want my Bubbe. I want my Bubbe!" as the adults roll up the car windows.

"Stop being such a baby!" snaps Liz.

"She is a baby!" Abraham says protectively. "She's only two."

"She's almost three," Liz retorts. "Oh, leave me alone, all of you!"

Jolene rubs and rubs her nose and tries to eliminate the horrible, sickening smell, but it won't go away. Abraham hands her his handkerchief. She blows and blows, but still, the stench remains. It stays, sticking to the inside of her nostrils, clinging to her gut, churning her stomach.

That smell remains long after they say goodbye to Grampa, his three blind house-mates, and Florence, the kind lady who promises to take good care of him. Even with closed windows, the emanation seeps in and remains after crossing the bridge again as they drive far away from Boyle Heights and Grampa.

Jolene doesn't ever want to go back again. But they do return. At first, they visit Grampa every few weeks, then every month, then whenever. The same drive, back over the bridge, smelling that pungent stink of decaying meat.

The impact of that odor imprints itself in Jolene's nostrils for hours each day and remains in her memory for life. Whenever she smells aging meat, it reminds her of Boyle Heights, that teeming, strange world in East Los Angeles, where dark-haired men wore long black coats, funny hats on their heads, and had long curls cascading down their cheeks. And the women resembled each other, too—with scarves covering their heads, carrying baskets, babbling in Yiddish with shopkeepers. Though the women were strangers, somehow, they had seemed familiar and comforting to Jolene, much like her Bubbe Sarah.

Chapter Six
1934

Without Sarah, Liz and Dan have to move.

They find a cheap room downtown on one of the steepest hills in Los Angeles. Their new address is on Third Street between Hill and Olive, below Bunker Hill, once one of the most expensive residential neighborhoods in Los Angeles. The wealthy no longer live on the hill. Years ago, they moved away, and the once beautiful Victorian homes are now boarding houses.

In 1901, Bunker Hill housed rich and influential people. They had so much influence that a cable-car system, called a funicular, was built just for them. They needed it, they insisted, to shop at Grand Central Market down the hill. Though the market was only one short block away, it wasn't easy to get there because it was 315 feet straight down. So, the former Bunker Hill residents talked city fathers into building the cable-car system. Then those privileged individuals went to the market, shopped, then rode the 315 feet back to their fancy homes. Imagine! City fathers spent an incredible amount of money so that a few, just a very few wealthy people, traveled one short block to market on a funicular system called Angel's Flight. Even though the rich are gone now, the two brightly painted orange and black cable cars named Olivet and Sinai are still there, traveling up and down, up and down that block-long steep hill every single day. And a rider can receive a thrill and a ride on the only cable-cars in Los Angeles.

It's not so bad walking downhill to work in the mornings. As Liz and Dan trudge up, up, up, that ever so steep hill toward their room after work, they look with longing at the cable cars passing by. Bending over in their exertion, they breathe hard, wishing they had a spare nickel to pay for a ride.

Without Sarah, arrangements must be made for Jolene.

Liz hears of a woman who cares for children. She seems pleasant enough, not expensive. When Liz hands her over to the woman, Jolene struggles, weeps, and tries to resist. Hesitating, Liz reconsiders until the woman promises to take good care of her, so Liz leaves.

The woman quiets Jolene and gives her a glass of milk. As she drinks, she watches the woman put on makeup, change clothes, put on a coat, and pick up her purse. Expecting to be taken for a walk, Jolene brightens. Instead of taking Jolene with her, she shoves her into a nearby closet. Shutting the door, she locks it and leaves.

Total darkness greets the young child—and a strange smell. Curling into a fetal position, thumb in mouth, Jolene cries and whimpers until, at last, she sleeps, the ragdoll Bubbe Sarah made for her clutched tightly to her chest.

Shortly before Liz arrives, the woman returns, unlocks the closet, pulls Jolene out. Carrying her to the bathroom, she cleans and changes her soiled pants. Frightened, Jolene whimpers and stays curled in a ball. Plunking her onto a kitchen chair, the woman places milk and graham crackers in front of her and commands, "Eat!"

Terrified, Jolene nibbles at the cracker watch as the woman removes her makeup and puts on the house dress she had on earlier. Bending over, she sniffs Jolene. "Ugh!" she exclaims. "You still stink! Close your eyes," she commands.

Fearing the worst, Jolene is surprised by a feeling of mist. Opening her eyes, she sees the woman spray herself with the cheap toilet water.

"There, isn't that fun? We're playing dress-up," the woman explains, nose close to Jolene's face. "That's what you tell your Mommy if she asks. You hear!"

Jolene says nothing, tears form.

"Is that all you can do? Cry! Cry! Cry! Can't you speak?" She grabs Jolene's head between her hands and squeezes. "Well, little cry baby! I'll give you something to cry about if you tell your Mommy we didn't play house. I'll squeeze your head so hard your eyes will pop out! Understand?" She squeezes Jolene's head even harder.

Jolene's tears turn into howls of distress.

Footsteps are heard. Then a knock.

The woman folds Jolene into her arms in a motherly fashion, patting her on the back as she opens the door to Liz, who shows dismay at Jolene's tears.

"Did she cry all day?" she asks.

"No way. Just a little, here and there, misses her Bubbe, that's all. We had such a good time, didn't we, Jolene? Just finished playing dress-up."

"Oh, is that what I smell?"

The two women laugh as they exchange goodbyes.

Jolene screams during the night and cannot be comforted. When Liz takes her to the woman the next day, she is terrified and clings to her mother.

"Is everything all right?" Liz inquires. "She didn't eat and had nightmares last night."

"Misses her Bubbe, that's all. Didn't you tell me she was acting up before…after your mother died? This is new for her. I'm new, that's all. She'll get used to it, to me. Don't worry."

Reassured, Liz hands the sobbing, resisting child to the woman. Her daughter's screeches follow Liz's footsteps down the hallway causing her to tense and stop. Then, all is quiet. She leaves.

The woman removes her hand from Jolene's mouth and shoves her toward the open closet inside the room.

The closet becomes Jolene's home away from home. She sleeps less, cries more, and messes in her pants more often, infuriating the woman. Weeks pass.

At home, Jolene has little appetite and clings to Liz or Dan. If they won't hold her, she curls into a ball, sucks her thumb, rocks, and rarely speaks, hardly ever making a sound. Liz is grateful for the silence. But at night, the silence is shattered, filled with Jolene's wild nightmares, screams, and inconsolable sobbing.

Liz knows Jolene misses Sarah, but this? Too much!

She considers looking for someone else, but the woman insists it takes time. Dan agrees.

Jolene's eyes have become accustomed to the closet's darkness now, so she explores and finds the source of the smell. They are balls. Tiny, white balls stored in boxes and bags. They become her toys—and her comfort food.

When Liz arrives later, the woman tells her Jolene isn't feeling well. Probably a cold, she offers. On the way home, Jolene convulses. Liz rushes her to the hospital and is shocked when the doctor tells her they have to pump her stomach. After emergency efforts are completed, the doctor admonishes her.

"She'll be fine, Mrs. Hartman, just fine. But you should be more careful about where you put mothballs when you have small children! Don't you know they're poisonous?"

Upset, Liz has no choice but to stay home. Where is she going to find a safe place for Jolene? As time passes. Bills aren't getting paid. She must go back to work. A young couple responds to a notice she posts at the local market. They have a little girl the same age as Jolene. Relieved, Liz visits their apartment. Their place is clean, and their daughter is friendly. Arrangements are made. The couple requests a week's advance to buy food, they say. Desperate and grateful, Liz agrees.

Liz brings Jolene to the new family the next day. Even the other child doesn't ease Jolene's fear. She clutches her doll and begs not to be left. With hesitation, Liz pays what they ask, tells them she'll be back by 5:30, and goes.

At 3:30, Liz receives a telephone call at the café.

"You, Mrs. Hartman?"

"Yes!"

"Is your daughter called Jolene?"

"My what? What are you talking about?" Liz asks, becoming alarmed. "Who are you?"

"I'm Sergeant Roche, Mrs. Hartman. You'd better come down to the station to pick up your daughter."

Later, a shaken Liz tells Marcus and Emma what happened. The family had abandoned Jolene. They took the money and her doll. They even took the dress off Jolene's back and left her sitting naked in the apartment.

"They just left her, those bastards. My Gawd! How could they do something like that? She could've wandered into the street, naked, been killed, or…"

The scenario is so horrific Liz can't continue.

Then, "A neighbor heard her crying and called the police. Thank God Jolene speaks so well, knows her name, the café. What if she couldn't…? What if she didn't…?" She breaks down at the unspeakable images she conjures.

"I wish we could take her in, Liz, really I do," Emma interjects. "But you know I'm working now too, and…"

"I know!"

"Life's full of bastards, Liz. You've got to be more careful," acknowledges Marcus.

"I know!"

Weeks go by before Liz finds another family. They seem kind and have two children, a boy and a girl close to Jolene's age. This time, Liz questions neighbors about the family. They reassure her. These are good people, they say. They are just having a hard time, with the husband unable to find work. Liz knows what that feels like. Still uneasy, she hears the boy cough. It's an unusual sound, like the bark of a dog.

"Is it contagious?" she inquires.

"Oh no! He gets that way every spring!"

Still apprehensive, Liz leaves Jolene with the new family. Hesitant at first, Jolene soon responds to the warm parents, the entertaining children. Within weeks her speech and appetite return, nightmares are fewer. One of the children's favorite games is trying to catch and eat the tiny black specks crawling over their bodies, clothes, and hair. Jolene is delighted with this family and fusses at the day's end when Liz comes to take her home.

Liz and Dan breathe a sigh of relief at their good fortune. Their comfort turns to anger a few days later when Jolene begins itching and scratching. Furious, Liz curses the family as she washes and plies each and every squirming louse and sticky egg from her daughter's head and hair. That is uncomfortable enough. But the worst part of it for Jolene is when she learns she can't go back and play with her new friends.

Upset, Liz refuses to look for another caretaker. Dan has a job now. She will stay home and care for Jolene. It will be challenging in that tiny room with no privacy for anyone. Dan and Liz are constantly at each other now, and it isn't easy to make up with Jolene underfoot.

Months go by. Dan's salary isn't enough to cover their expenses. Without her tips, bills pile up. The rancor in their room builds. And then it erupts one evening when he comes home and announces he's quit.

"You what?" Liz screams out in frustration. "Why did you quit again?"

"The boss treated me like dirt, Liz. Me! Who does he think he is?"

"Who in hell do you think you are?"

They scream back and forth at each other.

It's times like this that Liz remembers her mother's words loud and clear.

"Girls are cursed, Liz. Cursed and burdened!"

Jolene runs to the bathroom, hunches into a corner, covers her ears. Squeezing her eyes tight, she repeats the words to a game she learned from the friendly family, "One potato, two potato, three potato, four. Five potato, six potato, twenty…" trying not to hear Liz's escalating screams.

"Hey, it'll be okay," Dan says, trying to calm her. "Let me take care of the kid until something else comes up. Then you can get back to the café." He puts his arms around her and nuzzles her neck.

She pulls away. "Cut it out, Dan. This doesn't resolve anything." Then she looks thoughtful. She's going nuts in this room. Just her and the kid. Nuts! "It just might work until I can find someone else."

"Sure, baby, sure," he mumbles. Grabbing her backside, he presses her into him, rolling one of her plump breasts in his hand until the nipple hardens.

Liz's screams are heard no more. Moments later, the only sounds that can be heard are that of an old mattress spring, screeching out its distress in rhythm to thumping against a wall, and Liz's moans, soft at first, then rising, rising, rising…

Balling into a fetal position, Jolene sucks on her thumb and wonders why Daddy hurts Mommy so much that she cries out like that. She sucks, sucks furiously, until fear enshrouds her, uncontrollable fear that causes her to shake on the cold linoleum floor dampened with her tears. She is so afraid that her mommy will hurt so much that she'll go away, just like her beloved Bubbe did.

The new plan works.

Liz is happy to be back at work.

There is more money.

And Dan proves to be a great caretaker for Jolene.

He rocks her on his lap as Bubbe did and tells her stories about the stars. He cooks pancakes with her initials laid flat on a plate in the mornings, and he makes her laugh with his birdcalls. But she has the most fun when they take a bath together. That is when he lets her play with his toy. The little toy between his legs that grows bigger and bigger until it squirts water into the bathtub, just like a squirt gun.

"Our little secret," Dan whispers into her ear after he towels her off. Jolene giggles as he caresses her freshly scrubbed body. Sometimes it tickles. Then he touches, then he kisses. Touches then kisses. Jolene giggles and giggles. She feels especially funny when he kisses her between her legs.

"Our little secret," Dan always repeats. "Mommy would die, go away forever like Bubbe Sarah did if she knew how much I love you. If she knew I loved you more than anybody in this whole world. More than even her. She'd just die. So you must promise me you'll never, never tell Mommy about our little games. Promise!"

Mixed emotions flood Jolene. A deep, unsettling fear. Mommy mustn't go away! Mustn't! Then the fear is overcome with gratitude. She is so grateful for her Daddy's love and attention. Throwing her arms around his neck, Jolene repeatedly promises him that she'll never tell Mommy. Never!

Chapter Seven
February 1986 Therapy

I feel more relaxed today as I listen to Ramona discuss my situation with the therapy group.

"After years and years of role reversal, Jolene protecting her mom from harm instead of her mother protecting her, guess what?"

"Her mother always knew, didn't she?" states one of the women.

"Exactly!" Ramona nods.

I could feel the blood draining from my face. "How did…How could…?"

Ramona repeats her response, "Exactly! No big surprise, huh? She knew." With gentleness in tone and manner, she turns to me and asks, "Are you ready to share with us how you found out, Jolene? Can you share it now? How you found out your mother always knew and did nothing about it."

Hesitating, I nod in agreement. I try to speak after several deep breaths, but no words come. Sighing, I close my eyes, picturing that painful scene, as vivid to me now as when it happened almost five years ago. Opening my eyes, I begin.

"I was at Mom's apartment a few months after Dad walked out. I remember it was a bleak wintry day, unusually cold, windy. We sat at the kitchen table, drinking tea, crying, Mom and me. She was always crying after Dad left. I tried to help as much as possible but wasn't having much luck because menopause had hit me, and I was a basket case, crying almost as much as she was. But I wasn't sure why I was crying. I didn't know if my hormones were going crazy because I couldn't stand to see Mom hurting so much or because of a deep sadness in myself that I couldn't explain. I had no idea why I was crying. I didn't know. I only knew I couldn't make decisions, had unexpected emotional upheavals, and couldn't sleep due to the hot flashes and sweats that left me exhausted. I developed a lump in my breast after my doctor put me on estrogen, so that was out. He couldn't suggest anything else, and I became more and more depressed. Menopause was taking a heavy toll on my life, affecting my marriage, my relationship with my kids, my work, and everything else. As a last resort, the doctor suggested perhaps a therapist would help. When I went to one, you know what she told me?" I directed my question to Ramona.

She didn't respond, only shrugged.

"The therapist told me, 'Jolene, you're crying the tears you should have cried when you were a child!'"

"When I was a child, Ramona. Imagine! The tears I should have cried when I was a little kid. Isn't that something?" Unable to go on for a minute, I pause and take another deep breath. "Then she told me I'd spent so much time protecting my mother that I'd never built up protective walls for myself. She was frightened for me, she said. Frightened at how trusting I was of everything, Everyone."

"Trusting or naïve?" Ramona asks.

"Both, maybe."

"The therapist was on target, Jolene," Ramona agrees. "You spent your life protecting someone who not only didn't protect you; she sacrificed you to save her marriage. Don't you see, Jolene? Your mother was nothing more than a pimp!"

"…nothing more than a pimp!"

"…nothing more than a pimp!"

The words roll through the carpeted room like thunderclaps. They overwhelm me. I feel like I'm choking, and grab at my throat. The knot is so tight and painful; I can hardly breathe and can't respond.

Ramona repeats the words. The sounds pound and continue to wound my senses.

"It's true, Jolene. Your mother was a pimp!"

It's too much. Too much!

"No!" I gasp, finally able to speak. "No!" I don't want to hear what she's saying. I cover my ears and shake my head.

"No! No! Stop saying that, Ramona! You're lying! Lying! Mom loved me. She wasn't a pimp! She was just afraid."

"But she admitted she knew."

No! No! I can't hear this! I want to leave! My stomach hurts! My head hurts! Pressing my arms across my stomach, I try to ease the pain. The memory of my mother's words still burns in my brain. Even after so many years, those searing words of betrayal were the most painful words I have ever heard. I guess I moaned because Ramona asked, "Are you too uncomfortable? Do you want to stop?"

"No! I want to finish. Get it out already. I need to move on, Ramona."

"Then, just take it slowly, Jolene. There's no rush."

"Okay! Okay!"

Taking a deep breath, I continue. "There we were on that miserable day, both of us bawling away—with me, unable to comfort Mom because of my tears. I'd just come from a therapy session, and the psychologist's words, 'Crying tears, you should have cried like a child,' kept running through my mind. Suddenly, the question my mother kept asking jarred me from my thoughts."

"'What the hell do you have to cry about?' Mom kept blubbering through her tears. 'Why the hell are you crying? You've got a husband who loves you. Doesn't run around. Didn't walk out on you. You've got kids, a decent house, a career. What in the hell do you have to cry about?'"

"Before stopping myself, I found myself blurting out what the therapist had said."

"A therapist just told me I was crying tears I should have cried when I was a child, Mom! Do you have any idea what she meant by that?"

"My mother's swollen-eyed face had whitened. Abruptly, her tears stopped. She blew her nose and began to question me, 'What do you mean?' she kept asking. 'What are you trying to say to me?'"

"Even then, I couldn't expound on the subject. All I could do was keep repeating the therapist's words. I couldn't say anything else."

Murmurs are heard. No comments.

I continued, "At first, Mom looked like she had no idea what I was talking about. Then, all of a sudden, her eyes had widened. She'd gasped, shoved a handkerchief to her mouth, and mumbled, 'Oh, my Gawd! My Gawd! I always knew, Jolene! I always knew! But I was afraid to say something. I was afraid he'd leave me if I said anything. I had no idea it hurt you so much. No idea.'"

"It didn't sink in at first. Then I was filled with horror. Such unbelievable horror that I felt like someone had shoved a hot poker right through my heart. At first, I could hardly breathe. Then I became accusatory."

"'How could you? How could you?' I kept asking repeatedly? 'How? How? How could you let Daddy do…? Oh, my Gawd, Mom. How could you?' I could hardly go on. She just sat there crying."

"Then, I calmed down because I could see I was getting nowhere. I just wanted to know the truth and asked calmly, 'How could you allow something like that to go on, Mom? To your own child? Your daughter? How could you do it?'"

"And you know, she still said nothing. Absolutely nothing. She just sat there, no matter how long I questioned her, hoping for some answer. I just wanted something, anything, that could make some sense out of this nightmare. And I got nothing. As I railed on and on, Mom cringed at first. Then she sat, totally impassive, not moving a muscle. That was when I saw the most amazing thing happen. I saw what was almost an invisible curtain drop down in front of my mother's face, an invisible curtain. I tried to get her to talk, to answer a question, but now all she did was stare back at me, almost with a look of surprise, still saying nothing. Then, suddenly, she began to cry and asked me why I was attacking her? Attacking her? Can you imagine?"

"'Why are you trying to hurt me?' she kept asking."

"That's all she'd say that day. And, in the years to come, no matter what I said or if I brought the subject up, she'd look at me like I was crazy or ask me why I was trying to hurt her. Me, hurt her. She never spoke the truth about the subject again. Her invisible curtain remained. That curtain of denial. It was and has been Mom's perpetual armor against reality. And that protective shield remained with her for the rest of her life. There was never another acknowledgment of the truth again."

Exhausted from the telling, I began to cry, then continued, "I know Mom wasn't deliberately trying to hurt me, Ramona. She didn't have the strength to…"

Interrupting, Ramona asked brusquely, "When will you wake up, Jolene, and accept the truth? When are you going to stop defending your mother? And your father? You have a right to be angry with them, you know, even to hate them, Jolene. It's about time you stop lying to yourself."

Even though Ramona's tone of voice has softened, I still feel like I am being attacked and sob as I respond. "Ramona! You don't understand. I am not a liar! Never have been. You have no right to accuse me. I've always been honest. About this. About everything. I've never hidden things from people. Never! I told Charlie about Dad, some of my friends…"

"And your mother?"

"My mother?"

It's difficult for me to speak now. My voice is almost inaudible to the other women who sit listening and seem uncomfortable with my discomfort, yet none reach out to assist or comfort me.

"How could I tell my mother, Ramona? Why would I want to tell her? I protected her all my life. I was always afraid she'd be hurt or die if she found out the truth. I had to protect her…no matter how much I hurt." My sobs are muted now, almost like that of a wounded animal. "And when I married…had my own family…Mom and I became such good friends, Ramona. Why would I want to hurt her? It doesn't make any sense. Why cause more pain? It was in the past. Done with!"

"If it's done with, then why are you here?"

Why does she keep attacking me? I wonder. I feel like I'm being assaulted, pricked by a thousand needles from the internalized pain she's causing by her probing.

Ramona is well aware of the physical and emotional discomfort I'm experiencing. "You're here because you're still hurting, Jolene. Hurting a lot!"

Sighing deeply, I acknowledge the truth of her words. "I know. I know. I just didn't realize how much, Ramona. And I still don't understand how my mother could have…? I don't understand how any mother could…?" I cannot repress groans that come deep from within me as I rock back and forth. My groans become moans. "Oh, Ramona. I just wanted Mom to love me. I always loved her so much. And I miss her so…"

"I know. I know. You were a good daughter, Jolene," Ramona acknowledges my feelings. "Better than she deserved. Now it's your time to heal. It's time you understand how you were used and manipulated by your father and your mother."

Blowing my nose, I find my soaked handkerchief and ask for a tissue. One of the women pushes the box toward me. Thanking her, I pull out several, dab at my eyes, blow my nose again, and finally respond. "I know you're right, Ramona. I hear you. But…I still don't understand how any parent could do this to their child."

"Life creates strange paths for people, Jolene," Ramona responds. "Some children are welcomed into this world and coveted. Some are not!"

Chapter Eight
1934 Continued

Things are working out well in the Hartman household until Jolene develops a cough...like a barking dog.

"It was contagious!" screams Liz when Dan tells her Jolene is sick. "Damn! They lied!"

The diagnosis is whooping cough.

Sick as she is, Jolene remembers the disgusting smell again as her parents drive her to County General Hospital, located near Boyle Heights, which is the only hospital in Los Angeles with a contagious ward.

Liz reacts, too. Not to the smell, but to guilt, as she realizes she hasn't seen her father in ages.

Jolene screams when she is taken from Dan's arms to be placed in an oversized crib with high metal bars in the isolation ward. Liz and Dan are told they cannot go near her until she is well. So they peer down the long hall, wave at the iron bars, and shout, "We're here, Jolene, honey. Down here! Don't cry, baby. Please don't cry."

But Jolene isn't crying. She's hysterical, screaming, kicking, screeching, shrieking, and calling out again and again for her Bubbe Sarah. She continues to vent her anguish until, at last, her tiny voice gives out. It is then that the kind nurse gives her something to make her sleep. It is the only escape she receives, the only refuge from those unrelenting cold bars, the abandonment, the raging fever, and barking cough that racks her body for two whole weeks.

During that time, Liz does a lot of thinking, feels guilty about the situation, confirms her awareness of why she never wanted to be a mother. "I'm a lousy mother," she agonizes. "Lousy!" She recognizes that kids have no place in her life and thinks how things would have been better if she'd gotten rid of the baby the way Dan wanted. But she didn't want to die from bleeding like the girl down the street had done. She didn't want to die young, not like that girl, not like her friend Barbara. Liz wanted a chance at life. A chance to be somebody. Then she snorted in disgust. Who is she kidding? Dan was right. They shouldn't have had the kid, but they did. And now they're stuck. It wasn't so bad when Sarah was alive. But now… It's almost impossible to get someone decent to care for Jolene. It seems hopeless. Liz continues to ponder the situation, feeling trapped. Then, she brightens. Maybe there is a way out of this dilemma. She calls her brother-in-law Arthur.

After the perfunctory greetings, Liz comes right to the point, "Arthur, I know how much you and Lottie have wanted kids," she tells him. "And you…you like Jolene, don't you?"

"Of course, we like Jolene. What a crazy question. You know we love her. What're you getting at, Liz?"

"Well…do you… do you think you would be willing to…adopt her?"

The question stops Arthur. Rarely does anything surprise him. For a moment he thinks, then tells Liz he'll discuss it with Lottie that evening.

Arthur and Lottie are heavy drinkers.

Their days begin with a Bloody Mary and end with nightcaps. This day has been no different. They arrive home late in the evening, after having consumed many drinks. As they go at each other in a not unusual vitriolic battle, Liz's offer has yet to come up.

"Proper *shiksa!*" (non-Jewish female) Arthur lashes out at Lottie during their drink-induced verbal bout. "Proper schools! Proper parents! Proper everything! Don't you ever get tired of being so damned proper?"

"Don't you ever wish you were a man?"

Lottie is Arthur's fifth wife, yet he's never fathered a child, so her remark cuts deep.

They retire in anger, their satin-sheeted bed unable to soften the hurt. Yet, Lottie adores Arthur. He is her Prince Charming, handsome, generous, and exciting.

In his way, Arthur cares deeply for her as well. She is the most beautiful of his wives; witty, warm, and she gives him access to the kind of people he needs to bankroll his movies now that he's no longer a high-rolling bookie.

They awaken in the morning, turn toward each other, kiss, and reach out for their first Bloody Mary brought to them by Roger, their butler, the drinks having been discreetly placed on a silver tray next to the morning newspapers.

Remembering his sister-in-law's offer, Arthur tells his wife, "Liz called yesterday."

"Um…"

"She asked if we wanted Jolene."

"For the weekend?"

"No!"

"Longer?"

"Yes."

"Really! How long?"

"Permanently!"

"You're joking!"

"I'm not! She asked if we'd like to adopt her."

"How interesting."

"That's what I thought."

Later, Arthur calls Liz.

"We'll do it!"

Dan rages at Liz, "Are you crazy? How can you stoop so low? How can you embarrass me like this? My brother has everything I don't have, and now you want to give him my kid? No way! No way! And don't you ever bring up the subject again!"

"Dan. Be reasonable. We didn't want her, don't want her, and can't take care of her. They love her and want kids. They can give her everything we can't, all kinds of things."

"We're her parents!"

"Then, dammit, act like one! If you want to be a parent, get a decent job. And stay with it!" She stops, uncomfortable, surprised at her bluntness.

Dan smarts from the impact of her words, "Look, Liz, I'm sorry about quit—"

She stops him, "I don't want apologies or excuses anymore, Dan. I want actions. And your word."

He stares at her. Much as he hates being tied down, he loves Liz, needs her, and doesn't know why, but she's the core of his life. "You have my word, Liz."

She calls Arthur, "We've changed our minds, Arthur. Uh, we're her parents, you know. She's our responsibility!"

"Lottie's going to be disappointed, Liz. But I understand. If there's anything I can do?"

"No! No! Thanks, Arthur. Thanks for your offer."

"Well…Good luck, Liz. You'll need it."

Dan keeps his word.

Reuben hires him to work at his unfinished furniture store. Liz stays home and shops carefully for a new caretaker. In time, she finds, what she believes, to be the ideal family:

Ronny McPhierson, a fireman, lives in Inglewood with his wife, Nell, their daughter, Annie (close to Jolene's age); and a son, Seth, a year older. Liz likes the family but hesitates about the distance. Inglewood is two bus transfers from where they live.

Dan doesn't like the situation, period. He doesn't like how far it is and is against Jolene staying away all week. His objections continue until Liz asks him if he'd mind taking care of Jolene every other weekend. She'll have to work those weekends, she explains, to pay for the extra cost.

Continuing to object, Dan realizes if Liz works, he'll have Jolene all to himself two days every other week. Inwardly delighted, he appears calm as he approves the arrangement.

Liz is surprised at Dan's change of heart but is relieved that he agrees.

Inglewood is different. Yet, all the houses and yards look alike. Perhaps there is another color on a door; a rose bush or a tree. Otherwise, alike. The children are the same, too. They are white-skinned blondes with blue eyes. Most of the boys have short hair. The girls have silken, golden tresses which look like their mothers brushed them a hundred times each morning.

Jolene feels uncomfortable, out of place with these children. She knows she looks different, too. Her hair is short, cut in a Buster Brown haircut with bangs. It almost looks like her father had used a bowl when he cut it. And her hair isn't golden either. It's dull brown unless the sun strikes it. Then it shines almost red like Dan's, with highlights. She doesn't have clear white skin either. No! Freckles cover her round face. Instead of blue eyes, her almond-shaped eyes are speckled yellow-green like her mother. Some of the boys tease her, call her freckles.

Living with the McPhiersons is terrific, though.

The parents are kind and treat Jolene like one of their own. Annie becomes like a sister.

It is almost perfect except for Seth, who hates all girls, even his sister Annie. Now, he has to put up with another girl. Too much! Hoping Jolene will go away, Seth does everything to make her miserable. Standing on the garage roof, he drops bricks and dead birds on her head as she passes by and trips her every chance he gets. He also tries to get her in trouble.

Despite Seth, Jolene can never remember being so happy.

Chapter Nine
1935

Jolene loves the McPhierson family, even Seth, when he isn't mean. They love her in return and show it, especially one afternoon. That was the day when they put a blindfold over her eyes, and Annie led her into the dining room. When she uncovered her eyes, Jolene saw a large, green Jell-O mold, brimming full of sliced bananas, sitting on a table.

The McPhierson family and neighboring children shouted, "Surprise!" All of them, standing there, waiting to share the mold, the green Jell-O mold Nell made for her fourth birthday.

Jolene remembered her first birthday party forever.

That weekend, after Dan and Liz repeatedly hear details of the party, they decide to do something special for her. That afternoon the three of them take a ride on Angel's Flight. Up and down, up and down Bunker Hill, two times, while eating strawberry ice cream cones.

More content than she has been since Bubbe Sarah died, Jolene hardly remembers her anymore. Even when Liz shows her pictures, her grandmother looks more and more like a stranger.

Jolene also enjoys her weekends at home, especially when Liz works. Her daddy keeps her so busy. Sometimes they work on his stamp collection. Or, he teaches her card games and how to read. He also teaches her about boys:

"Never let a boy kiss you, Jolene," he warns, "or you'll have a baby! If you want kisses," he tells her, "come to me. I'll give you all the kisses you need. Remember, don't let boys kiss you, Jolene. Promise me?"

Always she promises. To anything he asks. Anything. And then they play Daddy's favorite new game, 'Little Mommy!'

First, he stands her on the bed and removes her clothing. Then, he dresses her in one of her mommy's nightgowns and calls her his 'Little Mommy.' She giggles when he touches her and kisses her entire body. On those weekends, she experiences her first orgasms, though she is too young to understand that her young body's wrenching with pleasure after her daddy's bouts of kissing and sucking has such an exotic name. And yet, she dreads the 'Little Mommy' game because he insists she sucks on his toy. She doesn't like it because it makes her gag. And often, he gets angry if she vomits. So she uses all of her willpower to keep from throwing up as his toy gets bigger and bigger. When it is ready to explode, he pulls it from her mouth, grabs a nearby towel, and squirts into it. But sometimes, some of the fluid gets into her mouth, and try as she will, she still vomits. When this happens, he shakes her so hard that her teeth rattle, and she feels like her head is about to fall off. Then he warns her to be a good girl, or he'll send her away to a bad girl's school.

Send her away! Bad girl's school!

Terrifying thoughts. But, most of the time, the game isn't frightening. Jolene loves pretending to be Mommy and a grownup. Loves it. And she loves the attention. She wants to make him happy. She loves him more than anyone in the whole world. And he loves her more than anyone in the entire world, too, even more than he loves Mommy. Not a game goes by that he doesn't tell her just that. And he always reminds her to never, never tell Mommy. Always she promises. Especially after he asks her, "You don't want your mommy to die, do you? Go away forever, as Bubbe Sarah did?"

Mommy go away, forever?

Her dread becomes intense. A lump forms in the back of her throat, so painful she can hardly breathe. As she lies in his arms, jumbled emotions and thoughts often careen through her head. She loves him, loves him so much. But she's terrified, too. What if she accidentally says or does something that reveals their secret? Then her mommy might die, go away forever.

Sometimes though, a new thought enters her head.

What if...what if Mommy did die?... Go away forever...? She'd have her daddy all to herself. She could be his 'Little Mommy' forever, even become his 'Big Mommy' someday. But what if...What if Daddy got mad at her for killing Mommy, sent her away?

Overwhelmed and overcome with these jumbled and painful thoughts, she feels unbelievable guilt and self-loathing. Oh, what a bad, bad girl she is! Bad! Bad!

Chapter Ten
1936

Before she is five, the McPhiersons enroll Jolene in kindergarten. In class, they are seated in alphabetical order. The boy behind her taps Jolene on the shoulder on the first day. She turns. Without warning, he plants a wet kiss on her lips. Remembering her father's warning about boy's kisses giving her a baby, she bites right through his lip. Shocked, the teacher removes both of them from the classroom, taking the boy to the nurse and Jolene to the principal's office. Then the McPhiersons are called.

No matter how often they ask, Jolene refuses to say why she bit the boy. Her punishment is to sit in a corner until she agrees to apologize. After sitting a while, Jolene apologizes to the boy and his parents but never reveals her reason for biting him.

Expecting a baby to come, Jolene waits and waits.

Daily she checks the mail, looks on the doorstep, peers out of the windows, and looks into the closets. No baby appears. In time she forgets the incident. She and the boy become good friends after he heeds her warning, no more kisses.

Jolene loves school, excels in her studies, makes friends easily, and gets along with students and teachers, except when she talks too much.

When weekends come, Jolene doesn't want to go home. School activities, kids' parties, any excuse will keep her with the McPhiersons. Saturdays are busy with friends and parties. Sundays, there is church and the McPhierson family dinner. Jolene hates to miss all the good times. There is so much more to do at the McPhiersons than at home. Liz is relieved to have a few weekends alone with Dan to help their relationship. It works, sometimes. Sometimes not. He still disappears for days at a time.

As time passes, Jolene spends more and more weekends with the McPhiersons. She has never been happier, though sometimes her body aches, longs for the pleasure her daddy brings to it. But she's beginning to have mixed emotions about their games now. She notices how different Ronny McPhierson treats Annie. He kisses her on the forehead or cheek, never on the mouth, as her daddy does to her.

When she asks Dan if all fathers have 'Little Mommies,' he acts disturbed and questions if she's ever mentioned it to anyone, then seems relieved when she tells him "No." He continually tells her that it's their special secret and she must never tell anyone. So, she always promises. But she is puzzled and wonders if it's wrong to be her daddy's 'Little Mommy.' However, when she's in his arms, all doubt disappears because she is so grateful for his love.

Reuben is upset. Dan isn't showing up for work.

"Liz, if Dan wasn't family, I'd…" And lets the subject drop, seeing her face. He doesn't want to cause her more pain. He also doesn't want to listen to her make excuses, never facing the truth about her husband.

"Reuben, it's hard on Dan," Liz tells him. "You know, both of us working so much. Just work, work, work. No fun. Maybe, if we didn't have to pay the McPhiersons, we'd have more money and could go places. That would make a difference. Don't you think? I'll talk to him."

"Sure, Liz. Sure! Whatever you say."

Liz brings the subject up that night, "I've been thinking, Dan. All work and no play. What kind of life is that?"

"You're not telling me anything I don't know."

"Jolene's getting older. She's in school most of the day. Maybe she doesn't have to stay with the McPhiersons anymore. She could stay with us, be more of a family."

"Since when have you become motherly?"

Ignoring his sarcasm, she persists, "We could use the money we'd save. Maybe see a movie, go dancing, have some fun. What do you think?"

"I'm not arguing. But there's no room for a kid here, Liz."

"I know."

"So? What are you talking about?"

"We could move."

"Where?"

"I don't know. If you're willing, I'll look."

"Sure! Go ahead. It might help. Anything would be better than this dump, this life."

A few weeks later, they pick Jolene up, saying they have a surprise for her.

Even after they transfer to a second trolley, Jolene's parents refuse to say what it is. Bombarding them with tales of school, her friends, activities at the McPhiersons, Dan and Liz smile, seem distracted, and hardly listen.

The three disembark at Vermont and Santa Barbara near Exposition Park and the Coliseum, home to the 1932 Olympics. Large ornate buildings stand amongst park trees.

"Museums," Dan tells Jolene. "One building is full of stuffed animals."

"Stuffed like Annie's teddy bear?"

"No! Life-sized! Big! Real-looking animals. Dinosaurs, tigers, lions, whales, monkeys!"

"Like in the zoo?"

"Sort of. Except some of these animals lived thousands of years ago. They're so real looking; if you went up and touched them, you'd think they would bite." He pinches her arm. She laughs.

Liz watches them, pleased.

"Except you can't touch 'em cause they're behind glass."

"Is that where we're going? To the museum? Is that the surprise? Is it?"

"You'll see."

They walk, not toward the museums but past them. Then they pass the park, cross the street and turn into a nearby residential block. There, multiple dwellings greet them; duplexes, triplexes, apartment buildings. Occasionally, a single-family residence is squeezed in with a rare garden. And there are a few trees.

As they walk, Jolene skips backward. "How far is it? Does the surprise have four legs? What color is it? Can I wear it?"

"Gawd, Dan! Can't you shut her up?" Liz pleads, losing patience, and wonders if this was a good idea. They continue to walk, turn west on 36th Street.

"Look!" Jolene shouts. "There's a school. Ugh! It's ugly."

Dan and Liz exchange a look.

Children play on the school grounds hitting a ball against a wall.

Jolene stops and stares. "Mommy! Mommy! Look! Look at those kids. Some of them are so dirty, and their faces even look dirty."

Liz snaps, "How can you be so stupid, Jolene? They're not dirty! They're Negroes. That's the color of their skin, Jolene. Black. Those are Negro children. Haven't you ever seen a Negro child before?"

Tears well in Jolene's eyes. "Black skin? Negroes?" Jolene sulks. Of course, she knows Horatio, who works at Uncle Reuben's store. He has dark skin, but nobody called him black or a Negro. And she's never seen a small black person before. And now her mother is mad at her. Eyes downcast, she slips her hand into Dan's, walks silently, not understanding this strange place, those peculiar children. She hates this surprise trip and wants to go back to the McPhiersons.

"I want to go home!" she blurts out.

"You are home!"

She looks up.

"Here we are! Here's the surprise! Well, what do you think?"

They now stand in front of a modest triplex across the street from the school where the children had been playing.

They play no longer. Now the children stand, making imprints against a chain-link fence, as they stare at Jolene, Liz, and Dan.

"This is the surprise?"

"Yes! This is where we'll live, Jolene, all together!" Liz strides down the path to the unit in the middle, takes out a key, and unlocks the door.

When Liz brings Jolene back to the McPhiersons, she tells Nell, "Jolene can stay until the semester end. Then she'll be living with us."

"Well, we love her, we really do. We'll certainly miss her," Nell responds.

Annie and Jolene cling together, sobbing.

"Don't let her go, Mommy. Say something."

"Please, Mrs. McPhierson, please!"

"I'm sure it's for the best, Jolene. You'll be with your Mommy and Daddy every day soon. Doesn't that sound wonderful?"

Jolene isn't sure. She's seen so little of her parents this past year. She snuggles into Mrs. McPhiersons' arms. "I guess so."

Hugging her close, Nell reassures her but can't hide her sadness. Even Seth is upset.

The semester ends.

Nell packs Jolene's few belongings. Liz and Dan arrive in Arthur's car.

"You'll bring her back for visits, won't you?" Nell asks.

"Of course!"

Annie makes Jolene promise, "You'll spend Easter and Christmas with us, won't you? And you'll be here for my birthday. Right?"

"Sure!" They hug repeatedly.

Nell hands Jolene a small box of stationery, "To write."

"Every day!" Again, hugs.

Seth hands her his most prized possession, his Olympic hat, "If anyone drops bricks on your head."

Jolene bursts into tears and hugs everyone again.

"Enough, Jolene," Dan insists. "Time to go."

But Jolene lingers. Dan picks her up, drapes the weeping child over his shoulder, and says their goodbyes.

Jolene doesn't know it, but she will never return to Inglewood to see the McPhierson family again. There will be a few letters, cards, Christmas greetings, and then nothing.

Arriving at her new home, Jolene asks, "Where am I going to sleep?"

"In here. You're going to sleep on the couch."

Jolene looks around the small living room at the old slipcover couch taken from the Sorkin's household, "Why?"

"There's only one bedroom."

"Why?"

"It's all we can afford right now."

Not hiding her disappointment, Jolene looks at what is to be her new home. Besides the couch, there is a lamp, two dismal overstuffed chairs, a dining room table, and four chairs. Everything crammed into this small space is all from her grandparent's place. Though it is midday, the room is dark. Two small windows reveal a triplex facing them—the only barrier is a low shrub. Paper-thin walls permit sounds from both sides, like uninvited guests.

"I wanna go back to the McPhiersons."

"I don't want to hear it."

"Annie and I had a bedroom. I had my own bed."

"You were lucky."

"I want a bed!"

"That'll do for now."

"No! I hate it here!"

"You'll get used to it!"

Mimicking her mother's words and tone, Jolene repeats the phrase, "You'll get used to it. You'll get used to it."

"Stop it, Jolene!"

She repeats the phrase, this time louder.

"Jolene! If you don't stop this minute, you'll be sorry."

Ignoring her mother's warning, she shouts, "You'll get used to it…You'll…"

Unable to control her frustration, Liz whacks Jolene across the face. She reels from the impact of her mother's hand.

Stumbling out of the house, Jolene holds her burning cheek. Running up the path, she sobs, "I hate it here. Hate it! Hate it! And I'll never like it. Never! I don't care what she says."

As she runs down 36th Street, Jolene continues to sob, with her hand still pressed to her enflamed cheek. She slows and begins to walk, passing several duplexes and a triplex, then stops in front of a house that has a tiny garden. In the earth, young chives sprout new growth. Bending down, Jolene pulls a chive out of the ground and smells it. Umm, it smells like an onion. She tastes it. Umm, delicious. Reaching down to pick another, Jolene stops when she hears shouts and sees an older man angrily shaking a cane at her on the porch shouting obscenities. Dropping the chive, Jolene hurries by, forgetting her cheek, her anger. She rushes past more buildings resembling her new home and sees no one.

Breathless, she stops to enjoy the shade of a tree, a lone tree, carelessly releasing leaves in front of a deteriorating apartment building. Relaxing, she hears rustling, the caw of birds. She sees nothing until dark shapes swoop down at her, screeching their rage. Blackbirds, protecting their young from the unknown, dive down repeatedly, pecking at her head, face and hands as she rushes screaming, seeking protection into the building's entrance.

Cowering in the doorway, she sees nothing but blackness as her tear-filled eyes try to adjust from daylight to the dark interior.

"Ooooooooh! I'm dying!" she wails, "I'm dying!" Rubbing her cut hands together, she tries to ease the pain and frustration. Wanting to go home but afraid of the birds, she hugs the door frame, distraught.

"What's wrong?" A voice projects out of the darkness.

"Who's that?"

"Who are you?"

"I'm Jolene. Who are you?" She looks and looks, still sees nothing but darkness.

"I'm Flora!"

"I'm Fiola!"

Two sets of smiling white teeth appear across the dimness, "We're twins. Identical, Marm says!"

"Twins?"

"Yep. Oney way tell us apart. Fiola has four fingers onna left hand. Me. I have five."

Curious but still frightened, Jolene backs out of the doorway into the sunlight. Angry caws force her back in. Scared, she begins crying again.

"Why you cryin? You hurt? Lost?"

"Yes. No. I…I…just moved in. Down the block. The birds…" She turns and looks outside. "The birds won't let me go home. They hurt me, hurt my head, my hands."

"Them's mean, those blackbirds. Always like that when they got young'uns in the nest. Marm says so. Says keep away 'til they young'un big enuff to fly. Says keep away."

"Well then. How do you go to school?"

"We wears a hat." The twins giggle, then break into laughter.

Jolene finds herself laughing in unison despite her discomfort. Peering into the darkness, she sees two shiny grins approach her. Then, two figures about the same size gradually emerge. They are identical, absolutely identical.

Upstairs, Jolene meets the twin's family: Marm, their mother; Gramma Adams; Uncle Herman, his wife Twila; and their three-year-old daughter, Samy. They all live here in this tiny apartment, smaller than Jolene's new home. Smaller, noisier, and to Jolene, a lot more fun.

Marm cleans Jolene's cuts, wipes her tears, and pats her head. Gramma Adams stuffs her with milk and cornbread. Then they return to what they were doing before the twins brought her to them. Fresh piles of shirts, underpants, slips, and hankies are everywhere. As Marm and Twila iron, the twins and little Samy fold finished garments into neat stacks. Gramma Adams goes back to her cooking. Herman makes music.

Sitting in a wheelchair because of his twisted, funny, useless little legs, Herman strums a banjo and sings. Marm sings along as she works. The others join in. Even little Samy's body sways in rhythm. Jolene listens, watches, is enthralled.

"Won't your mother be worrying, Jolene?" Marm inquires.

Jolene nods, wondering.

Wearing a hat loaned to her by the twins, she leaves a few moments later, her emotions mixed about this day. On the one hand, she hates the thought of going home, fearful her mother is still angry. On the other hand, she is thrilled at this household of new friends.

Self-conscious, Jolene stands as her teacher, Mrs. Allen, introduces her to the class. She knows she is ugly, wearing one of the two stiffly starched cotton dresses she owns, white cotton socks which droop around her ankles, and her brown high-cut shoes with lifts holding up her weak arches. Ugly and different. Even though her eyes are downcast, she knows everyone is staring at her.

And she's right. Every child in the room has its gaze fixed on her, staring in silence.

She hates being stared at, feeling ugly, feeling different again. But she is more unlike these kids than she was from the kids in Inglewood. There, at least her skin color resembled theirs. Looking up momentarily, she glances at her new classmates. Every single face looking back at her is black. She looks down again.

'It's not fair,' she thinks. 'Why couldn't I be in one of the other classrooms, where there are some white kids? I hate being stared at, feeling ugly! Not fair!'

She hates her parents for making her come here and hates the teacher and every black face in that room.

Those first few weeks are hard.

"Freckles!"

"Freak!"

"Teacher's pet!"

"Whitey!"

Even Seth's hat doesn't protect her. There are no bricks, but there is still pain. A push, a leg out, tripped, falling, skinned knees, bruises, hurt feelings. She hates going to school. Hates it! Until the day the twins come to her rescue.

"Leave her alone. She ain't done nothing."

"Bug off, Fiola. None a yore business."

"Make it my business, you ugly lil nigga, you!"

The twins lunge at her assailants from different directions. After that, confrontations are fewer. In time, she is one of the children bouncing balls at the playground, bouncing balls against the wall at the 'ugly school.'

No more balls. No more kids. No more playtime. It is dinnertime.

It's time to cross the street and go home. Mommy gets home late, Daddy even later. Jolene doesn't like going home to their empty house, waiting, always waiting, always alone. But it's only an hour or so. She lets herself in with the house key hanging on a string around her neck. She is one of the 'latch key' children described in the newspapers.

Liz has instructed her, "Never let anyone in when you're alone, Jolene. Not even the twins."

So, if the twins can't play, Jolene hangs around the schoolyard or sits alone.

She and Dan don't play 'Little Mommy' very often because Liz is home most weekends. Sometimes she feels funny and wishes her daddy was able to make her 'feel good.' But she has learned if she holds a pillow between her legs and rubs and rubs, it makes her shudder a little. It's not the same pleasure her daddy brings her, but it does release the pent-up desire she is developing.

There are more family activities now. Some days, the three of them go to Uncle Marcus's house for dinner or her Uncle Arthur's house. Sometimes they even go to a movie. Liz is working hard to make life better for all of them, making things work.

Even though the house is empty, it doesn't frighten Jolene because she knows her new friend, Eddie, the school janitor, is watching. He watches, making sure she is safe. Safe when she crosses the street and safe when she gets home.

Tall and dark, with skin as black and shiny as her daddy's pointed shoes, Eddie lives in a tiny corner bungalow at the end of the playground. He calls the children at 36th Street Elementary School, "his children."

"My children," he'll say with affection as he watches over them, protects them, teaches them responsibility.

If a child drops something, there's a tap, tap, tap on the shoulder. Eddie's long, pronged, trash pick-up stick is his gentle reminder. Quickly, the item is retrieved, and the wrong is righted. Eddie's children aren't afraid of him. No, they are not scared. Just aware and in awe. Because Eddie has a shotgun, a gleaming shotgun, he cleans every weekend as he sits on the steps of his bungalow. And each week, several children congregate around him on the porch steps and watch silently as he dismantles and polishes each piece of that shiny gun. Jolene is one of those children.

As he cleans the gun, Eddie tells stories, tales of his childhood in the South, how he hunted for possum and rabbits, and how 14 members of his family lived in a two-bedroom shack. He tells of working hard in the cotton fields when he was little. But what Jolene enjoys most is when he speaks of the music of his childhood. He says, "We always had our music, no matter how hard things were."

After gun cleaning is done, Eddie takes his gun inside and returns with a harmonica. This is the part Jolene loves best when Eddie plays his harmonica, trilling rich melodies. Sometimes he shows the children how to play. He teaches Jolene the song, "Oh, Susanna," and says she has natural talent. These are special days for Jolene when Eddie cleans his gun and she gets to play the harmonica.

"A shotgun!"

"Your friend Eddie has a gun!"

Her parents are upset, and both agree she's never to go near his bungalow again.

"Not fair," Jolene complains to Liz. "The other kids get to go."

"Maybe their parents don't know he has a gun."

"Yes, they do!"

"Well, I can't help it if they don't care. We do! And you're not going there anymore."

"Not fair!"

"Enough! I don't want to hear about it again!" But she does hear about it.

Jolene continues to complain until Liz finally explodes. The slaps shut Jolene up for a while, but not for long. Punishing her by putting her in a corner doesn't work either. Liz is beside herself.

"She's so persistent, Dan," she complains. "I don't know what to do with her."

"Ignore it," he tells her. They argue. Sometimes, the disagreement escalates to the point that he leaves. Any provocation gives him license to depart. Often, he doesn't come back for days. Liz cries softly in her bed when he's gone, thinking Jolene can't hear.

But Jolene does hear. She agonizes over her mother's tears and knows it's her fault her mommy is unhappy. Her fault Daddy left. What a horrible person she is. Horrible, horrible, horrible!

She doesn't mention Eddie again.

Instead, she fantasizes about having a big brother.

A big brother, Jolene imagines, is someone who will protect her from Mommy's slaps, Daddy's shaking, kid's teasing. Her brother would never make Mommy cry. He would make Daddy proud. Then Daddy would never leave. Her big brother would be waiting when she got home from school. And he'd take her everywhere with him. She'd never be lonely again. Oh, how wonderful it would be to have a big brother, she thinks. Someone nicer than Seth, though. She'd like someone like Eddie, a big brother with a shotgun, who could make music.

There he is. Jolene sees Eddie down the block, watching her, sitting on his porch steps. She waves. He waves in return. Noting it's getting dark, she hurries to her place, unlocks the door, goes inside.

Dan returns a few days later, and no questions are asked, even though he reeks of cheap perfume.

It is weeks before the subject of Eddie comes up again.

"Mommy?"

"What?"

"Can I go to Eddie's now? All the kids…"

"Stop bothering me. Do something."

"There's nothing to do."

"Find something."

"What?"

"She's at it again," Liz complains to Dan. "She never gives up with this Eddie thing."

"She's unhappy, Liz."

"So? everyone's unhappy. Who gets what they want in life? She might as well get used to being disappointed."

"God, Liz! You're beginning to sound more like Sarah every day."

Liz flushes and turns away in anger, "How come you always take the kid's side?"

"Maybe I remember what it was like to be a kid!"

"Maybe you haven't grown up yet!"

"Lay off, Liz! I just think she's alone too much, that's all."

"She has friends."

"They're busy, have families. Why don't we get her a pet?"

"A pet! That's all we need! You know we can't afford one."

"How 'bout a small dog?"

"No way. We're not spending our hard-earned dollars on something so stupid. End of discussion!"

Liz always ends an argument with that statement when she knows she's about to lose.

A few days later, the three of them are having a meal. Liz sits sideways on her chair in her usual position, always ready to respond if Dan needs something. She doesn't have long to wait.

"Ketchup, Liz! How can I eat this without..."

"Coming!" She's up, out of her chair, rushing to the refrigerator and back again, placing the ketchup bottle in front of him as a deep, resonant voice fills the room.

"The New Deal offers an opportunity for every American who can..."

Cheering drowns out the rest of the sentence.

"He's right, Liz," Dan enthuses, "Roosevelt's New Deal creates more jobs and income. Our luck's bound to change..."

"That would be nice."

"Aw, come on! You know I'm lucky. I chose you, didn't I? You're the best of the lot!" He rises and walks behind Liz's chair. Bending over, he kisses the back of her neck, grabs her buttocks, and squeezes. Running his hand into her lap, he begins to rub. She laughs coyly, "Dan, stop it. Not in front of the kid."

Jolene watches, emotions mixed.

On the one hand, she's happy that they're getting along now, not fighting. Yet, part of her wishes Daddy wouldn't grab Mommy in front of her. Jolene doesn't mind when they kiss in front of her unless they kiss a long, long time and start rubbing bodies. Sometimes, she wants Daddy to show Mommy how much he loves his 'Little Mommy. Then terror sets in, and the lump forms in the back of her throat. No! No! How horrible! she thinks. Mommy would die. She'd go away like Bubbe Sarah. Daddy says so! Oh! Oh! What a bad girl I am. What a bad, bad girl.

Overcome with guilt, Jolene goes to the bathroom and stays there until her parents insist she come out and finish her dinner.

Dan is back in his chair as Jolene re-enters the room and sits down.

"Roosevelt's a real winner, Liz. You'll see. We're in for some good times." He sits down, starts to eat again, stops in disgust. "Get me a sharper knife, Liz. This thing is like…"

Liz jumps up again.

Why can't Daddy get what he wants himself, Jolene wonders? Why does Mommy treat Daddy like he's a king or something? Jolene determines when she gets married, she'll not wait on her husband. They'll wait on each other.

The President's voice resumes.

"Prosperity is just around the corner, fellow Americans. Every worker, every single man or woman willing to work, has the right to a weekly paycheck and…"

Cheers override his voice again.

President Franklin Delano Roosevelt is a familiar name in the Hartman household. His every speech dominates their small rooms. Her parents hang onto every word, speak of him, almost with reverence. Jolene has never heard them talk that way about any other. She also listens to the President's speeches, not understanding a word of it, but likes how his voice sounds. She feels like the President is talking directly to her. That, her mother says, is some of FDR's magic. He makes people feel special and safe.

"Like Eddie?" asks Jolene.

Liz sighs, looks at Dan, and shakes her head.

Christmas is coming.

Liz and Dan decide to splurge and buy a tree since it's the first time they've been together as a family in their own place. Jolene is beside herself with excitement.

What an adventure, shopping for a tree, as the three of them pushed through row after row of pungent-smelling fir trees. Liz protests over the prices. Dan bargains. The choice is made. Jolene cannot hide her disappointment. Such a tiny tree. Hardly more than a large branch. Seeing her disappointment, Dan tells her, "It will be magical, Jolene, I promise."

He sets up a card table at home and places two light bulbs into a holder underneath it; one blue and one red. Then, he throws a white bed sheet over the table. Putting the tiny tree on top of the sheet, he hands Jolene a box of tinsel, the one luxury they allowed themselves. His enthusiasm engulfs Jolene and Liz. They laugh and joke as they place each silver strand after another on the few sparse branches. Finishing in a few moments, they stand back. The little tree still looks tiny, sad.

"It doesn't look magical to me, Daddy!" Jolene whimpers, on the verge of tears. She remembers the beautiful McPhierson trees, glittering with handmade ornaments, sparkling lights topped with a porcelain angel. And Uncle Arthur's giant tree reaching up to the ceiling.

"Let's pop some corn, Jolene," Liz suggests, trying to maintain the rare family unity they've been feeling. "I'll teach you how to string it. Then we'll put it on the tree. That'll make it more festive."

"Good idea, Liz!"

While they work in the kitchen, Dan makes adjustments under the table. After finishing, he turns off the overhead light and flicks a switch. The darkened room fills with flickering red and blue shafts of light shimmering off the tinsel. Pleased, he calls out for them to join him.

Standing in the doorway, mouths open, their faces show disbelief, then extreme pleasure. This time, Dan has kept his promise. The tree, and their small living room, have become magical. Jolene rushes to Dan, throws her arms around him, and gushes, "Oh, thank you, Daddy! Thank you! It's the most beautiful tree in the whole world."

Christmas arrives.

Jolene opens her presents in the morning. There is a paper doll cutout from her parents, an envelope containing a dollar bill from Uncle Reuben, a handkerchief stitched by Auntie Emma, a hand-painted mirror from Auntie Lottie and Uncle Arthur, and a snow-filled glass paperweight from Aunt Pola.

"I wish I could meet Aunt Pola someday, Daddy. Is she ever coming here?"

"Only God and ole Rivka know," he responds.

"That was some Christmas, Jolene," Liz comments. "You like your presents?"

Jolene hugs Liz. Her mother doesn't hug back. Then she embraces her father. "Ooh, yes! Thank you! Thank you so much. Can we cut out the paper doll now?"

"Sure," says Liz.

"Not yet," Dan tells them. "Wait a minute." He leaves the room and goes outside. A few moments later, he hands Jolene a shoebox with a lid. Inside the box, there is the sound of rustling.

Tentatively, Jolene lifts the lid and squeals, "Ooh, Daddy! A baby duckling!"

"A baby what!" screams Liz, giving Dan a dirty look.

"It'll be company, Liz. You'll see. Make her more responsible."

"It'll crap all over the place."

"I'll make a cage."

"Sometimes, I think you need a cage."

And the bickering escalates. Too engrossed with her new pet, Jolene is oblivious to the fighting as she picks up the yellow ball of fluff and gushes, "This is the best Christmas ever!" Being careful not to squash her precious cargo, Jolene hugs both of them again. Despite her misgivings, Liz is caught up in Jolene's delight. This child, her daughter, made happy with so little. Just a tiny yellow duckling, a duckling she names Oscar (not knowing the duck is a female).

Both parents' predictions come true.

Oscar does dirty the carpet and everything else she waddles over.

And Jolene does become more responsible, cleaning up after her.

Chapter Eleven
1937

Jolene lets herself in. "Hi! I'm home! Anybody here?" Always hopeful, never greeted.

Her daily ritual begins.

First, she pours a glass of milk. Then, she chants "Eenie Meenie" to decide between graham crackers and cookies. Making a choice, she takes the snack outside, sits on the back porch stoop, and begins talking to Oscar.

"Hi, Oscar. Want to know what I did at school today?"

Oscar ruffles her wings and repeatedly quacks in greeting.

"Good! Well, I," a pause then more happy quacking as she runs through her day, telling Oscar her innermost thoughts and feelings, slipping bits of the cracker to her attentive audience, who quickly gobbles them up as she talks.

Snack finished. Time to clean cage, put fresh water, hold Oscar, cover her with kisses. Now it's time to walk. Attaching a leash to the duck's collar, it's out and onto the street as Oscar quacks her expectations.

Walking…walking…Oscar quacking, past the older man's garden, now with radishes. Jolene checks to see if he's home, doesn't see him, pulls a radish out of the ground. Giving the roots to Oscar, she eats the radish with glee and walks past the blackbird tree, undisturbed.

"Quack! Quack!" Flapping her wings, Oscar scares off an approaching dog, always protecting Jolene. Walking, walking to the corner. No people on the street, none. They cross the road and walk past Eddie's bungalow slowly toward the fenced, now empty schoolyard.

"Quack! Quack!" Oscar warns of an approaching car that slows and pulls alongside the curb, the motor still running. The driver of the vehicle is a middle-aged, balding white man. Leaning toward her, he calls out through the open car window, "Hey there, young lady! You know Diane Runyan?" He speaks softly, too softly for Jolene to understand.

"Diane, who?"

The man poses the question again, even softer. Jolene looks confused and responds, "Didn't get the name, sorry!"

In a louder voice, the man calls out, "Come closer, closer, so you can hear me."

Jolene steps close to the car and leans on the open window.

"Do you know where Diane Runyan lives?" he repeats. "She likes to play with this." He glances down.

Jolene follows his gaze, stares, transfixed. He holds what looks like Daddy's toy in his hand, but much bigger, much bigger, almost like a giant snake, waving back and forth, back and forth.

Frightened, she screams, starts to pull away, but can't. She can't because he grabbed her hair and arm and held on tightly, trying to yank her through the open car window. She continues to scream, scratching at his hands, trying to resist.

"Quack! Quack!" Oscar flaps her wings as she runs in circles, squawking her agitation, as she continues to rage, trying to protect Jolene, "Quack! Quack! Quack!"

Hearing the commotion, Eddie emerges from his bungalow, sees what is happening, runs back in, and returns, shotgun in hand.

Seeing Eddie, the man lets go of Jolene. Falling to the sidewalk, she sobs as the car shoots forward, Oscar pecking at her to see if she's okay.

Eddie aims his gun at the moving vehicle. A loud blast. One tire is gone. The car skids momentarily, then weaves down the street, tire flapping. Regaining control, the man straightens the careening car and continues down the road out of sight.

Scooping Jolene into his comforting arms, Eddie soothes her tears and fears, reassuring her that the man will never return, never harm her. Never! And he, Eddie, will be there to protect her. Always.

Calming Oscar, who is still agitated, Eddie takes both of them home and waits 'til Liz arrives. After he and Jolene tell the story, Liz and Dan are ever so grateful that their daughter has a friend, such a good friend as Eddie, and ever so thankful that Eddie has a shotgun.

Almost every Saturday night is poker night.

The players are Liz, Dan, Liz's brothers, and their wives. Reuben also has a bride, an odd lady named Anne, whose high-pitched voice drives them crazy. Reuben and Anne had what her mother described as a "shotgun" wedding. No one ever took the time to explain what that meant. Jolene does know that the baby cousin she was told she would have never appeared.

Saturday night poker games bore Dan.

They are the highlights of Liz's week because her brothers are her best friends and the only people she can trust, especially Marcus.

Always her best friend next to Barbara, Marcus gave vent to Liz's daring side. He shared dirty jokes and taught her how to smoke, drink, and swim in the ocean.

Some of Liz's happiest memories of her youth were spent with Marcus, riding on the back of his motorcycle to Venice beach, where they could smell the salty crush of sea air, blocks before they'd arrive. Once there, they'd spend hours swimming back and forth beyond crashing waves. The only time they came out of the water was to eat. They'd wait the designated hour before they re-entered, taunting each other, wrestling, and laughing, then race back into the surf. There they'd stay until it was time to towel off and return home.

Pals, Liz, and her brother were. She even lied for him sometimes. Like the day they came home with bloody scratches on their arms and a massive bump on their forehead. She lied that day to their mother.

"A wave threw us into the pier!" she told an upset Sarah. "Barnacles cut us."

Not knowing what barnacles were, Sarah put iodine on their injured arms, an ice pack on her head, told them to be more careful, and that was that.

But the events of that day bonded sister and brother for life because a wave hadn't caused her injuries. No! It had been a wall, a brick wall.

Marcus had drunk one too many beers before they left the beach that day. Driving too fast, he had lost control of his bike, and they'd run smack into a brick wall. Liz was thrown to the ground and knocked unconscious. Several minutes had gone by before she'd opened her eyes. When she saw Marcus's look of concern and gratitude, she knew he'd be there for her always, and she for him.

Jolene doesn't have much fun when poker games are at Marcus's house. The reason is that she has to play with her cousins. She gets along okay with

Selma, the older one, but Alicia, born six months before Jolene, is a different story.

A beautiful child, graceful and delicate with her father's quick and sometimes cruel wit, Alicia's idea of play is to taunt Jolene.

"How come you have only two dresses, Jolene? Are giants like you hard to fit?" Jumping up and down on a bed, Alicia would squeal with laughter.

Alicia attacks again if Jolene pretends not to hear and doesn't react.

"Why is your hair so stringy, Jolene? You so poor, Auntie Liz can't buy you a hairbrush?" Again, shouts of laughter.

Jolene runs from the room when it becomes too much and snuggles under Dan's arm. Trying not to cry, she pretends to be interested in the game.

"What's wrong, baby?"

"Nothing."

"Then go back and play."

"Don't want to!"

"What is it?"

"Alicia's mean."

Liz doesn't like the game interrupted. "She's just teasing, Jolene. Ignore her. Let us have some fun. Okay?"

"Okay! Okay!"

Later that night, cousin Alicia is the subject of the conversation as Reuben drives them home.

"She's got Marcus's wit," Liz comments from the back seat where she sits, and Jolene lies, her head in her lap. Liz continues, "Alicia's so lovely, too, with a great personality. She's got everything going for her, that's for sure."

Dan adds, "You're not kidding, Liz, sitting in the passenger seat. She's a beauty. Bet she'll be a movie star or something when she grows up."

Reuben nods his head in agreement but says nothing.

Looking down at Jolene, Liz sighs and says, "Isn't it a shame Jolene's so, so...awkward?"

"She'll grow out of it," Dan defends.

Reuben comments, "Ugly ducklings grow into beautiful swans sometimes, Liz!"

"Sure! Sure!" Liz retorts, looks down again, "...and dollar bills grow on Christmas trees, too!"

Even Dan joins in the mirth that engulfs the occupants of the car.

No one notices the silent tears rolling down Jolene's cheeks because no one knows she's been listening to the entire conversation.

But poker games at Jolene's house are a different story. She loves Saturday night poker games at her house for two reasons. First, her cousins don't come. They stay with Aunt Emma's parents. Second, she feels important because she gets to be the banker. For a quarter, she gives each player four dollars' worth of chips. Raises are limited to a quarter. On a really good night, winners can win a whole dollar. Or, if luck is down, they can lose up to two.

Jolene watches the game and learns.

She can tell when someone bluffs and learns to keep a straight face while peeking at their hands. She even becomes a good-luck charm if she sits or stands behind one of them when they have a winning hand. Jolene is so integrated into the Saturday night poker games at her house that she's even the butt of some of their jokes.

"That little 'broken rubber' of yours has a nice spring," Marcus comments when Jolene jumps up from her chair to retrieve a dropped chip.

Everyone roars, including Jolene, feeling essential and very grown-up, even though she still has no idea what a 'broken rubber' is.

Saturday night poker games at her house are just about perfect. Except when she's threatened with an early bedtime.

"Gimme a Coke, Jolene!"

"Get the pretzels, Lil 'broken rubber'!"

"Need more peanuts…"

"I'm outta ice, girl! Fetch! Fetch!"

Laughter.

Sometimes Jolene balks, "How come I have to say 'Please' when I want something, and no one says it to me?"

"Don't smart mouth, Jolene!"

"I'm not, Mommy…I just wanna know why—"

"Another word, and it's bedtime for you!"

And so she shuts up.

Poker nights at her house are just about perfect, a good balance for her unpleasant experiences on some mornings before leaving for school.

On weekdays Liz awakens, puts the coffee on, then wakes up Dan. As soon as he gets out of bed, he grabs a crossword puzzle and pencil, enters the bathroom, and shuts the door. Then Liz wakes up Jolene. After she puts away her bedding, splashes water on her face, and brushes her teeth at the kitchen sink, Jolene puts on the dress she will wear all week unless she accidentally gets it dirty. Then, she sits down at the table, dreading the spoonful of cod liver oil Liz offers to her before she eats her breakfast.

"Protects you from all ills," Liz reminds her daily.

The orange juice is gulped down quickly to eliminate the oil taste. Then Jolene drinks her milk, eats a slice of toast, and plays with her cooked cereal. Frequently, she glances toward the bathroom door, "Gotta go, Mommy."

"He'll be out soon," Liz reassures her as she busies herself with dishes and lunch preparation.

Squirming, "Ask him, Mommy. Please!"

"Hold on, Jolene. It won't be long now."

"Please!"

"Kid's got to use the bathroom, Dan," Liz yells at the closed door. No answer. Jolene gets up and knocks on the door. "Gotta go, Daddy. Please!"

They hear the sound of flushing, yet no answer, no open door.

Jolene pleads, "Daddy, please, please!"

Still no answer.

Screams out, "Daddy! Gotta go!"

"Don't shout at me," Dan responds behind the closed door. "I'll be out when I'm out."

Liz hollers back, "Give the kid a break, Dan! She's only human." Then softer to Jolene, "Hold it in, Jolene. He'll be out soon."

Squirming, Jolene sits, experiences stomach cramps, shows tears of frustration. Clasping her arms across her belly, she begs, "Pleeeease, Daddy!"

Flushing sounds again, still no open door.

Frustrated, Jolene doubles over, face scrunched in pain, jumps up in anguish. "Can't hold it, Mommy. Can't!"

"Oh, for God's sake." Taking her daughter's hand, she rushes her to the back porch, hands her a yellow bucket, and swears, "Damn! Damn!"

Mortified, Jolene pulls down her pants, squats over the bucket, cries, "Sorry, Mommy. Sorry."

Dan emerges from the bathroom, sees them on the back porch, reacts in disgust. "Christ, Jolene! I told you I was coming out. Even animals know better than to crap in the kitchen. When are you going to grow up? Get a little self-discipline?"

Too angry to respond, Liz carries the bucket to the bathroom when Jolene finishes. Pouring the contents into the toilet, she flushes it and calls out, "Come here, Jolene. Get some paper. Clean yourself up."

Embarrassed and still sobbing, Jolene holds her dress high above her head to keep from soiling it. She hates her smell, herself, the yellow bucket, the ever-present yellow bucket.

Dan leaves the room.

"Sorry, Mommy. Sorry."

"Oh, stop saying you're sorry, Jolene. It's not your fault. When you gotta go, you gotta go, that's all."

Jolene wipes herself and flushes the toilet. Liz pats her on the head. Grateful, her mother isn't mad at her; she wraps around Liz's legs. Disengaging herself from the tearful child, Liz tells her to wash her hands and takes the bucket to the back porch.

Water is heard as Liz says, "Took me years to control my bowels, Jolene. Years! And I did such a good job of it that I'm constipated all the time now. All the time." She laughs bitterly. "You're lucky, kiddo! We didn't even have a yellow bucket in my house when I grew up. Not one damn bucket. Just one lousy bathroom, and one inconsiderate father, just like yours." She re-enters the kitchen.

"Wish we were rich like Uncle Arthur and Uncle Marcus," Jolene says wistfully. "Then we could have two bathrooms as they do."

"How true, how true," Liz agrees, thinking how much easier life would be if...

Then she sighs with resignation as she thinks how ironic her life has become, from wanting to become somebody to wanting two bathrooms!

In his way, though, Dan is a good father.

He teaches Jolene more involved board games: checkers, Monopoly, Chinese checkers. He teaches her so well that she even beats him sometimes. She also learns about the world when she helps him with his stamp collection.

"This country doesn't exist anymore, Jolene. See!" he tells her. And they search for it on the map.

Dan is usually right. Even though he only had a fifth-grade education, he knows many things, but not enough about anything to be good at something.

He's also a perpetual storyteller, filling her head with fantasies and promises he rarely keeps.

Like when he shows her a stamp and tells her not to touch it, stressing its great value.

"This stamp is worth a lot, Jolene," he'd say. "Someday, this collection is going to be worth a fortune."

"What's a fortune?"

"A lot of money. Enough to buy a car. To buy you a different dress for each day. Maybe two dresses a day. And a coat. A coat with fur around the collar. And shoes. Shoes to go with every dress."

"With these ugly heels?"

"No! Not with ugly heels. Pretty shoes."

"But, Daddy! Where would I put all the clothes and shoes? We only have one closet."

"Dan! Stop filling the child's head with garbage."

"Liz. If you don't dream it, it doesn't happen! We'll buy a house, Jolene. A brick house with a winding brick path leading up to it. There will be colored flowers on each side of the path. The house will have crisscrossed windows all over the front. It'll be two stories, have three bedrooms! And each bedroom will have two closets. Will that be enough room for your clothes and your shoes?"

He laughs at her wide-eyed expression as she nods, picturing her room with two closets.

"Daddy?"

"What?"

"Will we have two bathrooms?"

"Two!" bellows Dan. "No! Not two!"

Disappointment floods her face.

"Not two bathrooms, Jolene! Our house will have three bathrooms! One for each of us!"

She throws herself at him. "Oh, it's perfect, Daddy. Just perfect."

Involved in her endless household chores, Liz looks at them and mumbles under her breath.

"Three bathrooms! What a joke. We'll be lucky if we have enough money to get out of this dump, let alone have three bathrooms."

When Eve works, Dan takes Jolene to the new Observatory in Griffith Park after playing 'Little Mommy.' It is there he dreams and shares his special place with her. Peering through a giant telescope, he speaks to her of the future, about things he reads about in science fiction magazines when he hangs out at the local barbershop.

"Someday, men will fly machines with blades above them, Jolene. They'll land on top of buildings, in parking lots, everywhere!"

And they sit and wonder about such things, peering down at Hollywood, picturing machines with blades landing on top of those buildings, in parking lots, everywhere.

"Policemen will talk to each other through wristwatches, Jolene," Dan continues. "They'll talk into things called walkie-talkies. There'll be spaceships, rocket ships, and someday, Jolene, men will even live on the moon."

Mouth open, she believes every word he says as they stare up at the sky and search for the moon, even though it's daylight. Imagine men living on the moon.

Slipping her hand into his, Jolene knows she has the best father.

Jolene isn't the only one who thinks Dan is the best father. The twins never knew their father. So they agree wholeheartedly with Jolene, especially when he entertains them, whistling songs or making bird calls. They giggle, laugh, tell Jolene how lucky she is. Clapping and shouting, they beg him, "More! More!" causing him to remember...

How he used to stand on street corners, the Regina snow up to his knees. He was just a couple of years older than Jolene, whistling bird calls and popular songs and doing a few dance steps. Hoping people would clap and reward him, shivering, smiling, performing. And saying his thanks if someone dropped a coin into the can at his feet. Sometimes he'd earn as much as 15 cents a day.

Once, he won second prize in a radio show contest, whistling, imitating bird calls while drinking a glass of water. His award was a dollar, a whole silver dollar. He didn't get to keep the money. It went to ole Rivka. But the applause, that rewarding sound of applause in the auditorium. That was his. His forever! He could still hear that applause bouncing off the walls, the ceiling, surrounding him, filling him.

He knew it would happen again when he got to Hollywood, to America. He'd become famous, be applauded again, be somebody.

Instead, when Dan arrived in America, he went to work for his brother and became a runner (one of the guys who picks up bets people make on the horse races). Instead of being the successful businessman that he presented to his Canadian family, Arthur (his fancy, high-living brother) was nothing more than a bookie. Arthur made a lot of money. And the people who worked for him did okay, too, including Dan. Dan had bought expensive suits, smoked Havana cigars, and had money in his pocket in a couple of years. He could wine, dine, and dance the evenings away with women of his choice. And he did, almost every night.

It was a great life until the night Dan didn't 'run' fast enough. Arrested, he spent the night in jail. That experience terrified him and caused him to do some serious thinking. Being put in prison wasn't why he had come to America. Not to be a runner for a bookie, either, even if it was his brother. Dan had dreams. In jail that night, he made a decision. Arthur understood when he told him he was quitting and even got him some work at Paramount Studios as an extra.

Dan appeared in several films in the next few years. There were 13 jobs as an extra and three walk-ons. He was in heaven, being on a studio lot, being part of the Hollywood scene. That was what he'd always dreamed of, where he belonged. Dan loved show business, the excitement, drama, beautiful young starlets. But the excitement and dreams didn't pay the bills. And they were mounting as he wined and dined the starlets. Trying to supplement his income, he worked odd jobs. As always, they were hard to come by. In short order, he was broke. Bill collectors were knocking at his door. There was no choice. Dan went back to work for his brother again.

Then something happened that changed all their lives.

Betting became legal.

Arthur stopped being a bookie and started bankrolling motion pictures. It was still gambling but legitimate. It wasn't too long before Dan's brother had a new career as a flourishing motion picture producer. Now, he and Lottie were living the high life.

Dan continued to be a 'runner' for Arthur, but it was a different job at the studio.

His new duties require running errands instead of gathering bets. Now, he was called a 'gopher.' Embarrassed over the unimportance and title of his new job; Dan lied as he'd always done and told everyone he was a producer's assistant. In a way, though, it was the truth. He did 'assist' Arthur and everyone else on the set. Dan was indeed called upon, whether it was getting people bagels and cream cheese, lunch, coffee, cigarettes, or anything else they wanted all day.

"Go for this, Dan! Go for that! I want…"

But it didn't make any difference to Dan. He was happy just being on a movie set and earning a paycheck. He knew he'd be discovered, get a chance to 'be a star.'

In time, as always, Dan believed his own fabricated stories of the magical days he worked in the motion picture business.

Maybe Dan wasn't lucky with his jobs. But he sure didn't have trouble with women. With women, Dan was always a winner.

He'd see a woman he wanted, charm her, woo her, chase her, and seduce her. Once he won the chase, he'd walk away. It was the chase that excited him, then the conquest. He knew he pleased almost every woman, young or old, married or single. He could, and did, excite them, entice them, bring them ultimate satisfaction and then leave them before they became too clingy, too demanding. With women, Dan was the winner.

When Dan first saw Liz at the café, he knew this was a woman he wanted. She was different; Liz was. She was a challenge and voluptuous, yet part of her was dead. He wanted to re-awaken her, break down her walls, own her.

"Just call me Dan," he told her, doffing his Fedora.

"Why should I call you anything?"

"Because you're the woman I'm going to marry!"

No one laughed louder than Liz.

"You're mad!"

"Maybe! Find out tonight! A movie?"

"Thanks! But no thanks!"

"Why not?"

"I don't date short guys. And I hate red hair!"

Dan became a fixture in the café, showing up every day. On the odd day when he didn't appear, customers and waitresses missed him. Even Liz would look up expectantly each time the door opened.

Although she continued to say "No!" she enjoyed the attention but was annoyed at his possessiveness if a male customer slid his hand along her hip or buttocks. It was just part of the job as far as she was concerned. She'd remove the hand, make some joke and accept a generous tip.

But Dan stopped all that. Furious if anyone touched her, he'd blow a fuse, tell the guy off, no matter how big or small he was. In time no one touched her. No one.

In time, she finally said "Yes!" to a first date, a first kiss, his seduction, his lust, awakening hers…

"I don't want kids, Dan!"

"You're the first woman I've met who's practical, Liz."

"Good! We agree, then!"

"Right!"

Liz proved to be his most incredible seduction and his biggest mistake. Six months went by. Dan surprised himself and everyone who knew him. He was still with her, wanted her company, her body. Still trying to break down her wall, he wanted her to care for him, not just his lovemaking.

He heard himself say 'I love you!' and mean it for the first time.

"Don't, Dan. Don't!"

"Tell me, Liz. You love me too, don't you?"

"It's not in the cards, Dan!"

"Say it!"

"What difference does it make if I do?"

"A lot!"

"Then I do! I do! There! Does that make you feel better? Are you happy now? You have permission to quit, to go chase the next one."

"Cut it out, Liz!"

"Oh, come on, Dan! Everyone knows you take off once you conquer. Okay! You've conquered! Now go!"

Instead of going, he proposed.

They were married by a justice of the peace, and their honeymoon was an afternoon at the Orpheum Theater downtown. They were so engrossed in their lovemaking that they missed most of the double features and vaudeville acts performed that day.

Reality set in when they returned to the Sorkin's to sleep on the pull-out couch in the living room.

Sarah was beside herself.

Living under her roof and not married by a Rabbi? Sinners they were! In her eyes and the eyes of God!

"Ach, Poo! Poo!" she cried out daily, trying to ward off the evil spirits she was sure they had brought into her household. The frequency and sounds of their sexual desire drove Sarah crazy. She prayed, nagged, and ranted at them to have a Jewish wedding. To stop her harassment, they relented. In the third month of their marriage, a Rabbi re-married them under a canopy in the Sorkin living room, with immediate family members attending.

This blissful physical desire blinded them to their financial condition and inconvenient lodging for another three months until…

Liz felt a burst of heat in her vagina.

Angrily she pushed him away. "Damn you!" she screamed. "You told me you were protected!"

"I was. I am. I…I don't know what happened!"

"Well?"

He examined the condom and paled. "The rubber. The damn rubber split, right down the middle."

"You can go to hell! You and your broken rubber!"

Chapter Twelve
1938

Liz and Dan are miserable, but hundreds of thousands of Angelinos are unhappy, too, due to the destruction caused by the worst flood in the history of the City of Angels.

On March's first and second days, two storms released their fury, dumping almost 14 inches of rain on L.A. The Los Angeles River, which meandered haphazardly throughout the City of Angels from the San Fernando Valley to Long Beach, became so swollen that its banks overflowed. The floodwaters destroyed bridges, cars, homes, crops, businesses, and oil fields. More than 115 people died.

L.A. had been flooded before in 1914 and 1934, but never as bad as this. People were outraged and demanded that something be done. City fathers agreed, and that was the beginning of the concrete channeling of the L.A. River. During the next 20 years, contractors rerouted and retrofitted the entire 278 miles of river and its tributaries and built 300 bridges using 3.35 million barrels of cement, 147 million pounds of steel, and placed 460,000 tons of stones.

Dan's hardly home now. "Working!" he tells them.

Evenings, his meal sits on the table waiting. When he does come home, Liz doesn't ask where he's been. She doesn't want to know. She screams more and is apt to slap Jolene with little provocation.

One night Dan shows up late carrying presents; for Jolene, a lace hair bow, and Liz, her favorite, a box of chocolate-covered cherries.

When he hands her the bow, Jolene tries to put it on in her baby-fine hair. No matter how many times she tries, the bow slips off.

"A hair bow! Candy! Why Dan?" snaps Liz. "We hardly have enough money to buy the lousy orthopedic shoes Jolene needs. Why this?"

Ignoring her, Dan questions Jolene. "Can't you say thank you? Show your appreciation?"

"What's appreciation?"

"It means you're glad someone gave you a gift."

"Well, I'm not glad," she exclaims, bursting into tears. "I'd rather have nothing than pretend I like something when I don't! And I don't like this stupid bow!"

"The two of you," Dan explodes. "You're too much! Her sniveling! You always screaming every time you're on the rag. It seems like you're always on the rag lately!"

"That's right," Liz yells. "Lay the blame on us. Like I don't know what you're doing, where you've been."

"Reuben call you?"

Jolene runs outside yet can still hear her parents arguing as she gathers Oscar in her arms and tells her they're going for a walk. Oscar quacks her delight at the unexpected outing.

"I don't need Reuben to show me lipstick stains!" Liz screams. "To get rid of cheap, stinking perfume on your clothes!"

"Tone it down, Liz!"

"Don't you tell me what to do," yells Liz as she bursts into tears.

Jolene hears her mother's sobbing and her father's consoling words, "Don't cry, Liz," as she puts the leash around Oscar's neck and escapes to the street.

Later, Jolene leads Oscar to her cage, kissing her repeatedly on her beak, then lingering in the safety of her feathers as she mumbles, "I love you so much, Oscar. Do you love me?"

Oscar angles her head as though she understands, quacks, rubs her beak against Jolene's cheek, then waddles into her cage.

Entering the kitchen, her parents are no longer fighting. The only sounds she now hears are her mother's moans coming from behind the closed bedroom door, accompanied by the familiar squeaks of the mattress, and the steady bumping, bumping, bumping against the wall.

Sitting silent, Jolene eats her cold dinner and waits, knowing her parents will come out soon, and her mother won't cry anymore, for a while, anyway. And she also knows that her Daddy will come home for dinner at night, for a time anyway.

Usually, Jolene goes to the Adams' place after school. She is like family now. She helps them fold clothes, plays with the twins, sings, dances to Herman's music, and often has dinner with them. Meals at their house are highlights of her life. She smells what Gram is cooking when they enter the stairwell and walk down the third-floor hallway; collards, tart at first, sweetened with honey; crunchy fried chicken, squirting when bitten into; hominy grits, smashed smooth as mashed potatoes; or sweet potato pie. Jolene's mouth waters even before she gets to the door.

The Adams family shares everything with her. It doesn't make any difference how little they have.

"Hollow leg," Gramma Adams nicknames her. "If I didn't know better, I'd swear you was black, lil gal. Havin' all that rhythm and such an appetite."

The family laughs and tease, laughing harder when they see her blush.

Liz's feelings are mixed about Jolene spending so much time with the Adams family, eating their food. She's grateful her daughter has friends, someplace to go when she's working, but still... She knows how little money they have and so many mouths to feed.

"Jolene! There's plenty of food here. You don't have to mooch at the twins so often," she reminds her daughter.

"They don't mind. I don't like eating alone. Besides, it's more fun there. And..."

"All right. All right. Drop it!"

Liz resolves her conscience another way. She brings boxes or bags of leftovers home from work for Jolene to share with her friends. They enjoy day-old strudel, doughnuts, a chocolate cake, apple pie, or bagels, some so hard they are broken with a hammer.

"They'd just throw the stuff out if someone didn't take it," she says, shrugging off Marm's thanks.

It's Sunday again.

Liz is in the kitchen, cooking for the week.

"Can I help?"

"It's easier when I do it myself, Jolene."

"Can't I do something?"

"Yes! You can stop pestering me."

Ignoring her mother's warning, Jolene picks up a bowl of peas. She drops several on the floor, trying to shell them like she's seen her mother do.

"Jolene!" Liz grabs the bowl from her.

Sulking, Jolene wanders out of the room.

"Want to play checkers?" she asks Dan, who is doing a crossword puzzle.

"When I finish this," he doesn't look up.

"When's that?"

"When I finish."

Jolene looks. He has just started.

She drapes on the arm of his chair and asks, "Why are Jews God's chosen people?"

"Who told you that?"

"Preacher Buncie."

"Little he knows."

"Marm says Preacher Buncie knows just about *every*thing. Says Jews are special 'cause God said so."

"Everyone to his own opinion."

"So, why are Jews special?"

Dan shoves the pencil over his ear, showing displeasure.

"Jews are special, all right, Jolene! They're special targets for every miserable gentile in the world. Jews are so special, they can't get work, can't get into schools. Yeah! Jews really are God's chosen people. God chose us to take crap every time we turn around!"

Surprised by her father's outburst, Jolene still doesn't understand. "But why…?"

He picks up his pencil and writes in a word. "Enough, Jolene. Enough! Find something to do."

She wanders back to the kitchen, "Can I go to church with the twins?"

"Why?"

"Marm says I can. Anytime. Can I go? Can I…"

"Go! Go!"

A hand-painted, stained-glass window showers occupants with ever-changing light in this small converted store. A choir sings, shouts, and claps their hands in the front. Gram Adams sits in the second row, one of the most enthusiastic singers.

Some of the congregation sways as they clap in rhythm. Jolene is one of these. The only white face in the room, Jolene, shows her enjoyment of the moment by clapping and shouting louder than anyone.

But she, and everyone else, become frightened if Preacher Buncie points his finger at one of them and accuses them of being a sinner. The accused presses against the unyielding wooden pew and begs forgiveness, saying anything to get the Preacher's accusatory finger to point elsewhere.

"Yes, yes, Lord. I've sinned, sinned! Oh, Jesus, forgive me, forgive me!"

Satisfied, Preacher Buncie will move on, find another victim, another sinner, and point that long finger. In his eyes, everyone is a sinner.

Later, during his sermon, Preacher Buncie shouts out, "We're all one, you sinners! One color under the skin. All people are the same. Black!"

"If you want to live in the glorious Temple of the Lord, you've got to repent your sins. Repent! Because all good folks who follow Jesus will live in the Temple of the Lord!"

"Hallelujah!"

"Sinners, hear me! If you want to meet up with good colored folks, you gotta repent, you hear. Repent!"

"Repent! Repent!"

"Repent, and you'll live in the Temple of the Lord!"

"In the Temple of the Lord!"

"Where all good folks is one color."

"One color!"

"Black! Black, you hear me. Black! All good folks is black as the night sky. There is black, black, under lily-white skin, yeller skin! Black!"

The congregation goes wild, moaning and swaying. "Hallelujah, dear Jesus! Hallelujah! We good black folk are saved, dear Jesus. Saved!"

"One color?" Puzzled, Jolene turns to Flora.

Flora shrugs.

After church, Jolene questions Marm, "Why does Preacher Buncie say we're all one color, Marm?"

"Preacher means all folks is special, Jolene. In the eyes of the Lord."

"Is everyone black, like Preacher says? Even me?"

Marm laughs, "Specially you, lil gal. Specially you!"

"Why?"

"Cause you're so nosy. Askin' questions all the time."

Confused, Jolene looks disappointed.

Laughing, Marm pats Jolene's head with affection. "I'll bet my boots yore skin's black as coal 'neath those lil brown spots," she says, tapping the freckles splayed across Jolene's nose.

The twins follow suit. They tap Jolene's nose like their mother did, then run away. Jolene chases after them, shouting, "I'm a good black folk, too. I'm a good black folk, too. And I'm going to live in the Lord's Temple! Amen!"

Jolene arrives home after school the next day, lets herself in, begins her daily ritual, then stops. Instead of going outside to Oscar, she stares at the freckles sprinkled over her arm.

"Kisses of the sun," her mother calls them.

"Why does the sun kiss me more than other kids?"

"Guess the sun loves you more, Jolene."

"Do you love me as much as the sun?"

"Find something to do!"

And the conversation ends, never with the answer, Jolene wants to hear.

Jolene touches a freckle on her arm and wonders, am I really black?

She begins to dig at the freckle with her fingernail. It hurts! The skin reddens, a welt appears. She explores another freckle with the same result. There is more pain, reddening, another bruise. Disappointed, she rubs her arm. Searching through a drawer, she removes a knife, scratches at a freckle with it, experiences more pain, another welt. Not to be daunted, she pulls out a breadboard and lays her arm flat on the board the way she's seen her mother do with an uncooked chicken. Lifting the knife high in the air, she chops down at a freckle on her arm…

"Aaaaaaiiiiiiiiiiiiiii!"

Blood! Bright red blood squirts everywhere.

Shrieking, Jolene runs from the house to the comforting arms of Marm.

Cleaning the wound, Marm sends one of the twins to a neighbor who has a phone to let Liz know what happened.

After Liz arrives, Jolene tries to block the blows her near-hysterical mother rains on her, not hearing her explanation of why she did it. Liz repeatedly strikes out, so engulfed is she in memories of her mother's death.

That horrible scene flashes again and again in Liz's mind. Her mother's suicide. The overwhelming smell of gas. The unforgettable vision of Sarah. The open oven door. Her mother, Sarah, when she killed herself. And now her daughter is trying to do the same thing. Too much. Too much.

"No! No! It can't happen again. No! I won't let it. No!" Furious, overwhelmed, she continues to strike the cowering child.

In time Marm calms Liz, sits her down, and reasons with her. "It was jus a small cut, Miz Liz. Got fixed up right away. Such an inquisitive lil gal, that one is, thass all. Just has to know everything. She meant no harm. No harm at all."

"But why, Jolene? Why? Why would you do something so stupid?" Liz repeatedly asks, still not believing the explanation her child gives.

When she finally understands, Liz shakes her head in disbelief. Holding her daughter at arm's length, she tells her, "Promise me, Jolene, that you'll never do anything so stupid again. Promise! Promise me!"

"I promise! I promise!"

Most nights, Jolene sleeps first in her parent's bed, then later, when they're ready for bed, one of them carries her to the couch. To Jolene's surprise, Liz holds her long and tight, tighter than she can ever remember, before tucking her in and turning out the light. At the door, she reminds her to say her prayers.

"I will, Mommy. I promise!"

Lights off, the door closes. Jolene climbs out of bed and kneels to pray, as she learned at the McPhiersons, not in bed the way Liz instructs her.

She begins her nightly prayer, "Now I lay me down to sleep. I pray the Lord my soul to keep. If I should die before I wake…I pray the Lord, my soul, to take. God bless…" and she blesses everyone she knows, especially Oscar. Her prayer finished, Jolene climbed into bed and began her nightly conversation with God.

"God! Why was I born? Mommy and Daddy don't want me. They have each other. Why was I born?"

Waiting, she receives no answer, unknowingly repeating the actions of her mother and grandmother. Then she giggles and looks up toward heaven.

"Well, I guess you're not going to talk to me tonight, but thank you anyway, dear Lord. Thank you for making me black!"

She knows she is black. She knows because she looked underneath the bandage on her arm when she got ready for bed. She saw black, right where the knife had cut into her skin. There was deep, dark, black blood. Underneath her skin, she is black. Black! Black! Marm was right. She, Jolene Hartman, is black. She's just like the twins. Black as coal. Black as Eddie. Preacher was right. Everyone is black under the skin. Even white folks, and yellow folks, he'd said.

Happy and pleased with herself, Jolene hugs her bandaged arm until she falls asleep, thrilled with her new secret. Her discovery that she is black. For the first time since leaving the McPhiersons, she has a sense of belonging again.

It is Jolene's seventh birthday.

An outing is planned, and the twins are included. They sit across from Liz and Dan, riding a trolley downtown. With eyes wide and expectations high, the three seven-year-olds pop gum, a birthday treat. They chew, pop bubbles, giggle, and tease all the way downtown.

As they disembark, Dan warns them, "Stay together!"

Grabbing hands, they are swept along by a pushing, pressing crowd. Pushed, pressing, shoved toward barricaded 24th Street, open only to pedestrian traffic. The sea of humanity continues to plow forward, block by block, until they can no longer move forward and are stopped by an unmoving human wall lining Flower Street across from Children's Hospital, where a band plays.

"Oooooooooh!"

"Aaaaahhhhh!"

Wild clapping. Laughter.

In the middle of the street, elephants, clowns, jugglers, ladies in sparkling costumes atop horses.

Eyes wide, Jolene asks, "What is it?"

"A circus. The Al G. Barnes Circus," Dan tells her.

"What's it doing here? Where are we?"

"We're at Children's Hospital. Since those children across the street can't go to the big tent to see the circus, it comes to them each year." Dan points across the street.

Jolene looks. Groups of children watch with enthusiasm, though many are in wheelchairs or crutches. Some children are being held in the arms of staff members. Others lean into, what Jolene assumes, are their parents. Becoming upset, she remembers her hospital stay, the metal bars, the isolation.

"Do the children…do they have to stay there forever?"

Sensing her discomfort and not wanting to ruin the birthday outing, Liz makes light of it, "No! No, Jolene. Not long. Most of them go right home."

"Good!"

When the circus ends, they walk back toward the trolley.

Jolene holds onto Liz's hand. "This was the best birthday, Mommy. The best!"

Liz says, "It was fun, wasn't it?" Unexpectedly, she bends down and kisses Jolene on top of her head.

Overcome, Jolene begins to skip. She can't remember being so happy, sharing this special day with Mommy and Daddy and her best friends.

Dan and Liz hold hands, watching with pleasure as Jolene and the twins joke around, laugh, and giggle all the way back to the trolley stop.

As they wait to board an approaching train, a young woman pushes her face into Dans.

"What a surprise, Dan! Didn't expect to see you in town this weekend."

Not another word, and she disappears.

"Even in front of your kid," Liz hisses to Dan.

His response is unheard, overpowered by the shrill whistle of the oncoming trolley.

They board and find seats. The trolley jerks them forward, yet no one speaks. The ride home is quiet. Dan looks out the window. Liz remains rigid, trying to stifle her anger. Jolene blows bubbles to distract the twins and tries to keep them from feeling the tension between her parents.

Reuben calls Liz at the café.

"He quit, Liz! Just like that. Dan asked for his paycheck and walked out. Just walked out. You okay, Liz? Liz?"

Silence, then only a buzzing…

When Jolene comes home from school that afternoon, she sees a blue convertible parked in front. Behind the wheel sits the same young woman from the trolley stop. The front door to their place is open.

Surprised, Jolene calls out, "I'm home. Anybody here?"

"In the bedroom, Jolene, in here!"

Dan slams a suitcase shut as she enters the bedroom.

"Thought I'd be gone before you got home, baby."

He sits on the bed and pats his knee. Jolene goes to him and sits on his lap.

"I'm going away for a while, Jolene. I'll call. We'll go to the observatory soon. And remember…Keep the boys at bay, baby. They're up to no good."

He wipes tears away from her face as he speaks, kisses the top of her head, and leaves.

Weeks go by.

When Liz isn't working, she cooks, cleans, or cries. Works, cleans and cries. Unknowingly, she is duplicating her mother's life without the prayers.

Jolene tries to ease her mother's sadness. She asks if she can help or if she wants to play games, even teases, anything to get her mother's attention. Nothing works, absolutely nothing.

Liz doesn't scream, doesn't slap, doesn't respond to anything. Life seems to hold too many burdens and hurts too much. She begins to understand why her mother took her own life. Sometimes life seems too harsh, so tough. And she wonders why she continues to go through the motions of living. But she's not a quitter like her mother was. She'll never quit.

"Mother was right after all," she tells Jolene between sobs as they pick at their dinners one night. "Girls are cursed! Cursed because men come into their lives."

"What's cursed mean?"

"You'll find out soon enough," she sighs, rising from the table, removing the dishes. "What does it matter anyway? Go to bed, Jolene. Remember your prayers."

"But it's so early…"

"No buts! Do it!"

Jolene brushes her teeth, removes her clothing, kneels next to the bed, and ends her prayers with… "And please, dear God, let Daddy come home soon so Mommy can stop crying. Amen!"

Overhearing her daughter's last request, Liz's crying increases.

That night, a strange sound shatters the stillness.

Jolene awakens and wonders what aroused her. Then there is nothing except an awful silence. Frightened, she runs into the bedroom and climbs into bed with Liz. "Mommy, Mommy! Did you hear it? Did you?"

Alarmed herself, Liz folds Jolene into her arms. "Yes! Yes, I heard it. Some kind of boom of something. Like a blast. I don't know what it was, Jolene. An earthquake, maybe. No! Seems different."

Pondering, curious, scared, they hold onto each other, wondering. The window shade reddens from an outside glow, and sirens can be heard, first at a distance, then coming closer and closer. The sirens are so loud; the frightening sounds fill their tiny bedroom as brakes screech to a stop. Not in front of their place, no, a short distance away. Voices are heard, muted at first, then shouts. Grabbing their robes, they rush outside to find out what's happening.

"Stay close," warns Liz.

Outside, people mill about.

"Lordy! Somethings burning!"

"Where?"

"Down there. End of the block."

A neighbor points. Liz and Jolene look.

"It's Eddie's house," Jolene cries out! Breaking from Liz's handclasp, she runs toward the glowing sky.

"No, Jolene. No!" screams Liz. "It's too dangerous."

Too late.

Jolene rushes past police cars and shouting officers trying to keep order. A maze of curious bystanders swallows Jolene as she presses into the crowd. Pushing, pushing, pushing, she plows her way ever nearer to the smoke and flames bursting from Eddie's tiny bungalow. Finally, she maneuvers to the front and stands there, breathless, watching as yellow-coated firefighters wrestle hoses and force thundering streams of water toward the resisting crimson flashes. These brave, smoke-smudged firemen remind Jolene of her former friend, kind Ronny McPhierson.

Two firefighters emerge from the burning building, half-carrying, half-dragging a badly burned person who can hardly walk between them. As they pass in front of her, Jolene realizes the person is Eddie.

"Eddie! Eddie!" she cries out. "Are you okay?" She reaches out, trying to touch him as they pass by. For a moment, his eyes open. He tries to smile but can't. Eddie can't smile because his beautiful, shiny black skin has been burned so severely that it looks like green ashes, delicate, wispy green ashes.

Jolene calls out again. This time there is no response. Eddie's eyes have closed for the last time.

Jolene's teacher, Mrs. Allen, asks her to remain after class a few days later. When they are alone, her teacher sits across the aisle from her.

"I know you and Eddie were good friends, Jolene."

Jolene nods.

"I'm sorry you had to see such a thing."

"Why did he die, Mrs. Allen? Why...? How...?"

"I don't know, honey...There was a gas leak or something. Things happen."

"Why to Eddie?"

"I don't have an answer, Jolene. I wish I did. But I know Eddie thought a lot of you."

"How do you know?"

"He told me so several times. And he also told me that he taught you how to play the harmonica. Is that right?"

"Sort of."

"Said you were pretty good at it, too."

Jolene nods, unable to respond.

Mrs. Allen removes an object from her pocket and holds it out. Eddie's harmonica, slightly dented but still shiny, lies in the palm of her hand.

"A fireman found it, Jolene, and gave it to me. I shined it up as well as I could."

She continues to hold it out toward Jolene. Seeing no response, she pulls Jolene's hand toward her and places the harmonica in her palm.

The harmonica feels cold but warms slowly as Jolene's fingers curl around it, though she can hardly see it because her eyes are brimming with tears. Rolling the musical instrument repeatedly in her hand, Jolene marvels at it through the watery haze, not believing, not quite understanding.

"Whenever you play it, Jolene, you'll think of Eddie," Mrs. Allen tells her. "That way, he'll always be with you." A hug, a gentle push. "Now, go. Join the others."

After Eddie's death, Jolene becomes quiet, overcome by what has happened.

Liz is jarred from her lethargy and depression by her daughter's haunted face. The pain she sees in Jolene reminds her of when her best friend Barbara died. She understands the emptiness Jolene must feel, the despair, the questioning. Feelings Liz has buried since her friend died years ago. No one had ever replaced Barbara or come close to that special lost friendship. She wonders if Jolene will always have the emptiness she's felt since Barbara died.

With the loss of Barbara, joy and hope had left, too. Liz had become numb, going through motions but feeling nothing. Laughter and bantering had continued at the café, but she didn't participate. Her job became routine. She didn't even feel the hands placed on her buttocks or react to the leers down her bosom. She didn't care about anything. Nothing buffered her silent pain, encompassed her grief. Her parents' insatiable needs, anger, lost dreams, and hopes didn't matter anymore. Nothing mattered.

Years blurred and passed.

Liz buried herself in work, became a bawdy storyteller, and escaped into books and reading until she finally fell asleep. Then she'd awaken to another repetitious, torturous, unfeeling day the following morning. She rarely dated didn't want to feel or think.

Marcus badgered her to have more fun.

"Go out, Sis. Lighten up. Life isn't made up of work, work, work. How 'bout getting on with your life?"

"What am I supposed to do about the folks?" she'd ask. "Want to take over?"

Quickly changing the subject, Marcus would offer to buy her a beer or start to tell a joke. And, for a short time, Liz would 'lighten up.'

Those hours with Marcus, those dirty jokes, and a few beers became a weekly routine for the brother and sister until Marcus caused a woman to go flying.

The lady went flying on a Monday because Marcus didn't work on Mondays. He was a liquor salesman, and that was his day off. That day was no different from most other Mondays when he'd have a few beers with buddies, then race downtown on his motorcycle to do some shopping for Emma. Then Marcus would speed down Broadway toward Sixth Street to head home when he finished. He was happy, happy, listening to the engine's roar as he rode his bike as fast as possible. Roaring. Roaring. Roaring. Feeling the wind on his face. Speed. Sound. The wind. That was what his bike was all about.

Nothing was different that Monday, except for a small woman in her sixties. A woman who went flying, carrying her bundles, a whole day's shopping. A woman who went flying into the air.

At the corner of Sixth and Broadway, the woman stepped into the street and his bike path. She stepped right out from the front of a streetcar that had hidden her from sight.

Marcus wanted to avoid her, tried to avoid her. There was no place to go. People were everywhere: the waiting zone, the sidewalk, everywhere. There was no place to go except…

The woman's death was listed as accidental.

The police smelled Marcus's breath and knew he'd been drinking. They knew he'd been speeding, too. But the many witnesses swore he wasn't at fault. There was no way he could have avoided her, they said. He couldn't avoid hitting the tiny woman carrying a whole day's shopping.

Marcus sobbed in Liz's arms that day at the police station. He cried and sobbed.

"She looked so surprised, Liz," he kept repeating. "Looked so surprised…when my bike caught her skirt, pushed hard into her body. Caused her to go flying, flying, flying…"

On that day, brother and sister vowed never to drink again. They kept that promise, too, the only exceptions, perhaps a glass of wine or champagne on a special occasion.

Liz wants to comfort Jolene.

What can she do? What can she say? No words come. For her, an activity works better.

"The movies? We're going to a movie?" asks Jolene, not quite believing.

"Why not?"

They take the streetcar, transfer twice, then walk several blocks to reach Hollywood Boulevard, the magical street where numerous flashing marquees announce the titles of movies shown that day.

Jolene clings to her mother and tries to avoid the crush of people who press against them as they stand in line at one of the theaters, waiting to buy tickets. Then they hurry with the crowd toward the entrance, where an attendant takes the tickets, entering another world—a magical world of make-believe.

For one of the rare times in her life, Jolene is speechless. Her head swivels. There is so much to see; chandeliers, murals, statues, everywhere. Swarms of eager filmgoers, the sound of their conversations engulf them. As Liz leads her across the lobby toward a curved staircase, she tries to take in everything at once. It is impossible. And it is not until they walk down, down, down the deeply carpeted staircase that she finally finds her voice.

"Are we...are we in a castle, Mommy?"

Laughing, Liz tells her, "No, silly! No! This is the Pantages Theater, where they show motion pictures."

They arrive at the restroom. Entering, Jolene stands, enthralled. Here is a world of mirrors and multiple images. In front of her are mirrors, mirrors everywhere. Then mirrors within mirrors, reflecting images of her staring and her mother, laughing at her reaction. Delighted, Jolene makes silly faces. Her antics cause other patrons to laugh.

Amused, Liz watches for a while, then nudges her toward a row of shiny marble stalls.

"Enough already, Jolene. Enough. Go pee!"

Entering one, Jolene sits, enchanted, pretends to be queen of the Land of Mirrors, and shouts to Liz, who occupies the next stall. "Wouldn't it be heavenly if we had one of these?"

"Yes, yes. Hurry up. We'll miss the movie."

Then the thrill of squirting scented soap into her cupped hands from what looks like a perfume bottle, watching bubbles disappear as water gushes from a carved brass figurine to land in a shiny onyx basin. Such elegance. And the final touch. Almost too much for her to handle. A uniformed Negress hands her a warm towel, offering to help her dry her hands. When she hands the towel back, the woman asks her, "Y'all goin tah see the movie or play down heah, child?"

"Play? Where?"

She points to an adjoining room.

As Jolene turns and looks through the door, she sees an enormous sandbox on the floor filled with toys and a few children. Standing nearby, a uniformed caretaker calls out to the children in a foreign-accented voice.

Upset, Jolene turns to Liz, "I thought you said we were going to a movie!"

"We are! We are! Those children are too young, but you're not. Let's go."

Relieved, Jolene follows her mother upstairs to one of the balconies. Liz tells her to hurry, then explains what they are about to see. "The movie is called *Snow White,* the first full-length movie made from a cartoon. Come on, Jolene, you'll love it!"

They sit, part of a vast audience a few moments later, waiting for the show to begin in one of the largest theaters in Los Angeles, where 500 people can be seated downstairs and 200 – 300 in the balcony. Jolene stares up at the intricate wooden ceiling above them as they wait. Then she studies the audience of mostly chattering children and their mothers below. In time the lights dim. On stage, crimson velvet curtains part. As the audience quiets and the movie begins, Jolene sinks deep into her plush seat, eyes wide open. Her eyes remain wide open until the evil queen confronts Snow White. Then, she squeezes her eyes shut and hunches close to Liz as she hears two loud shrieks echo throughout the theater.

Without warning, Jolene is jerked out of her seat and pulled up, up, up the darkened aisle. Protesting, not understanding what is happening, she begins to cry.

Confused, she keeps asking, "But why, Mommy, why? Why can't we stay? Why can't we see the movie?"

What Jolene doesn't realize is that she is the one who screamed. The evil queen had frightened her so much that she had screamed twice.

Nightmares begin. For weeks, the wicked queen visits Jolene nightly. She boils Oscar in a pot, blows up Eddie, kidnaps her daddy, and kills her mommy.

Berating herself, Liz fumes. It never turns out right no matter what she does with this kid. Some women are born mothers, she decides. She certainly isn't one of them. And she was never meant to be one, either. She might as well give up trying. Yet, Jolene's ongoing discomfort and misery tug at Liz's heart.

A few weeks later, she decides to try again.

This time Liz plans a beach outing.

During the ride to Long Beach on the big red streetcar, Liz shares stories of her childhood days at the beach. The reminiscing stops when they arrive and begin to walk along the boardwalk.

"Breathe in," Liz instructs Jolene. She inhales, too. "My favorite smell, the saltwater. The best," she tells her.

Jolene is happy to share something so special with her mother. She repeatedly inhales as they walk toward the blinding white sand. Foaming breakers can be seen in the distance. Suddenly she stops, mouth open, "Look! Mommy! Look!"

"I know."

They stare at what seems to be a never-ending wooden pier, braced by hundreds of weathered pilings. On top, a giant roller coaster zooms on tracks covering steep inclines and dips, its cars hugging the curves of what is known as America's fastest ride. Floating screams emitted from the coaster's occupants mingle with shrieks of seagulls and crashing waves.

"Are we going on that?"

"Nope! I don't think so."

Relieved, Jolene removes her shoes and runs to the sand. Testing it, she realizes it is too hot and puts her shoes back on until they are about 20 feet from the surf. Liz fans out a blanket and places their lunch and personal items on it. Removing her dress, she reveals a discreet one-piece bathing suit. Putting a rubber hat over her head, she hands Jolene an empty coffee can and a tablespoon, then instructs her, "Here! Play with these until I get back. Don't go near the water or talk to anyone. Promise!"

Nodding, Jolene sits down and watches her mother race toward the ocean. Liz runs like a young girl set free. When she reaches the water, she shudders as she dips down repeatedly, careful not to get her face wet. Braving the temperature, she finally immerses her body, head held high, and begins to swim, taking her beyond the breakers.

Playing in the sand, Jolene checks the ocean now and then to watch her mother swim, making sure she can see her head bobbing in the sea, stroking parallel to the shore beyond the breakers.

In time Liz returns to the shallow water and calls out for Jolene to join her. Afraid, Jolene holds back. Liz comes out of the water, pulls her along into the surf. Terrified, Jolene fusses and holds Liz's hand as she listens to her mother's advice.

"When the wave comes, jump. Jump sideways so that the water won't go in your mouth."

Liz is right. When Jolene forgets and faces the wave, she is knocked down, chokes on the water, and wants to get out.

But Liz won't let her quit.

"You must learn to respect the ocean, Jolene. Always! Don't be afraid of it. Don't fight it. Relax! And always, respect it!"

In time Jolene does as her mother tells her, relaxes more. She begins to enjoy herself almost as much as Liz does. She even tries to learn the fundamentals of swimming.

Liz's strong hands hold her belly while she paddles, pretending to stay afloat. If Liz releases her, she immediately sinks, swallows the water, and becomes frightened. Liz's hands hold her again, allowing Jolene to overcome her fear. She starts paddling again. The lessons and laughter continue.

They return to their blanket, exhausted.

Liz brings up the subject of Eddie, which is difficult for her. Comparing his loss with her friend Barbara, she tries to let Jolene know she understands.

"Do you...? Am I making myself clear?"

"I guess so." Jolene shrugs, then she asks, "Does it ever stop hurting, Mommy?"

Liz has no answer as they pack up to go home.

Jolene asks, "Did you love your friend Barbara?"

"Yes, very much!"

"Did you ever have another friend like her?"

"No! Never! There are friends and friends!"

Jolene looks confused.

"I mean... A person can know lots of people have lots of acquaintances. But friends, real friends. Well... You can count real friends on the fingers of one hand." She holds out her hand and counts out one finger at a time. "There are usually lots of fingers left over." Staring out of the window, she says softly, "Lots! A person is lucky to have one special friend, even one, Jolene. Even one."

"I'll never have another friend like Eddie!"

"Maybe not...But you'll have other friends. Not like Eddie, perhaps, but others. You like people, Jolene. People like you. You'll have more than one friend, I'm sure." Then with envy, "Sometimes I wish I was more like you, Jolene. I really do. You're so, so open, so trusting. I hope life doesn't hurt you too much." Unexpectedly, she hugs her as the trolley approaches.

Thrilled at her mother's affection and exhausted from the day's outing, Jolene leans heavily against Liz's body and falls asleep after they sit down. Content with the day's outing, Liz nods off too, thinking, "At last, something went right!"

Well, almost...

That night Jolene's sunburn turns into sunstroke. Liz bathes her repeatedly in a vinegar bath until the chills and fever leaves.

Since Dan left, it's quieter because there's no fighting, but Liz cries more now. Even playing with the twins doesn't bring Jolene out of her lethargy.

And now, no Eddie. No Eddie!

Eddie told her he would always be there. Always protect her, sing songs to her, play the harmonica.

No Eddie! No Eddie! It's not fair! Such emptiness. Such sadness.

Now, Jolene's main companions are Oscar and Eddie's harmonica. Hour after hour, she talks to Oscar, crying into her solid feathered body. Then she practices the harmonica. Sometimes Oscar tries to run away when she hears the sound. But most of the time, as Jolene plays, Oscar, her best friend, quacks along.

Chapter Thirteen
August 1986 Therapy

Instead of seven women, today, there are eight of us in the therapy session. As we have every week for the past several months, we have come to discuss our past sexual nightmares in the hopes of finding understanding and new self-images. Ramona, our facilitator, nods at the new member hunched on a chair next to me.

"Ladies, this is Holly."

I extend greetings, but there isn't much interest on the part of the other women until Ramona looks at Holly with admiration and says, "Ladies! Holly is one brave young woman. She is suing her father for sexual assault!"

That gets everyone's attention. A few women murmur acknowledgments. Some nod. Others still say nothing, but I'm impressed, so I give her a thumbs up and say, "What a courageous thing you're doing, Holly. What prompted you to take action?"

She completely ignores me, like I don't exist.

One of the other women comments sarcastically, "Good luck to you, little lady! You'll need it! Going against this macho-dominated society which seems to think men can get away with anything, including rape because they don't believe there is such a thing. How can there be rape, they ask? Why, ladies, we all know, every female asks for it. Wants it!" Then she hisses with bitterness, "Years ago…when I told my first therapist that my father had raped me, he responded with, 'Well, you certainly must have been a sexy little thing.'"

All of us, except Holly, groan in unison and respond somehow.

"Sexy!"

"Oh, my God!"

"Damn!"

"Stupid bastard!"

Ramona turns to the new member and asks, "Would you like to share your story, Holly? I'm sure everyone is interested."

We nod in agreement and are curious to know why she's suing.

Tensing, the girl, who couldn't have been more than 19 or 20, doesn't make eye contact with anyone. Instead, she wets her lips as though she's going to speak, then says nothing. Her fingers rub against her thumbs, unconsciously, incessantly.

"That's all right," Ramona acknowledges. "If you don't want to share today, you don't have to."

Face hardening, Holly spits out, "I know I don't have to. I don't have to do anything I don't want to today or any day! I know it!"

Taken aback momentarily by the ferocity of the girl's response, Ramona sits back, then agrees, "You're right, Holly! You're absolutely right. You're in charge of your life now, aren't you?"

Laughing bitterly, Holly retorts, "In charge? What a joke."

"If you don't want to speak of the past, can you share why you're suing?" Ramona asks.

"Why?" Holly stares down at her hands, unaware of the constant activity of her fingers, "Why not? He's a bastard and has to be made accountable."

The word "accountable" hits home in my mind...

That terrible day was etched in my memory when I tried to get Dad to be "accountable."

I'd arranged a luncheon meeting with Dad because of an incident at our house a few days before. My folks had been over for dinner. Afterward, we were all sitting in the family room, schmoozing. Dad entertained us by whistling, then pretending he had a bird in his hand. Enchanted, my first girl, who was just barely two, had approached him and climbed onto his lap. To everyone's surprise, I had jumped up and snatched my daughter away from him so quickly that she began to cry. I'd made no excuses that evening to anyone when they questioned me. I couldn't. All I could do was grab my little girl, run from the room, and hold her tightly to my bosom, wanting to protect her from him and the world as I slowly appeased her frightened tears.

After that, I knew I had to confront my dad. Make him promise to stay away from my little girls. That's why I had called him. But he didn't know the reason. He was just pleased with the invitation and said he looked forward to having lunch with me. But I didn't dare to face him alone, so I asked Charlie to come along.

Surprised by my husband being there, Dad seemed uneasy at first, then was his old charming self. After the usual small talk, I got up the courage to broach the subject. I told Dad I held no grudge about the past. But I wanted him to stay away from our daughter. Charlie said nothing but held my hand under the table to support me.

"What do you mean, stay away from my granddaughters?" my dad had asked, looking confused. "What are you talking about, Jolene?"

"Dad!" I pleaded with him. "Please don't make me give specifics. Just don't go near our girls, okay! Please! Promise!"

I tried so hard that day to make Dad "accountable." I guess I even hoped he might say he was sorry. If he had, I would have forgiven him. I always loved him. But it was a mistake, having Charlie there. Perhaps Dad would have said something if we'd been alone. Perhaps. I don't know. Maybe it would have turned out differently. Bitterly, I remember my dad's reaction and realize it probably wouldn't have been any different, with or without Charlie.

That day Dad had not only acknowledged my request but had also laughed at and derided me.

"Such a vivid imagination, Jolene! Such a good storyteller!" And he'd turned to Charlie, smirking, "Where does your wife get these fantasies, Charlie? She should be the writer, not you." And he'd continued to laugh and laugh as though enjoying a good joke.

We didn't join him in his laughter.

Dad's reaction forced me to keep an ever-constant eye on my daughters and all of my children from then on. They were never alone with my father, and they never slept overnight at my folk's place. I showed respect to my parents because I was afraid my kids wouldn't respect me if I didn't. I adored Mom and had a wonderful friendship with her. But, I kept Dad at a distance. To all appearances, everything seemed normal, but there was always a watchful wall of anxiety and fear on my part when he was present. And that wall, just like Mom's invisible curtain, never came down until my children became adults.

I'm curious about this new member, the youngest in our therapy group. "How did you get your father to admit what he'd done?" I asked her, the frustration of my dad's non-committal attitude still rankling me, even after all these years. "Mine never did!"

Holly directed her gaze at me for the first time, and I could distinctly see her features. Mousy, poorly shorn hair hung limply around her pallid face. Her thin mouth turned down at the corners. Early creases already were apparent at the outer corners of her steel-gray eyes, almost hidden by untamed bangs. My heart ached for this young girl, with a face so aged and pained beyond her brief years.

"Admit it?" She scoffed. "How could he forget what he did?" Haltingly, she uttered words that hit the room like bullets, "He destroyed...my brother!"

Then she spoke in monotone without any emotion.

"I want my father to pay for everything he did to us. I want him to pay for all therapy, any therapy. And my education, too. But what's more important is that he's got to see that my brother gets the best care there is because..." She pauses, anger now accentuating every word. "...my brother's going to be in a mental institution for the rest of his life...because of what my father did to him! And I want the law to force my dad into therapy, too, force him to face up. I'm going to see that he accepts responsibility for what he did to us, the rotten bastard! The bastard!"

There are no tears. Only silent rage fills the room.

I want to fold my arms around this young girl and comfort her. Oh, the poor soul, I think. As I lean toward her, Ramona stops me with a hand gesture.

"Do you want to continue?" Ramona asks her.

In clipped words, anger still seething underneath, Holly's story unfolds.

"He's an alcoholic, Dad is! It started when I was eight, a year after my mom died. My brother and I shared a room. One night, my dad came into our room smelling like a distillery, ripped my gown off, and threw himself on top of me. That first time he had to hold his hand across my mouth to keep me from screaming from the pain and waking up my little brother. But I learned fast. I learned not to give the bastard the pleasure of knowing he hurt me. He kept trying to get me to show something, but I got so I said nothing, felt nothing. All I could feel was hatred, a red hot hatred that filled me up every time he breathed on me or tore into me. I learned to handle it."

I listened and watched intently as some women relived their own nightmares. Some felt empathy, I guess. I know I was so overcome my tears flowed.

"But I'm not suing him for what he did to me, not for that," Holly continued. "It's what he did to my brother. He's got to pay for that. Big time!"

Noting her rising agitation, Ramona offers, "You don't have to share anymore if it's too painful, Holly."

Again, defiant, brittle tones confront the therapist. "Too painful?" She smirks, "Nothing is too painful today. Or any day! Nothing!" Holly looked defiantly around the room. "You want to know why I'm suing the bastard? It's because he sodomized my little brother for six years. Six lousy years, right in front of me!"

Shock! Dismay! Disgust! Everyone in the room reacted.

Ignoring the reactions, the girl continues. "He'd take us into the bathroom. That's where he'd do it. He'd make me sit on the floor and watch. I'd have to sit there and watch him torture Davey, that sweet, angelic child. See the silent screams in him welling up. I'd get slammed around if I tried to stop him. I'd beg him to take me, not Davey. But he'd laugh, get rougher with both of us. When he'd finish with Davey, he'd drop him on the floor next to me. Then he'd urinate over the two of us, saying that's all we were good for. Sometimes he'd even…"

Shocked at what isn't said, we have different reactions. A few try to adjust their seating positions, seem unable to get comfortable again. Others stare out of the window as though wanting to escape from this recently unfolded drama. All of us, including the therapist, are visibly shaken. My motherly instincts take over after my initial horror and thoughts of wanting this foul man dead rather than sued.

"I must assist this damaged child," I think. "I want to hold her, tell her she'll be okay. Comfort her as I've done so often with my children when they were young and hurting, hugging them and telling them, 'You'll be all right! You'll be all right! Mommy is here. Mommy will fix it.'"

And most of the time, I could fix it.

I wondered how anyone could fix such a terrible wrong? How? Tentatively, I reached out and took her hand. Though she didn't respond, she didn't pull her hand away either. I tell her how sorry I am and that I'm here for her if she wants anything. Her cold hand continues to lie in mine, impassive. Squeezing a little, I am pleased to feel her fingers relax, warm to my touch. As we sit there, hands entwined, Ramona addresses me.

"Now, Jolene," Ramona says, "do you want to share today?"

I can't believe what I'm hearing. Shaking my head in wonder at the therapist's stupidity, I tell her, "After what we've just heard, Ramona, you expect me to discuss my situation? What happened to me is so trivial compared to Holly. I'd be embarrassed to..."

"Forcing sex on a child in the name of love is more insidious than what Holly's father did!" Ramona says with authority. "Put things into perspective, Jolene."

Shocked, the attention of the group focuses on the therapist.

"Why don't you put things into perspective, Ramona?" I respond defensively. "What you're saying is insane! There's no comparison. There was only oral sex with my dad. He never once forced intercourse on me. Never once. He didn't enter, rape me, Ramona. He never hurt me like..." I stop and look at Holly.

"Don't you think stealing a child's innocence hurts them?" Ramona asks. "When a person forces sex on a child, whether it's touching their genitals, kissing them in sexual ways, or raping them, it all boils down to one thing. That boy or girl has had their childhood stolen. A child's innocence has been destroyed! If the child is very young, sometimes they have no idea that something is wrong if it doesn't hurt. Particularly if it gives pleasure like you had, Jolene. But in time, guilt, shame, addictions, lack of self-esteem, all kinds of socially disabling patterns can develop, which many of you have experienced. Often, people don't realize how much an unhealthy sexual encounter at an early age can affect a person for the rest of their life because they bury it. Or," she looks at Jolene, "a person can think as you did. 'I wasn't raped. It wasn't much compared to Holly's experience.' Jolene, I disagree! It is a 'big deal'! All inappropriate sexual advances are a 'big deal' and should be dealt with by professional incest therapists. That's why I'm glad you're here, Jolene. Even at this late age. Don't you see? You're here to finally release the pain of what your father did to you, to release the demons you buried and carried with you for so long."

"But I didn't bury..." I respond defensively again. "I always remembered what happened. I just went along with my life, that's all. What occurred in my childhood is in no way as traumatic as what Holly went through. No way!"

"Jolene! You don't have to be raped to suffer the consequences of sexual misbehavior. When an adult who is supposed to protect you uses you as a sexual object, don't you think that's damaging?"

"Of course it is. Of course. Only you don't understand, Ramona. My dad didn't use me just as a sexual object. He truly loved me. He was the only one who…"

Losing patience, Ramona stops her. "Jolene! When are you going to stop defending him? When? We know he loved you and your mother didn't. He could have given you that love without sexual demands, couldn't he?" She looks at me.

I don't have an answer for that one.

"Of course, he could have if he hadn't been such a sick, sick man!" Ramona continues. "And so is Holly's sick father. Sick! Sick! Sick! I don't care whether someone drinks or says he loves you or needs you, or he will die if you don't give him what he wants. Anyone who uses a child for sexual pleasure is a mentally sick person! And it's about time society faces up to it and does something about it." She pauses and says with sadness, "It all stinks, ladies. It all hurts. I'll repeat what I said before, Jolene; whether you believe it or not, what happened to you in the name of love is more insidious than what happened to Holly in fits of drunkenness, violence, or rape."

Some women are as confused by Ramona's statements as I am. Others are visibly disturbed. Holly is impassive. Still shaking my head in disbelief, I'm very uncomfortable over where this is going and am grateful when Ramona's attention returns to Holly.

"When a child is sexually molested and feels anger or hatred like you did, Holly…like you do," Ramona says, "that child has an outlet for the outrageous actions that have taken place. It's not a contest here, Jolene. For you," she looks around the room, "or for any of you. All of you have been mistreated and damaged." She looks back at me. "Both you and Holly have experienced terrible injustices at the hands of your fathers. What happened to Holly and her brother Davey is heartbreaking and inexcusable. But that doesn't mean that what happened to Jolene is a small matter." She turns to me and says, "Jolene! Look at Holly!"

Having no idea what she is proving, I ignore her request.

Ramona speaks to me again in a commanding tone I cannot ignore. "Jolene! Look at Holly! See her anger! Have you ever felt anger like that toward your father, Jolene? Ever?"

Uncomfortable. I feel cornered and want to get out of there. Instead, I nod and say, "No."

"And you, Holly," the therapist turns her attention back to the girl. "Have you ever defended your father like you just heard Jolene do today?"

Holly snorts a half-laugh.

Then, something important happened to me, the 55-year-old woman, and Holly, the 19-year-old girl. We turned toward each other, and our eyes locked. It was then that as we both realized that age is no barrier to the bond we are forming as we begin to gain knowledge from one another in healing.

Ramona tells us our time is up. Most of us rise and begin to form a circle. Holly remained in her chair. The rest of us place our arms around each other's shoulders and perform the weekly ritual before leaving.

Ramona closes the session with, "As I've said beforehand," her tone is softer now, almost motherly. "You don't have to forgive anyone in this world…except yourself. You have choices. You can keep the person who has hurt you in your life if you want to. You can forgive them. Forget them. Bury them. Divorce them. Or, you have another alternative." She looks at Holly and smiles, "Or…you can sue them!"

In unison, we call out, "Amen!"

Chapter Fourteen
1939

Life without Dan is different.

Jolene feels closer to her mother now and shares things they've never done before. Her mother is crying less now, too, and not hitting her as much either.

But the significant difference since Dan is gone is how much time they spend with relatives.

It all starts on the day Liz tells her, "Grampa's going to stay with us a while, Jolene. Florence, the lady who takes care of him, has to go away for a few weeks."

"Why can't he stay with Uncle Reuben and Aunt Anne?"

"Their place is too small, so he's staying here, and that's that."

The Sorkins never finish a sentence when they mention Aunt Anne's name lately. There are only vague comments about "something missing up here" as they tap their heads.

That weekend, Grampa Abe arrives.

And that night, all the other Sorkins, except Anne, show up for dinner. Such fun that night. The house almost bursts with joviality. Even her cousin Alisa doesn't bug her that night because everyone is busting a gut, laughing at Marcus's or Grampa Abe's jokes and antics. Jolene and her cousins are fascinated when Grampa tells time because he has no glass on the face of his watch. Time is discovered by touching the hands with his fingers. Every few minutes, one of them tests him. And like clockwork, he's always right, then roars with satisfaction to the children's delight.

Jolene begins to enjoy having Grampa Abe with them. One reason is that he sleeps on the couch. That means she gets to sleep with her mother. He also loves to dance to music on the radio and teaches her the two-step, pretending they are dancing at a fancy nightclub.

But the most interesting thing about living with Grampa is taking a walk with him.

As Oscar pulls along on her leash, Grampa walks down the street, tap, tap, tapping his cane here and there. Checking, continuously checking for a curb, an oncoming car, a dip in the sidewalk, his cane sounding a warning, protecting him from a mishap. Oscar is also quacking, quacking her protective observations.

Some people stare. Others, trying to be polite, look away.

"Sometimes, I think my cane has eyes," Grampa tells her one day as they walk.

"Real eyes?"

"Of course," he tells her, delighted, and begins another joke, knowing he has a captive audience.

Weeks pass. One, two, then three. They pass quickly, but not quickly enough for Jolene because there's one thing about Grampa that drives her crazy.

It's the way he eats peas.

She becomes almost physically ill as she watches him smash every pea on his plate, pressing and mushing them flat. Then he picks them up with a spoon. Even though they are crushed together, he still makes a mess.

It is at the kitchen table that Jolene resents Grampa's blindness. She wishes he could see, pick up an individual pea, cut his meat, eat a salad the way they do, like other grampas. Much as she loves him, she is pleased to see him go when Marcus comes to pick him up that weekend to take him back to Boyle Heights.

It is a long, long time before she can eat peas again.

A few days later, the telephone rings. It is Uncle Arthur. "Coming by to show you my new car, Liz. Take you and Jolene for a spin," he says. "It will take your mind off Dan."

"Thanks, Arthur...but no thanks. I'm too busy. Perhaps another time."

"Come on, Liz! We'll have dinner afterward, a treat."

"Please, Mommy, please," Jolene pleads, overhearing the conversation.

Continuing to shake her head, Liz says an emphatic "No!" Besides being busy, her unspoken reason for not wanting to go is that Arthur drives like a maniac.

This is a family joke.

Arthur buys a new car every year. He doesn't buy a new one just because he can afford it. Either he burns the brakes out and doesn't want to replace them, or he drinks too much and totals the car.

"Cheaper than getting a new set of brakes!" he always jokes, laughing louder than anyone when they'd tease him.

A family joke, yes. But still, few want to ride with him. My mother was no exception. Except for the day when he called and told her he wanted to take us to the beach in his brand new Lincoln Continental convertible. As he described the new car over the phone, Mom's eyes had widened, and then she said, "Well…"

Mom and I were on the sidewalk a half-hour later when Uncle Arthur and Aunt Lottie drove up. The car was magnificent, maroon with a beige top, leather interior, and glistening chrome trim.

"Oooohs" and "Aahhhhs" were heard, not only from us but from neighbors who had gathered to watch Uncle Arthur park this splendid vehicle which looked like it came from another planet, while Aunt Lottie waved and shouted big "Hellos" to everyone.

"Isn't it gorgeous?" Aunt Lottie gushed.

That word hardly described the shiny vehicle. It was 1942. Henry Ford's son Edsel had come up with the idea of an 'elegant' automobile such as he'd seen on a European trip. The Lincoln Continental Cabriolet was one of the popular results. Because of the war effort, only a few over 1,200 had been built and purchased, and Uncle Arthur felt lucky to have been one of those buyers.

The Cabriolet was so elegant that it came with a radio, heater, power windows, a power-operated convertible top, clock full instrumentation, and was promoted as so quiet that occupants would feel like they were floating on a cloud.

After Mom and I climbed into the back to sink into the soft golden seats smelling of new leather, Uncle Arthur drove off.

"This is heaven!"

"I love it."

And it did feel like we were floating on a cloud, so we continued to pay no attention to Uncle Arthur's driving until…

"Oh, Artie! Bet you can't take your hands off the wheel," squealed Aunt Lottie in the front, giggling and drinking from a silver flask as we approached the almost empty Pacific Coast Highway.

Opening our eyes, we were horrified to see Uncle Arthur take a long drag from his flask and say, "Here we go, girls. There's no traffic, and this baby's a masterpiece. It can drive itself," and he held his hands up in the air.

Mom and I grabbed each other as she shouted, "Oh for Gawd's sake, Arthur, stop showing off. Put your damn hands on the wheel!"

Laughing and ignoring her words, Uncle Arthur and Aunt Lottie shrieked their delight, toasting each other as they finished off their flasks.

Frightened as we were, Mom and I began to watch with fascination as the Lincoln silently glided along like a magical machine, giving us a show of an overcast day, breaking waves, quiet beaches, and a few hardy souls playing volleyball.

Suddenly, we hit a bump.

The Lincoln, still silent, skidded off the main road, rolled majestically through a near-empty parking lot, and came to a soft stop in the sand to the shock and amusement of the few nearby beachgoers.

There were no seatbelts in those days, and we were lucky not to have been thrown from the car.

Uncle Arthur laughed and said, "Well, guess I won't need new brakes this time. Think I might keep this baby for a while."

Aunt Lottie's shrieks of joy joined his laughter. And though we were still shaken up, even Mom and I couldn't help joining in until strangers ran up and helped us out of the car.

But the best relative to show up came as a surprise a few weeks later when Liz received another telephone call. This time it was Auntie Pola from Canada.

"Pola! Pola! Where are you?" A pause, then her exclamation, "Hollywood! You're kidding!"

Jolene listening in, becomes excited and asks, "Is it Daddy's sister, Auntie Pola from Canada?"

Ignoring Jolene, Liz continues, "Yeah! He left about a month ago," and continues to tell Pola what happened.

Jumping up and down, Jolene pulls at Liz's skirt. "Can I talk to her, can I?"

Irritated, Liz gives her a look. "Work and pleasure, huh! How great! How long are you going to be here? A month! Terrific! How did you manage to get away from ole Rivka?"

A long pause, then more laughter. "Great! You deserve it, kiddo! Carl with you?"

Another long pause...

Jolene tugs and tugs at Liz, "When can we see her? When?"

Liz shoos her away, "Sure! Sounds good to me. Let me get something to write on." She hands the phone to Jolene and says, "Here, pest! Talk while I look for a pencil."

As she takes the phone, shyness overcomes her, and she says nothing. Liz returns and looks exasperated.

"Jolene! It's costing her. Say something, or I'm taking the phone back!"

Softly, so softly she can hardly be heard, Jolene whispers, "Hi!"

"Jolene!" a deep voice, sounding much like a man, booms out at her. "How's my only niece? You must be quite big now."

Still shy, "Yes."

"Looking forward to finally meeting you."

A little more confidently, "Me, too."

While they ride the trolley to Pola's place the following week, Liz thinks about Dan's family.

How his parents, sickly, 38-year-old Austrian-born Jacob Hartman and 18-year-old, Rumanian-born Rivka Neiman, ended up in the same small village in Eastern Europe. Their marriage was arranged too, just like Liz's parents. The main difference was that Rivka and Jacob fell in love. They tried to get to America, but the quota was full. So they ended up in Canada. The tiny grocery store they purchased provided food for their ever-growing family but little else. Rivka, ever pregnant, had one miscarriage, three dying at childbirth, and nine live births.

By the time Daniel, next to the last, was born, Jacob was bedridden with a weak heart. It was a hard life for Rivka; so much work, little joy, scrimping, trying to feed and clothe her big family. But her burdens were bearable because she had Jacob, her beloved Jacob.

When Jacob died, it broke Rivka's heart. She became bitter and angry, and those emotions remained with her for the rest of her life.

Rivka lost the store when Dan was four. How were they to live? The oldest child still at home was 13-year-old Pola. Mature for her age, she quit school, taught herself how to type and take shorthand, lied about her age, and was hired as a secretary at the local newspaper. By the time she was 20, Pola was Assistant to the Editor. At the age of 25, she was the Managing Editor.

Family members assumed that Pola would never marry. It was her responsibility to stay home to take care of Rivka and the boys, and she did. Then something unexpected happened.

Pola met and fell in love with Carl Romberg, a German engineering student at the nearby University. Carl wasn't Jewish, so they kept their relationship a secret until he proposed.

"What? Are you crazy? Marry a Gentile (non-Jew)! Never! Over my dead body, you will!"

Rivka's words lashed out at her daughter when she heard, accusing, condemning.

"No! No! Of course not. Carl will convert!"

"Convert? He steps in this house I die! You hear! I die!"

And true to her word, Rivka had a minor heart attack.

Carl never did cross the threshold of the Hartman household. And Pola never moved out. Even after the youngest child departed, Pola stayed and took care of Rivka.

Years passed. Neither Pola nor Carl ever married another nor loved anyone else. They were bound for life, if not in matrimony.

Carl went to work for the Canadian government, traveling worldwide, working on projects he couldn't discuss. Once, perhaps twice a year, they met somewhere, far from Rivka, far from accusations.

Liz's eyes misted, wondering what it would be like to have a man true to you like that, like Carl.

They arrived at Pola's place.

Jolene meets her aunt, and a loving bond forms at first sight.

Pola is short, stocky, raven-haired, and white-skinned. Her mouth, a slash of deep red lipstick, and dark circles under her eyes that no amount of make-up can hide. Jolene's attractive, no-nonsense aunt wears a dark business slack suit, white blouse, and comfortable shoes. Jolene learns that this outfit is her aunt's uniform, no matter where she's going or what she's doing.

Embracing both of them simultaneously, Jolene is amazed at the strength and warmth of the hug.

They share tea and jam-filled biscuits as they pore over a photo album filled with pictures of Pola and Carl in various exotic countries.

Liz exclaims, "Gawd, Pola! You've been everywhere. How lucky you are!" Then, with envy, "Here I am, 30 years old, and I've never even been out of the State of California."

"So, who's stopping you? If you want to do something, do it! Don't just sit there and moan about it," Pola states matter-of-factly, in her deep, resonant, determined voice, with broad A's and precise diction.

"Are you kidding? What could I do? How could I go anywhere?"

"You can do anything you wish if you want it bad enough. Just take off! Go somewhere."

"Where?"

"How do I know? Where do you want to go?"

"Well…I've always wanted to see this country, but… Who am I kidding? What would I do with the kid?"

"What would you do with Jolene? Let her stay with me."

"Pull her out of school?"

"Why not? I'll give her an education she can't get in a classroom. Guaranteed!"

Liz laughs, "I'll bet you could!" Becoming serious, she stares into her sister-in-law's face, "You really mean it, don't you?"

"Have I ever said anything I didn't mean?"

Liz shrugs, "You're something else, Pola. I know it's just a pipe dream, but thanks for the offer anyway."

But Liz's pipe dream becomes a reality.

With Pola's prodding, Liz borrows enough money from her for a ticket on a Greyhound bus and leaves on a trip that takes her across the United States and back. But the best part of it is that Jolene gets to stay with Pola for three whole weeks.

Pola's apartment is almost the same size as Jolene's triplex. Square footage may be similar, but they are as different as night and day.

Jolene's dark and depressing living room is crowded with her grandparent's old overstuffed furniture.

Light floods Pola's third-floor Hollywood apartment from a wall of windows overlooking Barnsdale Park. Minimal contemporary furnishings complement the small rooms designed more for eye appeal than comfort. There is a tiny kitchenette off the living room, a tiled bathroom with no bathtub, only a shower, and a bedroom commanding the same park view, plus paradise for Jolene—a tiny alcove off the living room. So little is the nook; it can't be called a room. Yet, it is perfect for the small cot Pola rents, just for her.

Sure she's died and gone to heaven, Jolene revels in having a room of her own for three whole weeks.

"No couch for you, kiddo! Only adult accommodations will do," Pola booms out as she hugs her, pleased at her niece's delighted reaction.

Rituals dominate Pola's life.

Her outfits.

And her mornings.

Each day begins early with the ringing of the telephone. Her aunt, already dressed, takes the call. Multi-tasking, Pola jokes and laughs as she converses while instructing an assistant. At the same time, she prepares Postum and jam-filled biscuits. The steaming beverage and biscuits are an integral part of this daily routine, as is the early phone call. To complete her morning ritual, she retrieves the newspaper in the hallway outside their doorway after she hangs up, places the food and paper on the table, then calls out to Jolene to join her.

Jolene also develops an early morning ritual.

First, she makes her bed. Then, she rushes to the bathroom, brushes her teeth, and turns on the shower, waiting for it to heat to the temperature she desires. Every day Jolene knows she can shower as long as she wants. She can do this, says Aunt Pola, because the hot water never runs out.

What a new and liberating experience!

To have hot water course down, cascading over her head, her face, covering her entire body. She revels in the experience, applying her aunt's scented soap and shampoo. As she showers, she daydreams; she is a fairy princess with a prince kissing her hand. She is Snow White, commanding the Wicked Queen to disappear forever. She walks hand in hand with Eddie, then her daddy. She has a big brother whose freckled face resembles hers. Only he's taller and more muscular. Experiencing these, her first showers, gives Jolene a sense of power as she stands, wasting water, wasting heat, feeling wicked, wonderfully wicked.

At the McPhiersons, she had to bathe with Annie. The water was always cool. She gets to bathe only once a week at home on Saturdays. Her mother hardly puts enough water to cover her legs, and it's always so cold. If she asks for more hot water, she will likely hear her mother say, "Waste not, want not, Jolene! Water isn't free, you know. We pay for water, for heat, too. You'll see how expensive things are when you're older when you have to pay the bills. You'll see..."

Then often, Liz stops mid-sentence, "My Gawd! I do sound more like my mother every day."

Indulgence! Indulgence! It is the first time Jolene has experienced such indulgence in her entire life. And she enjoys every moment. Hearing her aunt call out, she quickly dries her body, dusts herself with talcum powder, puts on one of Pola's robes, and with hair still wet, joins her.

Pola greets her with a bear hug and gravel-voiced, "Good morning, sunshine! Enjoy your shower?"

Her aunt's greeting warms Jolene's body and her heart.

Then they sit, sipping and eating, each taking a section of the newspaper, as Pola notes with amusement how Jolene ignores the comics and pores over the front page.

As she looks at a captioned picture of President Roosevelt attending the opening of the New York World's Fair, Jolene comments, "Have you ever heard President Roosevelt speak on the radio, Aunt Pola?"

"Several times. Why?"

"I like him. Don't understand what he says, but love his voice, don't you?"

"Most people feel that way about politicians."

"What do you mean?"

"Politicians often sound good, but they talk out of both sides of their mouths!"

Seeing her niece's confused look, she laughs, "They say what they think voters want to hear, but few mean what they say."

"President Roosevelt's not that way. Daddy and Mommy think that he..."

Jolene stops eating and looks sad. The painful lump begins forming in the back of her throat again.

Surprised, Pola asks, "What's wrong, Jolene? Did I say something?"

"No! No! You didn't. It's just that—we used to listen to the president when he spoke when we were a family and did things together and... Mommy was happier too, but since Daddy's gone, Mommy's been soo… Oh, I don't know!" She stares down at the table, eyes full.

"You miss him a lot, don't you?"

Jolene nods.

"Don't worry. He'll be back. When he hears Liz's carousing around the country, having the time of her life, he'll be back pronto. Dan knows a good thing when he sees it. Your mom's the best thing that ever happened to him." She rises, takes both cups, "More?"

Jolene stares down at the table, the lump hurting, restricting speech, nods in agreement.

Pola fills the cups, returns to the table, and sits down. "You know, Jolene, I agree with you. President Roosevelt does have a rich, comforting voice. He is a good man," Pola continues, "Certainly the best man who's been in Washington in a long while, don't you think?"

Jolene nods, still unable to speak, tears sliding down her cheeks.

Pola pushes one of the steaming cups toward her, "Careful. It's hot!" Then she looks thoughtful, "I agree with your parents a little, Jolene. Some of the things your president has done have been pretty bold. I have to give him credit for that. Though many wouldn't agree."

Although she is sad about her parents, Jolene is filled with wonder as her aunt talks to her like an adult, always respectful, ready to listen, and responds to anything she has to say or question.

The lump in her throat eases, "Why don't they agree, Aunt Pola?"

And they are off on one of the many informative conversations Jolene will have with her unique Aunt Pola during this magical, three-week visit.

Happy to share this time and finally get to know her niece, Pola, too enjoys herself as much as Jolene. Yet, she is surprised at her niece's deep sadness and unexpected maturity. Pola's heart goes out to her, assuming it is due to the upheaval in her parent's marriage, and Jolene becomes the child she was never allowed to have.

One of the most critical aspects of this visit turns out to be her aunt's supportive comments.

"Don't be afraid to speak out, Jolene," Pola will often say. "Question what you don't understand. You may be young, but you're bright. Don't let people intimidate you. If people are afraid of or angered by your questions, that's their problem, not yours. The only way to learn is to question. If people don't like it, then they're the ones who are being childish, not you."

And Pola never minds her ever-constant questions.

"What is inti...?"

Then her aunt's ever-patient explanation of a word or an observation.

Gaining confidence is not the only lesson Jolene learns during this educational experience away from school. She and her aunt explore nearby Barnsdale Park. They picnic on a sloping lawn surrounding Hollyhock House, the former residence of Aline Barnsdale, who once owned all this land before she donated it to the city to become a park.

"A woman to admire," Pola says, reviewing literature about the long-deceased owner. "She was one of Los Angeles' most liberated women."

"What's liberated?"

A detailed explanation follows, then...

"It says she worked to free India from British rule. Built this house so other women who fought for causes could live here, too."

"Why?"

Another question and answer time, another lesson about life, about courageous women.

Later, touring the house, they are told that Frank Lloyd Wright designed the building in 1917.

"Brilliant man, Jolene. He, too, was ahead of his time, like Aline Barnsdale. Both brave people. They took chances. That's what life is about, Jolene, taking chances, making the most of every moment."

Jolene wishes Aunt Pola was her mother. She's so different from Liz, and the opposite of her brother Dan, too. How can this be, she wonders? Brother and sister. One so direct, so supportive, so strong. The other is defensive, thinking life short-changed him because he didn't have a son. He feels sorry for Pola, too. She sure doesn't. It seems like her aunt has had an extraordinary life with many adventures. She'd like to have experiences like that too.

"Do you take chances, Aunt Pola?"

"Sure! Been knocked down a few times, too, a lot of times. So what! You just get up, dust yourself off, and get on with it. Life is a learning process, Jolene. Learn from your mistakes. Then you have a kick when things go well. And I've had a lot of kicks, too, Jolene, a lot!" Laughing, she gives her niece a playful kick in the behind. "But nothing comes easy, kiddo. I've had to work hard for everything. And I've been well rewarded."

"Do you…I mean, Daddy always says you want to live here but can't because of 'ole'… Excuse me, Aunt Pola. Daddy calls Gramma 'ole Rivka'. Are you unhappy living in Canada, working all the time? Being with Gramma? Daddy thinks you are. And he seems disappointed, too, in most of the things he does. Except when he's at the observatory. He loves that place."

"Your father's a dreamer, Jolene. Always has been! Some people never grow up, I guess." She hugs her. "And your father's wrong. I'm not unhappy. I love what I do, Jolene. Where I live," laughs, "Even 'ole Rivka,' as you put it. I thrive on my work. It's challenging, ever-changing. When you go to work, Jolene, don't just settle for money, kiddo. It isn't worth it. Go for how you feel here," punches herself in the gut. Then she places her hand over her heart, "And be happy here."

"You happy without Carl? Mommy says…"

"Out of the mouths of babes!"

For the first time, Jolene sees her aunt's face cloud. Pola looks away and bites her lip.

Now she's done it. She's made her aunt uncomfortable and doesn't know how to undo the pain she thinks she's just caused. Stammering, she blurts out, "Sorry, Aunt Pola, sorry… I always talk too much. Everybody says I do. Says I never know when to stop. I'm so sorry! Sorry! I didn't mean to…"

Recovering, Pola gives Jolene a playful punch, "Not to worry, kiddo. It had to come up sooner or later. I had no idea how much you knew. Hey! I told you I get knocked down just like the next guy. To answer your last question…"

"We can change the subject…"

Ignoring her niece's perpetual interruption, she continues, "I'm as happy as I can be without Carl. That's God's truth, Jolene. Happy as I can be."

But Jolene sees, deep within her aunt, an ache, an unfulfilled hunger she recognizes in her mother.

That hunger is more than fulfilled when they hear a knock at the door a few days later. And there stands Carl. Arriving unexpectedly, Carl lifts Pola off the floor and smiles as he tells her, "Surprise, my lady! Surprise!"

No one is more surprised than Jolene.

Somehow, she had pictured Carl as an identical twin of her aunt because Pola was the opposite of her daddy. How could they not be twins? They had this great love, Mommy says, even though they are apart.

So different they are, yet, Carl proves to be a counterpart to Pola. She is of short dark stature, powerful high energy, immediate decisions, and a deep voice. He is tall, slim, fair, soft-spoken, and deliberates everything.

After Carl is introduced to Jolene, he, like Pola, takes her into his life as a smaller person, not as a child. The three of them share days that etch themselves into her memory forever.

They attend a concert at the Philharmonic Auditorium, a vast, converted church downtown. Hearing the pianist playing Rachmaninoff's Piano Concerto in B-flat Minor fills Jolene with such delight that chills course down her spine.

"Oh, Aunt Pola," she gushes, tears of happiness flowing, "wish I could make music like that."

"If that's what you want, then you'll do it."

They see *The Wizard of Oz* starring Judy Garland. Jolene is old enough to enjoy the make-believe this time, and the movie does not terrify her. She memorizes *Over the Rainbow*, a song from the film, and decides it is her favorite. She sings it daily to the amusement of Pola and Carl.

Wandering through neighboring Hollywood streets, they explore curio shops, small cafés, and bookstores. And they talk, always talk, have discussions about everyone and everything they see, read or hear. There are no harsh words or arguments. Animated discussions and sometimes disagreements take place. If Carl and Pola disagree, she becomes more emphatic. He remains soft-spoken and calm until he makes his point.

Oh, so different from home, thinks Jolene again and again. So different. So loving, magical. Why…? Why can't they be my parents, she wonders over and over? Why?

Even in public, they are affectionate to her and each other, not pawing each other as Dan does to Liz. They hold hands and share gentle hugs and soft kisses, sometimes with light teasing and laughter.

They read Liz's daily postcards or letters in the evenings, sharing her adventures vicariously.

She writes of Las Vegas, where there are huge hotels with people gambling as her family does on Saturday nights but losing a lot more money. There are free meals at what Liz calls midnight buffets. And they laugh at Jolene's red face when they read about the show with naked ladies.

The Grand Canyon is a colorful gorge so deep Liz couldn't see the bottom. So deep, she writes, that she leaned too far over and almost fell in trying to see. A nice cowboy called Hank, also on the tour bus, pulled her back.

After that, every card or letter mentions Hank in some fashion, where they eat, walk, tour the Black Hills, or visit a cousin in Cleveland.

"Who knows?" says Pola, as she winks at Carl.

At night Jolene is tucked in, kissed goodnight by both. When they retire to Pola's bedroom later, Carl closes the door ever so softly, so considerate is he of Pola's young charge. After the door closes, Jolene snuggles deeper into the content of the bedclothes. To her, they are the perfect couple, Pola and Carl, just perfect. Even the noises they make behind the closed bedroom door are ideal. There are no squeaking springs, animal moans, or groans, just rustling sounds, occasional laughter, then quiet.

Jolene is going to be eight.

Liz's letter comes two days before her birthday, postmarked in New York. Inside two crisp $1.00 bills, instructions not to spend them foolishly.

It is the big day. Jolene rises, mopes about the apartment, and is disappointed that her parents aren't here to share her birthday. Pola tells her to get off her duff, shower, and dress. They take a trolley downtown, exit, walk half a block and enter a fantasy world.

Clifton's Brookdale Cafeteria.

Replicas of California redwood trees, waterfalls, brooks, chirping birds are everywhere. They wander through groves of trees, drop coins into a wishing well, follow a stream that fills their glasses with free lime water from a miniature waterfall. Then they get into a long line as they, and many others, wait in line to select a meal. Jolene couldn't believe her eyes. In front of her, what looks like miles and miles of gleaming stainless steel counters that look upon more food than she has ever seen in her life. The line moves forward.

"Choose as many dishes as you like," Pola instructs her. She and Carl watch in amusement as Jolene deliberates, chooses, removes, chooses again, removes. In time, all of their trays fill. But Jolene's tray is too heavy for her to carry. An attendant comes forward and takes her tray. They follow him to a table in the rainforest section. Sitting under a canopy, they watch raindrops pelt down every 15 minutes during their meal.

There is much activity around them. Jolene is as busy watching as she is eating. The artificial rain drips down, hundreds of diners dine. A singer, accompanied by a pianist, sings. While taking in all of this, Jolene also tries to converse with her aunt and Carl. To their surprise, she eats almost everything, finally stops, admits she's full.

"Too bad! You won't have room for…?" Pola teases, looking up.

Some waiters approach their table. One holds a chocolate cake covered with eight burning candles. Placing the cake on the table in front of Jolene, they sing the birthday song. Clifton's policy is to present free cakes to diners for special occasions.

Jolene giggles and glows as Pola, Carl, and nearby patrons complete the serenade, "Happy Birthday, dear Jolene. Happy Birthday to you."

Taking a huge breath, Jolene closes her eyes and silently wishes, "I wish…I wish the three of us could be together…forever!" After blowing out the candles, Jolene requests a big piece.

"Sure your eyes aren't bigger than your stomach?" asks Carl.

"They don't call me hollow leg for nothing," she retorts, causing much laughter. The joyful sound mingles with raindrops, clattering dishes, and chattering diners. Jolene closes her eyes and gathers the special moment and sounds forever into her heart and memory.

While Carl pays the bill, Jolene selects a sucker from a miniature castle next to the cash register. Such a perfect ending for a perfect day, marred only by a brief moment of regret that her parents couldn't share this happy event.

Carl is leaving.

There are no tearful farewells, just quiet words, a few sighs, tender embraces, and a last lingering kiss. Then he is gone.

That night Dan calls Pola, "I can't believe Liz is wandering around the country! How can she take off, leave the kid, and…"

Jolene hears Dan's accusation blast from the receiver as Pola holds it away from her ear. "And what? Why are you surprised, little brother? You think you're the only one who can have fun?"

Jolene doesn't hear Dan's response. But she does hear Pola lash back, "You're a jerk, Dan. An ingrate. You'll be lucky if she does take you back. A pause, Okay! Okay! Noon. She'll be ready."

Pola hangs up.

Jolene looks disappointed, "Didn't Daddy want to talk to me?"

"He not only wants to talk to you, my sweet. He's taking you to lunch tomorrow."

Jolene looks downcast. On the one hand, she's thrilled at the prospect of seeing her daddy. Yet, she hates it when he comes and then leaves, never knowing if he's coming back.

"Why the long face? I thought you'd be excited."

"I am sort of. But Daddy always says he's going to stay and makes promises, and then he…"

"Maybe this time he won't go, Jolene. Maybe he's come to his senses." Pola opens her arms. Jolene goes to her and wraps her arms around her aunt's neck, grateful for the warm, encompassing hug she receives in return.

"I love you so much, Aunt Pola."

"Ditto, my girl! And I'll always be here for you, Jolene. Remember that! Always!"

Aunt Pola was right.

Daddy didn't go away this time. After they have lunch, he stays in touch every day, sometimes reading Liz's postcards or letters, commenting on her descriptions of Niagara Falls, Washington D.C., New Orleans, and Texas. He becomes increasingly agitated at her continued references to Hank, her new friend.

When Liz calls and learns that Dan has returned, she sounds upset and is unsure she wants to see him, saying she's developed feelings for Hank and he's asked her to be his wife. Pola tells her to sleep on it, not make any decision yet.

Liz is coming home.

Jolene, Pola, and Dan wait at the bus station. They wait, not knowing what to expect. They all wonder, is Liz coming home alone or with Hank? Jolene watches as her father paces back and forth, back and forth, puffing, puffing nervously on his cigar, leaving a trail of smoke behind him.

The bus pulls in. Jolene's hand tightens in Pola's grip. Dan stops pacing, joins them, takes Jolene's other hand. His palm is wet. The three of them stand there, waiting apprehensively.

The bus stops, doors open, steps drop. People begin to disembark.

Jolene and Dan's hearts race as they wait, their mouths dry. Pola tries to reassure them that everything will be okay.

Liz emerges, suitcase in hand, and steps down, assisted by a man with a large Stetson hat on his head. There is a sharp intake of air from Dan and Jolene.

Liz kisses the man on the cheek, they hug, and he boards the bus as Jolene and Pola hear Dan's cry of relief. Liz waves and walks toward them, alone.

Grateful, they laugh and cry as they rush toward her shouting their greetings.

Pola returns to her apartment alone.

Dan, Liz, and Jolene return home together as though nothing has ever happened.

A few days later, it is time to say their goodbyes to Pola. This time, Liz, Dan, and Jolene stand at the Glendale train station and wave as the Santa Fe train disappears on the horizon.

Long after the train is out of sight, Jolene still waves, tears streaming down her face, as she repeatedly shouts, "Come back soon, Aunt Pola. Please come back soon."

Her parents tug and tug at her, but she remains steadfast. Jolene is so upset, so very upset that the train is taking her Aunt Pola away from her, back to Chicago, then to Canada. Back to Rivka, back to being, "As happy as I can be, without Carl."

Jolene and her parents settle back into their routine.

Dan goes back to work for Reuben. Liz returns to the café. And Jolene returns to school full of stories to share with her friends. But somehow, life is never the same again. She feels different from her friends and classmates. Somehow older, more worldly.

And she's not happy when her father reaches out for her now, either. It seems wrong. Her body craves the physical pleasure of orgasms, true. But her heart and conscience object now. Every time she is in his arms, she hates herself, feels dirty, so very dirty, and so guilty.

Frustrated, she masturbates more often and tries to avoid being alone with him. If he does manage to get her alone and she shows resistance, the shaking becomes more pronounced. Her headaches last longer now. Or he tells her to pack her suitcase, with the threat of the 'bad girl school' if she gives him any more sass. When she pleads with him not to put his penis in her mouth, he strokes her, calms her, reassures her how much he loves her, how happy she makes him. Gradually, he wears down her resistance. Dan, still the professional lovemaker, finally gets his way. She gags after his ejaculation, runs to the bathroom, spits out his semen, then dryheaves until her chest and throat hurt so badly; she can hardly talk.

It is late October, and it's so hot; the schools close down. Kids are sent home. Liz can't leave Jolene at home, so she takes her to work with her. Everyone makes over her at the café, commenting on her freckles, thick hair, unusual eyes. They ask about her scabbed knees, those ever-present bruises and scabs.

"Clumsy, clumsy, clumsy," Liz tells them after Jolene has hurt herself again.

Bumping, constantly bumping into something; tables, walls, tripping over stairs, furniture, or taking a fall. Her legs have grown so long they seem to arrive at every destination way before her knees are ready for it.

Jolene discovers that she isn't black during this physical growth. Her blood, like other white people, is red. All these years, she had been comforted with the knowledge that she was black. Devastated, she realizes that she is still white and doesn't belong anywhere, black or white.

As comments continue about her bruised knees at the café, Liz responds with, "Not the natural athlete her mom is, huh," and pretends a balled napkin is a basketball, looping it successfully into a wastebasket time and time again to cheers from co-workers and customers.

A week passes. The heat continues.

The radio announcer tells of car accidents caused by angry drivers, fights breaking out, even a few deaths. Newspapers show pictures of kids running through streams of water from broken fire hydrants to get relief from the sweltering heat breaking records.

As the heatwave continues, windows and doors are kept open, fans keep turning, but nothing helps. Homes have no air conditioning. There is no relief. No one sleeps. No one.

"Can't stand it, Dan."

"What can we do about it? We've already bought a fan."

"Cousin Selma rented a place at Venice Beach."

"So what! They've got a houseful already."

"I know. I know. But Selma said we could use their bathroom and share the kitchen."

"Where would we sleep?"

"You'll see."

Arriving at the beach that weekend, they join hundreds of families camping out on the sand who have come to seek relief from the heat. Most of them are relatives of the Jewish families who rent or own small cottages lining Rose Avenue, where it meets the boardwalk in Venice Beach.

Cousin Selma's place is six doors from the boardwalk. Such lovely people, Liz's cousins, all 16 of them, letting them share the one bathroom. Two families occupy the bungalow. Three families sleep on the sand. Even though there's always a line to use the bathroom, Jolene never has to use a bucket or pee in the ocean because everyone is considerate.

Dan doesn't like the situation, all the people, no privacy. He can't stay as long as he wants in the bathroom. He leaves in the morning: good riddance, one less to share the bathroom, the relatives' joke.

Her relatives have no children her age, so Jolene is again with adults. This doesn't bother her. Some of them have interesting stories, especially Cousin Sy, Selma's father.

"Professor Sy, the postman," they call him. Her mother says Cousin Sy has a college degree and could have been a lawyer but didn't want to work at a desk. Jolene loves the stories Professor Sy shares about being bitten by dogs, helping to deliver a baby, putting out a fire, thwarting a robbery.

Jolene and Liz enjoy the gypsy life, extended family, the ocean, and group meals.

On the third night, as they sleep, shouts are heard up and down the beach, "It's raining. Thank Gawd, it's raining!"

Jolene awakens to the feeling of moisture, raindrops forming tiny wet droplets on her face. Excited, she sits up, then is frightened as thunder crashes in the distance. The heatwave is over. Hurriedly, people pack, give their thanks, hugs, fond farewells, and leave for their homes.

Later, as they ride the trolley, memories of the past few days fill Jolene's thoughts; sleeping on the sand under the starlit sky, sharing food, one bathroom, so much laughter, so many hugs and kisses from so many loving relatives. She thinks how nice it must be to have a big family like that. Even if there is only one bathroom, it's not so bad when people don't do crossword puzzles or take too long. Smiling as she dozes off, Jolene can't wait for another heatwave to happen again. Then, maybe, she'll get another chance to sleep under the stars.

Chapter Fifteen
1940

Dan isn't happy working for anyone, even Reuben. He wants to be the boss. Always the silver-tongued salesman, he sells Reuben on the idea of loaning him money to open a store selling unpainted furniture like his store in Glendale. Reluctantly, Reuben agrees. Plans are made.

Jolene's ninth birthday is coming up.

She waits and waits for her parents to say something, do something. Anything! Nothing happens. They're so busy thinking about the new store they leave for work saying nothing. Nothing at all. Who can be so busy they stop thinking of birthdays? There is so much excitement, so much to do. Tomorrow is the opening of the new store.

"Not fair! Not fair!" Jolene yells at the empty rooms after her parents leave. "Why do they hate me so much? Why was I born? Why can't I just die?"

Throwing herself on her bed, she thinks of ways to get even. "If I hung myself in the closet, they'd be sorry. No! Maybe they'd be happy. They wouldn't have to bother with me anymore. How would I know if they were happy or sad? I wouldn't be here. I'd be dead! Nope! That won't work."

Feeling dejected, she mumbles about how lousy life is as she goes outside, puts the leash on Oscar, leads her up the path. Oscar quacks as the postman approaches and greets them.

"Got a package for you, Jolene."

Thanking him, she takes the wrapped box back to the house. Sitting on the stoop, she wonders what it is, who sent it? Ripping off the wrapping, she removes a greeting card and reads it aloud to Oscar.

"To keep beautiful memories and melodies alive. With love, hugs, and kisses, Aunt Pola."

Tearing at the crumpled paper, Jolene squeals in delight as she observes the gift—a ceramic music box. Removing it carefully, she sees it is etched with the Wizard of Oz characters; Dorothy, Scarecrow, Cowardly Lion, and the Tin Man.

"Look, Oscar, look!" Jolene exclaims, bubbling with pleasure. "Oscar, look!" She holds it up to the duck's head. "A beautiful music box, Oscar. Aunt Pola sent me a music box. Isn't it something?"

Twisting the lever on the bottom of the box, "Over the Rainbow" begins to play. Tears of joy appear in Jolene's eyes. "Oh, listen, Oscar. Listen! Isn't it beautiful?" She holds the music box up to Oscar's face and begins describing the characters. Suspicious of the strange noisemaker, Oscar quacks her disapproval.

"Oh, Oscar. Isn't Aunt Pola wonderful? She remembered," Jolene enthuses. "She remembered everything. My birthday. My song. Isn't she just something?"

Remembering Pola's words, "I'll always be here for you, Jolene. Always," she kisses the music box, then Oscar. Looking up at the sky, she shouts, "I love you so much, Aunt Pola, wherever you are. And I'll always be here for you, too."

Dan and Liz return home late that night. Jolene is sound asleep, the music box clutched in her arms. They have still forgotten it's her birthday.

The store opens the next day, and the party goes on all day. Momentarily, it eases anger and disappointment about her birthday. How thrilling it is to see the name, "HARTMAN'S UNPAINTED FURNITURE," printed on an enormous sign in front. There are balloons everywhere. People mill about. Family from both sides are there, friends, acquaintances, and a few customers.

Jolene has never seen her father look so happy.

Puffed up with pride, Dan cannot stop himself from looking again and again at the sign in front of the store as he tells Jolene, "This place will make us rich someday, Jolene." He points to the sign. "I'll buy you that brick house I promised you, and the clothes, and the shoes and…"

Interrupted by a well-wisher who comments on the size of the store, Dan turns from her and informs the man that the store takes up an entire half-block.

Jolene marvels. Wow! Her father said the store takes up a whole half block on this street called Olympic Boulevard, one of the busiest streets in Los

Angeles. Looking at all the traffic whizzing by, she is sure he is right this time. Soon, they'll be rich.

A week goes by before Liz remembers.

They take her to Clifton's Cafeteria with a bit of guilt, but it doesn't make up for the resentment Jolene still feels. Somehow, the cafeteria isn't as perfect this time. She doesn't enjoy the food as much, realizes the rain is fake, isn't surprised by the free cake or singers. Somehow, it's all too late. Too late! Sensing her disappointment, her parents splurge and decide to take her to a movie.

"It's called *Grapes of Wrath*," says Liz. "People say it's a great movie about a farm family."

Later, as they exit the theater, a red-eyed Liz hugs Jolene to her, "Makes us seem rich, doesn't it?"

Still crying, Jolene nods into the folds of her mother's cloth coat.

"Why didn't you find out more about it, Liz?" Dan accuses. "So damned depressing."

"Sorry, Dan, sorry!"

So sad a film that even he is shaken.

It is a long time before Jolene loses the image of those impoverished people. Every time she looks into the icebox and sees it so full of food, she thinks of the poor family in the movie, pulling turnips, dried weeds, anything out of the dusty earth, foraging for anything edible to make a soup.

Liz still feels guilty.

No matter how hard she and Dan try to make amends for the forgotten birthday, the incident hangs over their heads. It's not that Jolene accuses them. She says nothing. The guilt comes when Liz sees her daughter hunched over on the bed, holding the music box close to her ear, singing along, always smiling.

Gawd! Pola remembered! In Canada. And she got the gift here on the right day too. How could they have forgotten something like that? Even with the store opening and all. How could they have forgotten? These are questions Liz asks herself repeatedly.

She remembers how terrified Jolene had been when she was in that hospital crib, crying out not to be left alone. Liz had sworn then that she wouldn't let the kid down again. And now she'd done it. She'd done it again. Damn! Damn! What a lousy mother she is. Lousy. Lousy. Why does she have to be a mother, anyway? Why can't she ever do anything right? Why is it so hard to reach out, to comfort her own daughter? Why is she repeating every single lousy mistake her mother made with her?

Spring comes.

It's a wet spring, raining more than usual. Business is slow. Occasionally, someone parks in front, buys a desk, a chest, inquires how to finish it. Dan doesn't know how and calls Reuben for instructions.

"Give a class, Dan. That's what we do! Show them how. Then they'll come back for more," says Reuben.

But Dan can't give a class. There are never enough customers. Never enough money to hire someone who can 'show them how.'

Summer comes.

"We're moving!"

"Why?"

"More convenient to the store," Dan says.

"It'll be nice, Jolene, new friends, better opportunities," Liz tells her.

Hysterical, Jolene asks, "You mean I have to go to a new school? Again?"

"No! No! Not for a few months anyway. You'll have the whole summer to get acquainted with the neighbors and make new friends. You'll love it!"

"No, I won't! I won't! I'll hate it. I know it! You can't do this to me again. I won't go! I'll move in with the twins!"

They take her a few days later to see the newly rented house. Jolene is still lamenting the move and refuses to accept her new fate until they arrive and…

The new place not only pleases her, but she also loves it.

The small two-storied house sits on a hill in a dead-end street called Sanborn Ave. It is the second of three identical plaster boxes. Each has a steep driveway that leads into a one-car garage. Besides the garage, the first level has a laundry area and a large storage playroom. Dan has made arrangements to purchase a car on time. He needs it, he insists, to get them to work. Against her better judgment, Liz agrees. But every monthly bill brings stress and arguments between them.

Next to the driveway, a narrow stairway leads up to their new living room, kitchen, and bathroom. All of the rooms have views of Hollywood. And best of all, Jolene could hardly believe her eyes, not one but two bedrooms! Finally! She is going to have a room of her own.

This delightful small house, located off Fountain Avenue between Sunset Boulevard and Hyperion in West Hollywood, is near Silver Lake. Not a natural lake, Silver Lake. Instead, it is a large scenic reservoir storing drinking water for thirsty Angelinos. Contemporary homes designed by architects Richard Neutra and Rudolph Schindler jut out from neighboring hills surrounding this jewel of an artificial lake. Silver Lake was initially planned for upscale dwellers but didn't quite make it. The neighborhood never gained the status of Beverly Hills or Bel-Air. So the area's lovely homes remained modestly priced and allowed average-income families and professors who work at the nearby state college to occupy a number of the dwellings.

Even though Jolene loves having her own room, she is still upset at the thought of leaving the twins, the Adams family, her other friends. But, most of all, she refuses to believe she has to leave Oscar, her beloved duck, behind.

They have to leave Oscar, her parents insist because there is no yard, no place to house the duck outside yet. And Dan is too busy right now, working seven days a week to build a cage.

"As soon as I can, I'll build one, Jolene. I promise. Then we'll get Oscar."

Upset, she listens to them, then asks, "But where will he live until you build the cage?"

"Spoke to the man with the yard a few doors down, Jolene, Mr. Granger," Dan tells her. "Said he'd keep it 'til we can come. He has a pond, too. Did you know that?"

"Mr. Granger!" Jolene's stomach churns at the thought of that man taking Oscar. Mr. Granger is the man whose vegetables Jolene has been stealing. Oh, how he hates her, hates Oscar. What was her daddy thinking?

"But…"

"Promised he'd take good care of Oscar, Jolene. He's not such a bad old geezer. You'll see."

"But you don't understand, Daddy. He hates…"

"It's all we can do right now, Jolene. I've got enough on my mind without worrying about a duck."

"But, Daddy…"

Losing patience, he turns from her, "That's enough!"

"But, Daddy…" she howls to the now empty room.

On the day of the move, Jolene puts the leash on Oscar. She and Dan walk slowly down the street, leading the plump, waddling duck until they reach Mr.

Granger's house. They stop and stand in front of the house that will be Oscar's new home. She's terrified of Mr. Granger. Why is Daddy doing this to them, she wonders? Isn't there someone else who…? She continues to hesitate.

Gently, Dan nudges her. They walk down the path to the porch. Becoming apprehensive, Oscar starts quacking and pulls on the leash. Bending down, Jolene gathers Oscar into her arms, hugging and stroking her, trying to calm her. Kissing her on her beak, she tells Oscar how much she's loved and that they'll be back soon. But nothing works on the agitated duck as they walk up the stairs.

Dan rings the doorbell and steps back.

Then they wait. The door opens.

There he is, Mr. Granger, Oscar's new caretaker.

Jolene has never been so near to the man before. Up close, he is even more foreboding, with his tight, downward tilted mouth, slits for eyes, deep ridges rolling back and forth across his forehead, his voice, a deep growl.

"Whaddya want?"

She steps back in fear. Dan nudges her forward again. "I…I…"

The man grimaces behind the screen door, his demeanor changing when he sees Oscar.

"Ahah! You brought the duck?"

Snorting his satisfaction, he opens the door and reaches out. Quacking in agitation, Oscar snaps at him, again and again. Swearing, the man backs off, pulls a coat from a nearby rack, wraps it around his arm and hand. Reaching out with his protected arm, he jerks Oscar out of Jolene's embrace. The duck quacks, hisses, tries vainly to escape but is held firmly as the man places his coated hand over her beak.

"Oooooh, Daddy! Oscar's so unhappy. Please! We can't leave her here. We can't!" Jolene cries out, upset at Oscar's distress.

"Oscar will be fine," Dan reassures her. "We'll be back in a few weeks, Mr. Granger. I appreciate what you're doing," offering a bag of feed to the man.

"Leave it! Leave it! Got all I can handle here."

Dan lowers the bag to the porch.

"He eats vegetables, too," sobs Jolene.

"How well I know," he glowers at Jolene.

She backs off, frightened but begs, "Please, take good care of Oscar, Mr. …Mr. Granger. Please. Until we…" Jolene chokes up, unable to finish.

"Yeah! Yeah! You bet I'll take good care, little girl."

Mumbling something about, "I'll take proper care of…" he slams the door in their faces.

Howling, Jolene collapses into Dan's arms as she mumbles, "Oscar! Oscar!."

Even though Jolene loves her new bedroom, she is inconsolable about leaving Oscar. Nothing her parents say or do appeases her. Nothing!

More than a few weeks go by before Dan builds a cage, so he and Jolene drive back to 36th Street to pick up Oscar. Knocking on Mr. Granger's door repeatedly, they receive no answer. They walk around to the pond. But Oscar isn't in Mr. Granger's yard or the pond. Mr. Granger doesn't seem to be home.

They inquire of the neighbor.

"Gone to visit his sister," a neighbor says.

"But where's Oscar, the duck?"

The neighbor looks uncomfortable as he shakes his head.

They seek out the Adams family.

"Oscar's in the man's stomach, Jolene. Thass where he is. Had Oscar for dinner, he did!" Flora tells her shocked friend. "Him's lied to you, Jolene. Lied! Told the neighbors, got even for all the stealing you done. Got even, he said. Him's a mean-un, that one, real mean."

There is no way Liz or Dan can explain or comfort Jolene after what happened to Oscar that day or for months afterward. Liz is helpless, but Dan is determined the make it up to her.

Jolene's unhappiness is absolute until the day Dan arrives home with a black and white furball in his hands.

"The breed's called a miniature silver fox, Jolene," he says, handing the quivering puppy to her. "Going to need a lot of love and attention. Think you can handle it?"

Between tears and gulps, Jolene nods, holding the puppy close, squealing with pleasure as she feels tiny licks of affection attacking her face, neck, and ears.

"What are you going to call her?" Liz asks, grateful to finally see her daughter smile again.

"Twinkie! Because she's so twinkly," Jolene announces.

That tiny new friend sleeps next to her bed in a shoebox, complete with a ticking clock.

Dan tells Jolene to wrap the clock in a towel. "The puppy will think the ticking is its mother's beating heart," he tells her. "Then the puppy won't be lonely."

Jolene and Twinkie, those two young ones yearning for the love and comfort taken from their lives, console one another. Jolene learns to adapt, enjoy, and love despite life's hardships. The new puppy adopts Jolene as its mother and brings back the sparkle in her eyes.

Once again, Dan has proven that, in his way, he is a great father.

Business is brisker, but not much.

Dan can't understand it because Olympic Boulevard is such a busy street. There is so much traffic going by in the morning hours. Hundreds of cars and buses head east. They carry thousands of people downtown to work. In the late afternoon and evening, vehicles packed with those same commuters take them back to their homes. Why don't they stop, he wonders. Why don't they shop in his store, buy his furniture like they do at Reuben's place?

Dan hadn't realized that those thousands of workers passing by daily are on rigid time schedules, eager to get to work and eager to get home. Olympic Boulevard is a commuter street, not a shopper's boulevard. If people want to shop, they do most of it in their neighborhoods.

This time Jolene doesn't feel uncomfortable at her new school, Lockwood Elementary. She doesn't feel different, either, because there are so many different kinds of children here. Some are golden-haired, like the ones she used to know in Inglewood. Others are yellow-skinned with silky black hair and slanted eyes. They have names like Mori, Yamada, Keiko, and Sayuri. There are boisterous children with dark, wavy hair called Mario, Giovanni, Rosa, and Sophia. And last but not least, some children look like her cousins, named Ruth, Becky, Samuel, Abe, and Ronald. All welcome her, include her in their games, and offer friendship.

Fall comes.

Business drops off, and Dan can't afford to keep his helper. Liz quits the café to replace him. She dusts, helps move furniture, answers the phone, and worries about customers who don't come. But her biggest concern is about bills that aren't being paid.

"It takes time to get known, Liz," Dan reassures her.

Even though Reuben is worried, he agrees with Dan. "Sometimes it takes time, Liz, takes time."

Jolene sees little of her parents because they're so involved with the store, but they don't worry about her now. She seems preoccupied and happy with her new friends, Twinkie, and the school. She even won some contest, as Dan proudly tells his customers. His kid did a painting or something, a hand holding a lit match with the words, "Don't start fires!" He's told the framed picture hangs in the school hallway. A Fire Department commendation hangs next to it. He and Liz haven't seen it yet, but they will soon.

Somehow, they never get around to seeing it, which doesn't disappoint Jolene too much as she's used to being ignored by them, getting the positive feedback she needs from her new friends and teachers.

Jolene hates hospitals.

Walking down this stark, unfriendly corridor, she keeps her eyes downcast and holds tightly to Dan's hand as they follow Liz. The hallway is cold and has a heavy, antiseptic aroma. Her stomach turns. Why did they bring her here? Why? Without wanting to, she glances into every room they pass. Inside she sees older men lying in beds. Some sleep, others cough. Some moan and call out in pain. Most are alone. The scene is repetitious as they pass each open door.

Liz stops and glances into a room, "There he is!"

Jolene peeks in and sees her grampa in a hospital bed.

"This is his third stroke, Dan. Don't see how he can survive this one..." Liz whispers.

"He's strong as an ox, Abe is. You'll see, Liz. He'll be outta here in no time."

"Sure."

The small room is cramped with four beds, a few chairs, curtains to be pulled for a moment's privacy. In each bed was a sickly, smelly elderly man.

Forced greetings are offered with hollow gaiety.

"Abe. How're ya doing?"

"Hi, Dad."

"Hi, Grampa."

All tubes and sheets, Abe opens his eyes and sighs, "Ach! Mine kinderlach (my children)."

Kissing Abe on the forehead, Liz pulls Jolene to the bed. "Give Grampa a kiss."

She bends over and presses her lips upon his grizzled cheek. An objectionable stench greets her. Grimacing, she pulls back. "Something smells awful!"

The three adults laugh, "Probably the urinal."

"What's a uri—"

"Oh God, Jolene, no questions, please! Let us talk."

She hangs back and remains quiet, the urine smell still stinging her nostrils.

During the visit, her parents make small talk and joke, trying to get Grampa to laugh. But it is no use. For the first time that Jolene can remember, her Grampa Abe doesn't joke back. He doesn't laugh. Nothing but sighs come from him, then his quiet statement, "I'm tired, Liz, tired. Tired of living."

"Dad! Don't say that!"

That night Abe did what he wanted to do.

He quit living.

The next day Jolene tells her friends about her grampa's death. Rosa asks if she is going to the funeral.

"I don't know. Guess so," Jolene replied.

"Better not look him in the face," Rosa warns her. "My mom says if you look a dead man in the face, he'll jump out of his grave and haunt you forever."

A few days later, Jolene sits in the car at Forest Lawn and watches from a distance as her black-clad parents join other mourners dressed in black in front of a small building at the cemetery. Liz had told her to remain in the car because a funeral was no place for a kid, she'd said.

Jolene is grateful she doesn't have to go to the funeral. She doesn't want to see her dead Grampa and be haunted for the rest of her life.

But the casket wasn't open, so she wouldn't have seen him even if she'd been allowed to attend because he had already been cremated, and his ashes were to be placed in a marble vault.

Many men wearing white aprons over their dark suits filed into the building with the Sorkin clan, the Hartman clan, and a few friends.

Dozing off, Jolene is awakened later by voices and sees people milling around outside, some embracing, some saying farewells. The men wearing aprons remove them and shake hands. Then all disperse toward their respective vehicles. Her parents return to their car. Liz, red-eyed, blows her nose into a large handkerchief.

"Why were those men wearing aprons?" Jolene asks.

"They're Shriners, Jolene."

"What's a Shriner?"

"Name of a club, a club Grampa belonged to. They gave a nice service, didn't they, Dan?"

"Seemed strange, not having a rabbi."

"It's what he wanted."

"I know."

"What's a rabbit?"

"Rabbi!"

"Why didn't Grampa want a rabbi?"

"He was cremated, and the Shriners did…"

"What's cre—"

"Enough, Jolene, enough!" Liz screams as she turns around and slaps her across the face. "Gawd! Don't you ever know when to stop? Not one damn more word out of you, you hear! Not a damn word!"

Jolene sits, holding her smarting cheek, wondering if she is supposed to feel sad, too, cry like her mommy is doing. Like others she'd seen leaving the building. But she didn't feel sad. So, how could she cry? Grampa was 76 years old on his last birthday. And Daddy said older people always die. Then she wonders why they are acting so sad, especially about Grampa. They hardly ever saw him. And her mother was always complaining about how much it costs to keep him in Boyle Heights. Then, why is she crying, Jolene wonders? You'd think she'd be happy. Oh, well. Sometimes she doesn't understand why grownups act the way they do. But this time, she says nothing because she knows she'll get belted again.

Not another word is spoken in the car on the way home, not by anyone. The only sounds come from Liz, who sniffs and blows her nose, sniffs and blows her nose.

A new friend is in Jolene's life now. Her name is Keiko, and she lives next door. They have much in common because her parents also own their own business, a jewelry store in Little Tokyo, and they leave early in the morning and return late in the evening, just like her parents do. Keiko is bright, too. For the first time, another child challenges Jolene intellectually. It's a whole new, stimulating experience, talking to Keiko, exploring each other's minds, sharing interests.

But there is a world of difference between Jolene's home and her new friend's home.

First—the smells.

When Jolene enters her own home, she often smells garlic or onions. Scents are still present from her mother's cooking efforts the night before. Sometimes there's a musty smell from rooms being closed up all day. Or there might be the scent of Twinkie greeting her. The greeting reminds her to take Twinkie outside for a walk. A strong doggie smell reminds her it's bath time.

When entering Keiko's house, the smell of incense is always present, from some previously burned or those presently lit. But all constantly invade the nostrils.

Second—the furnishings.

Carpets cover all floors in Jolene's home, except the kitchen and bathroom. They have new furniture now, too. Liz couldn't wait to get rid of her parent's things. Their rooms are brighter now too, but there is no sense of plan or design in furnishing the Hartman household.

In Keiko's home, there are no carpets.

Each room mirrors highly glossed, sleek wooden floors polished so finely you can almost see your reflection when you look down. In the living room, everything is so tasteful, so special. A decorated silk screen sits in one corner. Perhaps a floral arrangement here, a carved figurine there. Pillows take the place of couches and chairs. Low wooden tables finish the decor. Bedrooms are almost bare, with mats unrolled at night for sleep. Wherever you look in Keiko's home, it is a visual feast, but simple, simple.

The families are different, too.

Keiko's parents are so polite. No one ever raises their voices in Keiko's home, not once. Keiko's father always dresses in a black silk suit, and his silky black hair is lacquered tight to his head. Her mother wears bright red lipstick, and her long, shiny, black hair is wrapped tightly in a bun. She wears different colored embroidered silken kimonos, which snugly encase her slim body, as do the tiny embroidered slippers on her feet. She is so beautiful, so delicate. Keiko's parents are so prim, proper, and lovely when they leave in the morning, and they still look perfectly groomed when they return at the end of their long workday. Not a hair is out of place, or a wrinkle appears in their delicate clothing as they bend down to kiss the top of Keiko's head, greet her quietly upon their return.

The conversations are never about work. They revolve around Keiko, her day's activities, interests, friends, accomplishments. If Jolene is there, polite inquiries about her activities also are included.

Sometimes, Jolene wishes she could live with Keiko, be her blood sister, be the daughter of these beautiful, perfect parents. But then, it is time to go home, to reality.

As her mother fixes dinner at home, Jolene chatters on and on about her day's activities. Liz gets a kick out of her daughter's stories. Nothing pleases Jolene more than making her mother laugh. Dan always needs something or demands her attention whenever Liz's laughter rings out.

So, no matter how tired she is, Liz brings Dan his slippers, fills his pipe, lights his cigar, empties his ashtray, does whatever he asks as she prepares the meals, sets the table, never allowing Jolene to help. Here, at least, when he's home, Dan is her man. She wants him to feel like a king.

And so it is that Jolene is often excluded from their world even in the few short hours that her parents are home in the evening. She then retreats to her room with Twinkie, the music box, Eddie's harmonica, talks with God, and dreams of living in Keiko's house until Liz calls her for dinner.

Liz sits in her usual sideways position during the meals, waiting to respond to Dan's demands. She tries incessantly to please him. But she knows, and Jolene knows, that it is impossible to please her father when it comes to food.

Dan eats not for pleasure but to survive. No matter what is placed in front of him, he gulps it down and hardly chews, unaware of what he's eating. And he can't understand why others dally over their meals. Her father often finishes his entire meal before Jolene has even downed her salad. And her slow chewing and incessant chatter become intolerable for him sometimes, like tonight.

Through with the meal, he wipes his mouth and looks with disgust at Jolene's full plate. "Why can't you just eat, Jolene? Do you have to yak, yak, yak all the time? Don't you ever know when to stop?"

"Aw, lay off, Dan. The kid was just…"

"Was just…Was just…All she does is talk, talk, talk. In that annoying voice of hers. Isn't there a limit to how much a person can…?"

"Sure, Dan, sure. Don't pick on her. It's not her fault that…"

And they go back to the day's failures, life's failures, the broken record, which goes on and on and…

"If I'd had a son, I'd…"

"If we'd never had children, we'd…"

"If I wasn't Jewish, I'd…"

"If I'd finished high school, I'd…"

"If we hadn't married so young…"

"If we had more money, we'd…"

"If…if…if…!"

It hurts Jolene's feelings when her father tells her he can't stand the sound of her voice. She doesn't understand. How can he dislike the sound of her voice so much and still love her? With the lump forming in the back of her throat, eating becomes an even slower process.

Ballet lessons take up much of Keiko's time. Dreaming of becoming a ballerina, she does pirouettes for Jolene and tries to teach her how to stand on her toes. So easy and graceful for Keiko. Impossible for Jolene. Rather than mock, their trials end up in laughter. Whatever they do, they make each other laugh as special friends do. The friendship grows.

Eating at Keiko's house is another adventure.

Keiko's parents teach her how to use chopsticks. Steamed rice, wrapped beef, pork, even raw fish—rejected at first—but tolerable with tasty sauces are plucked and directed to her mouth with the delicate wooden sticks. Then, sweet rice paste balls and green tea for dessert. Dining with Keiko and her parents is a joyful experience for Jolene.

There is a boy in Jolene's life now, too. His name is Harold. He walks her home from school every day, carries her books, and sometimes buys her an ice cream cone. Then they sit on her porch steps and talk and talk and talk. Harold wants to be a doctor. When they play doctor, she and Keiko are his nurses.

Twinkie is the patient. Three months older, Harold expresses his undying love and gives her a ring he found in a Cracker Jack box. They will marry when they grow up, he insists. He wants to touch her lips with his. Much as she loves him, Jolene remembers her father's warning and is still afraid of being kissed by any boy. Even though she now knows where babies come from, there is still a chance that her father's words are true, so Harold is content to hold her hand.

Liz laughs and is delighted when she learns about Harold. It is their secret. They do not tell Dan.

Rosa and Sophia, Jolene's other new friends, live next door down the hill.

Loud sounds emanate from their homes. People sounds—laughter, arguments, shouts, something called opera (where people sing different melodies simultaneously), and there are always hearty welcomes from their moms.

Large women, their moms are wrapped in enormous aprons, happy in their kitchens cooking, always cooking. They welcome the girls with warm words and loving hugs, encompassing all who cross their thresholds.

It is fun being in their homes. They play dress-up, smearing their faces with an older sister's cosmetics, clap around in high heels and bras. They also peek at the older sisters pressing against their boyfriends as they spoon when they think no one is watching. Jolene and her friends look and giggle until screams of "Out! Out! You little monsters!" are shouted at them if they are apprehended.

The overwhelming smell in Rosa and Sophia's homes is garlic, garlic, garlic. That spice permeates everything in the house, including their breath. Jolene can't wait to sit at her friend's food-laden tables, where everyone is welcome. There, tantalizing aromas make her stomach grumble in anticipation. She can't get enough of the delicious homemade Italian food. Her enthusiasm is so great that her nickname resurfaces.

"*Mama mia!* She must have a hollow leg! Look! Look! So much food. And she remains so skinny, skinny like a stick!" Envious, good-humored teasing from the ample mothers as they watch their daughter's friend eat like there is no tomorrow.

These families make her feel comfortable. They are so warm and loving, with so much laughter and music. Even though they are different in so many ways, they remind her of the Adams family.

Momentarily, pangs of remorse fill her.

Where are they, she wonders? Will she ever see her old friends Flora and Fiola again?

A refilled plate is placed before her. As she digs in, delight, laughter, friendship engulf her again, and the Adams family is forgotten.

Jolene loves the new neighborhood, having her own room, her new friends. Most of the time, she doesn't even care whether her folks are at home or not. And thankfully, Daddy is so busy now he hardly ever demands that she be his 'Little Mommy.'

Chapter Sixteen
1941

Because she is working so hard and worrying all the time, Liz slaps Jolene more often now and vents her frustration in the only way she knows. Jolene learns to duck, avoids some hits, doesn't cry when Liz's aim hits her target. Instead, a silent rage engulfs her. She stares, staring defiantly at her mother, not saying a word.

"You'll get another if you look at me like that!" Liz threatens but refrains from hitting her again. So surprised is Liz at the intensity of emotion confronting her. A young version of hers, those eyes look at her with unexpressed fury. The smoldering anger stops her from repeating the insult, from continuing to make her daughter the scapegoat for life's frustrations.

But now, Jolene is also the target of her father's anger and discontent. At the brink of failure again, Dan lashes out at anyone, anything, always avoiding his own ineptness.

Her mother's outbreaks Jolene can handle, having had them all her life. But her father's fury? This is new. This is painful. Where is his love, she wonders? His adoration and support? Why is she now his enemy? Now he says she's the cause of his bad luck. He blames her for everything; if a window shade tears, a tire goes flat, no customers show up, and their bills can't be paid. These things are her fault! Her fault! All because, "Jolene's a lousy daughter—a stone around my neck," he tells her. He often tells anyone, "How can I succeed if I only have a lousy daughter? Now... If I had a son, someone to carry on my name. Things would be different, I'm sure."

Jolene stays out of her father's way as much as possible. If things go wrong, he'll take it out on her. Shaking, insults, or threats occur. Sometimes he pulls her clothes out of drawers and the closet in his fury and shoves them into a small suitcase. Then, with the case in hand, he drags her to the front door and tells her he's taking her to the "bad girl's school."

Terrified, hurt, and not understanding, Jolene resists, cries, and begs not to be sent away. Resentful of being his target now, she sometimes becomes angry and fights back as she tells him, "I don't care, don't care! I'll call Aunt Lottie. She'll come and get me." Then she usually breaks down crying, "They'll take care of me," she sobs, "because they love me, even if you don't."

Furious, he'll yell back, "Good riddance, lousy daughter! Good riddance. Go! Go! Lousy ingrate! Who needs you?" Then he'll start to shove her out of the door.

That's when Liz intervenes. Upset and crying, she'll insist, "We must stay together, as a family. As a family." After she calms him, she takes the suitcase from him, unpacks it, tells them to make up. They must become friends again. She suggests checkers, or they can work on his stamp collection. They'll have a nice dinner together. She'll just go to the market, get a few things. Be back in an hour or so, and she'll leave.

Like a chameleon, Dan sheds the persona of the antagonist and becomes the charmer. Still smarting from the upheaval, Jolene often goes to her room, wanting to be alone. He always follows. She wants him to stay away from her but is afraid another tirade will occur. If she does resist his advances, he'll resort to mockery, "So big shot. So! So… Just because you're almost as tall as me now, you think you're too big to be my 'Little Mommy,' huh? When I say you do something, you do it. Understand?"

Wanting desperately to rebel, instead, she tries to please him. But she's so torn between fear, disgust, a longing to get away, and her need for his acceptance. For a moment, though, if she closes her eyes, sometimes she can recapture the feeling of being loved.

Caught between these two unhappy people, Jolene tries to excel at school, still be a good daughter, hope they will love her, appreciate her accomplishments. But nothing she does ever seems to work. Nothing is ever quite enough.

Like the day she brought home a report card, all A's and one B. Her teacher had commented on the bottom of the card, writing what an excellent student Jolene is and how proud they must be of her. But she had also given her an "N" because of too much talking. Jolene shows the card to her parents and asks for a signature.

Liz is pleased and laughs at the teacher's comment about talking, "So, what else is new?"

Dan is outraged. It isn't the "N" that bothered him. No! Instead, he blasts her with…

"What the hell is this? What's this?" he repeats again and again. "What's a 'B' doing on this card? How in the hell did you get a 'B'? Weren't you paying attention? How will you get anywhere if you don't pay attention?"

He raged on and on, shaking her steadily as he questioned her. So outraged was he that he never even acknowledged the many "A's" on the card.

The next day is Saturday.

Saturdays are just awful.

Her head hurts from the shaking. She wishes there weren't any Saturdays, ever, as she lies in bed, cushioning her aching head. Not just because she has a headache, but because this is the day when she's almost always alone.

Her parents work, won't take her with them, tell her she'd be in the way. They want her to stay home, clean her room, bathe Twinkie, and stay out of their hair.

Saturdays, Rosa, and Sophia help their mothers with household chores. Keiko takes ballet lessons and then goes to Little Tokyo to help her parents' store. Even Harold is busy, too. He's in Hebrew school.

Saturdays are just awful, she decides, just awful. There is no one and nothing to distract her from hurtful feelings or thoughts. Why can't she please her parents, she wonders? Why did she have to be a "broken-rubber" kid? Why wasn't she like Keiko, Rosa, Sophia, and Harold? Their parents love them, want them. And she hates hearing about her father wanting a son. Hates it!

"Why, why?" she asks God. "How come I wasn't a boy?" Unknowingly, she repeats the question her mother had frequently asked God as she grew up.

Yet, Jolene differs significantly from her mother in one respect. Whereas her mother hated being a girl and always wanted to be a boy, Jolene likes being a girl! She hasn't ever wanted to be a boy. But sometimes, life is unfair; she thinks and vents her frustrations out loud to Twinkie later.

Brushing him after his bath, she tells the small squirming animal, "Someday, I'll kill myself. Then they'll be sorry. I'll put my head in the oven like Gramma did. That'll make them sad…Umm, noo! I'll drown myself in the bathtub. That's better. I'll just lay down and swallow all the water. My eyes will pop out, and my stomach will get big. Then they'll be sorry." She ponders her decision for a while and shakes her head. "Nope! I can't do that. Mommy would cry and cry. What if she was so sad she died? Then, Daddy wouldn't have anyone. Oh, how awful. And my friends would be sad, too. I don't want to make them sad. Can't I do anything right?"

And she continues to fantasize, cuddle and share her innermost disgruntlement with Twinkie, her one and only constant companion.

One day Aunt Lottie calls to ask Mom if she would let Jolene spend Easter with them.

"Why Easter?"

"Easter was so important to me as I grew up, Liz. And Artie doesn't believe in Easter or Jesus. It would make the holiday special for me again if I could take Jolene to the sunrise services. Please."

"Why not? If you promise not to drink."

"Promise!"

And that's how Jolene ended up being driven by Aunt Lottie in their incredible new Lincoln convertible one Saturday afternoon.

Jolene sits tall and stares admiringly at her aunt's profile. Lottie's face is shaded by the large, black hat is held in place with a jeweled butterfly hat pin. Dressed in flowing chiffon and her always present pearls, her aunt's long, still-shapely legs are clad in silk stockings that show her manicured toes peeking out above her stiletto-heeled shoes. Jolene is sure her aunt is one of the most beautiful women in the world.

Cruising down Wilshire Boulevard, they pass some of Los Angeles's finest stores where windows display foreign automobiles, clothing, jewelry, items for the very wealthy. Wilshire Boulevard is such a beautiful street. Lined by slender-trunked palm trees swaying in unison, the trees bend in the wind, never breaking, remaining tall, like towering toy soldiers guarding royalty.

Lottie makes a quick right turn and pulls up to a columned entrance. Uniformed attendants rush to open the car doors and greet and assist them to the pavement. As she is escorted from the vehicle, Jolene feels like a princess.

"Be careful where you park it," Lottie instructs the attendant. Turning to Jolene, she asks, "Well, was my driving okay?"

Shyness overcoming her, Jolene does not respond. Instead, she stares down at the ceramic tile on which they stand.

Laughing, Lottie tells her, "Come on, Muffin. You don't have to answer." Taking her hand, she pulls her along and commands, "Let's shop!"

Entering I. Magnin's is a treat. It is the grandest department store in Los Angeles. Such an extraordinary place. Jolene's head spins this way and that, trying to take in everything at once. The slick marble floors, sparkling chandeliers, shiny glass counters containing exquisite merchandise, each item more beautiful than the next. Well-dressed, arrogant, and frozen-faced women stand behind the counters, ready to assist the moneyed clientele browsing the aisles.

Jolene clings to Lottie's hand, feeling so out of place. She's more aware of her scuffed shoes now, her drooping socks. The too-short velvet dress she is wearing exposes her ever-wounded knees to the eyes of the world. Feeling ill, she wants to vomit, knows she can't.

Pulling her alongside a cosmetic counter, Lottie sprays both with perfume and rubs lotion onto their hands. They sniff each other and laugh. Jolene's discomfort eases. As they wander through departments, Lottie first examines this item, holds something up, puts it down, and doesn't purchase anything. Reaching the handbag department, she points to a purse in a locked case. Oohing and Aaahing, she says, "It's alligator, Jolene," and strokes it reverently after the saleslady hands it to her.

Jolene has no idea what an alligator is, decides it must be very special as she sees her aunt sign the sales slip. The cost of the purse is $100.00.

"Now it's your turn," Lottie announces, pulling her niece toward a gilded cage. The cage, a golden elevator, is operated by a uniformed black man.

"Where to, Madam?" he asks.

"Children's department, please."

The golden cage pulls them upward. The doors open. On the next floor, they exit and are in another wonderland filled with elegant merchandise but in smaller sizes. Refined customers wander aisles, accompanied by their children dressed as well as the mannequins they pass. A few children snicker and point a finger at Jolene. One makes a nasty remark about her funny-looking shoes as they pass by. She feels ugly, different again. Oh, so very different.

"Aunt Lottie, I'm going to be sick."

"Here! Here, suck on this," commands Lottie. She hands her niece a mint. Ignoring her protestations, Lottie pulls her along to a dressing room, tells her to sit down, put her head between her legs, and breathe deeply. Informing her she'll be right back, she leaves.

Miserable, Jolene sulks and stares down at the carpet. Looking up, she sees multiple images of herself in the triple mirrored room. Hating what she sees, she drops her head again and remains in that position until Lottie and a saleslady return. In their arms is an array of children's clothing.

At first, it's fun trying on the clothes. Then, the feeling of ugliness returns. Everything looks stupid on her. Stupid! Especially dresses with ruffles. Her bruised knees stand out like gnarled tree stumps. She hates this shopping trip, these silly dresses, and the saleslady, gurgling non-sensical approval, her Aunt Lottie for making her do this. But most of all, she hates herself.

Bursting into tears, she wails, "I'm sorry, Aunt Lottie. I'm sorry I'm so ugly."

Nonplussed, Lottie holds out her handkerchief. "Here! Wipe your eyes! Blow your nose." Nodding to the saleswoman, she instructs her to leave. Turning to her niece, she asks, "Jolene! How old are you?"

Sobs, "Almost ten."

"Ten is tough, Jolene. Tough! You're not a little girl anymore, and you're not a woman, either. Your face and your body are confused. In fact... It probably seems like nothing matches, does it? Especially the feet and knees." Laughing, she taps one of Jolene's scraped knees.

Despite her emotional discomfort, Jolene smiles.

"But it'll all come together soon, trust me."

Rummaging through her handbag, Lottie removes two photographs from her wallet and hands one to Jolene. "Here! Look at this!"

The photo shows a gangly, buck-toothed girl clinging to a tall, elegant woman.

"That's me and my mom, Jolene. I was 11 years old."

Amused at her niece's surprise, she hands her the second photo and exclaims, "Now! See how I turned out. I was something, wasn't I?"

Jolene stares at the photo of her aunt, taken when she was a glamorous starlet. So taken by the transformation, she stutters, "You were...you were so..."

"Gorgeous! Yep! You said it! At 18, I was under contract with Universal Studios. Going to the top, I was. Going to the top! Instead, I couldn't handle the spotlight, hit the bottle, and slid right down."

She breathes deeply, looks much like she could use a drink, pops a mint into her mouth instead. "Well! What do you think? Wasn't I something?"

"You were..." Jolene's young mind doesn't have words to describe her aunt's breathtaking beauty. Instead, she hugs her and says, "To me, you're still the most beautiful person in the whole world."

Touched, Lottie hugs her in return. "My fan! My number one fan!" Cupping her niece's chin in her hand, she pushes her face into hers and says, "What I'm trying to say, Jolene, is for you to have patience. Wait! Wait! Your turn is coming. Give yourself some time. You're going to be a knockout, too. Trust me!"

"Really?"

"Really! I'm not lying." She crosses her heart, "Hope to die if I am."

"Better not say that 'cause Mommy worries when you drive and..." causing both of them to laugh 'til tears course down their cheeks.

When they recover their composure, Lottie embraces her and says, "Trust me, Muffin. I'll find something that looks good on you today. I promise."

Lottie kept her promise.

A few hours later, Jolene stands in front of the mirrors as her aunt checks her over from top to bottom, making sure everything is correct. The tailored, long-sleeved, navy-blue sailor's dress is long enough to hide her knees. Over the dress is a navy-blue wool coat to match. Both items have broad, stiff white collars. Unseen underneath, soft, silken panties and a silken under-slip cling to her young body. On her head, a navy-blue tam cocked to the side. Lottie adjusts it slightly. White lace stockings with elastic tops grab tightly to Jolene's calves. On her feet are black patent leather shoes with tiny black bows. And the final touch, a white rabbit's-fur muff, her hands tucked inside. Protected in the muff's zippered compartment were a small comb, a tiny change purse holding four shiny new quarters, and a lace handkerchief with an embroidered "J" in the corner. Everything perfect. Absolutely perfect.

Salespeople had responded to Lottie's every request. Her niece's first Easter outfit is complete.

Jolene now stares enthralled at the multiple images, thinking, can this be me? What stares back at her is a well-dressed, freckle-faced, bright-eyed, long-limbed, attractive child. Who is this girl, she thinks? Is it me? Wow! I'm just as pretty as those nasty kids who teased me earlier. Wish they could see me now. Sighing with relief, she no longer feels ugly or different. And she is forever indebted to Aunt Lottie. Forever!

Her old clothes neatly packed in bags, Jolene sits proudly next to Lottie as they drive a few blocks east on Wilshire and turn into a restaurant parking lot. Again, attendants rush to assist them from the car. Jolene stares at the unusual restaurant. The building arches high into the sky in the shape of a huge, huge, brown bowler hat.

"It's called the Brown Derby," gushes Lottie. "The 'in' place for Hollywood people, my dear." She pulls Jolene inside.

A tuxedoed gentleman greets them, "Ah, Ms. Lottie! So nice to see you again. And who is your young friend?"

"This handsome young woman is my niece, Henri. Her name is Jolene. Say hello to Henri, Jolene."

"Ah, as lovely as you, Lottie."

Unable to look directly at him, Jolene giggles, then blushes. The adults laugh.

Henri calls out, "Ramon! Ramon! Show Madam Lottie to her table."

Following Ramon, Lottie exchanges greetings with people as they pass, receives and gives pecks on cheeks, introduces Jolene, who becomes shyer by the minute. The brown leather-lined booth in which they are seated has a glamour shot of Lottie on the wall next to them. Sitting on her knees, Jolene stares and stares at the photo, at the signature at the bottom, "To Henri, my favorite maître d', With love, Lottie Carroll."

The waiter asks, "...the usual?"

Lottie nods and says, "And a Shirley Temple with two cherries, for my niece."

After the waiter leaves, Lottie turns to Jolene and speaks conspiratorially, "Our little secret, okay, Jolene? I know I promised Liz I wouldn't drink, but we must celebrate your first Easter outfit, mustn't we? Our little secret, okay?"

Jolene nods as she stares with curiosity at other photographs on the walls. "Who's that?"

"Joyce Pickford."

"And that, and that, and...?"

"Errol Flynn, Clark Gable, Lon Chaney, Douglas Fairbanks," the names roll off Lottie's tongue effortlessly as Jolene points. Her aunt continues to nod to people seated throughout the room. The waiter returns and places two long-stemmed glasses on the table filled with amber-colored liquid. One has one cherry. The other has two cherries and a straw.

"Mine's a Manhattan, Jolene. Yours looks like mine but doesn't have liquor in it. Cheers, Muffin!"

Lifting her glass, Lottie extends it toward Jolene. Holding on with both hands, Jolene raises her glass. Lottie pulls her glass away, "No! No! That's not the way a lady drinks. Like this, Muffin. Like this." Her aunt shows her how to extend and crook a baby finger while grasping only the stem of the glass with one hand.

Jolene tries to imitate her and almost topples her glass. Liquid spills. Embarrassed, she apologizes.

Requesting napkins, Lottie mops up, then tells her, "Don't apologize, Muffin. Try again. Try until you get it."

Repeated attempts, repeatedly, until spills become fewer, mop-ups unnecessary. Then finally, success! At last! Holding her Shirley Temple with one hand, baby finger crooked, Jolene clinks her glass to Lottie's Manhattan, exclaims, "Cheers!"

"Cheers!" Lottie responds.

They break into laughter, almost spilling their drinks again.

"Now, young woman!" Lottie addresses her niece. "Once you know how to crook your baby finger while drinking, the world will always know you're a lady." She winks as Ramon places another Manhattan in front of her, another Shirley Temple in front of Jolene. "Our little secret, Jolene. Right?"

"Right, Auntie!" Jolene responds. So used to keeping secrets, she has no trouble promising to keep this one, too, as she sips her second Shirley Temple, finger crooked, feeling very grown-up, very much like a lady.

It is Easter.

They rise, dress in their Easter finery, drive to the Hollywood Bowl, park, and are led to their seats. A darkened sky still offers a faint moon over the concrete amphitheater nestled in the Hollywood Hills. Clouds of steam rise from the mouths of hundreds of Angelinos, who have also arrived at this ungodly hour. They chatter, shiver, sip beverages, and huddle together, trying to stay warm.

Lottie and Jolene scrunch down, warmed by blankets, as they sit in canvas chairs placed in private cubicles three rows from the stage. Privileged seating, this is. Not like those freezing their bottoms on the tiers of cold, concrete benches, reaching high above them as far as the eye can see.

On stage, choir members chat amongst themselves. Musicians tune instruments. A magnificent grand piano stands in the corner, shiny black top thrust open.

Lottie points to the piano and taps Jolene's arm, "Artie is buying one for me, Jolene, a concert grand. Isn't it the most?"

Jolene nods, doesn't answer, is distracted by the giant white seashell she sees at the back of the stage.

"What's that seashell?"

"A sound buffer," Lottie tells her.

"What's a...?" she asks.

Lottie shushes her as the conductor, baton in hand, emerges. Applause fills the Bowl. Acknowledging the praise, the conductor beckons offstage. Formally attired singers enter and sit down. There is more applause. Then a minister walks onstage. Everyone rises. The minister offers the opening prayer. All close their eyes and pray silently until they hear, "Amen." In unison, all say "Amen," then sit. As the conductor raises his baton, it becomes quiet, deadly still. The baton is lowered...

The amphitheater fills with glorious music.

When piano sounds emerge unchallenged, chills ripple down Jolene's spine. It is the same reaction she had experienced when she attended the concert with her Aunt Pola and Carl. Leaning into Lottie, Jolene whispers, "Oh, Auntie, don't you think the sound of the piano is the most delicious sound in the whole world?"

Thoughtful, Lottie looks at her niece.

Easter services are wonderful, just wonderful. Then comes the magical ending. Hundreds of white doves are released. Given their freedom, the doves fly into the sun's reflection as it rises at the crest of the hills.

Jolene's heart feels full. She tries to capture this incredibly beautiful moment forever as she watches the doves fly higher and higher, higher and higher, until every last one of them disappears. Disappearing into the now-glowing, red-orange sky.

As Jolene and her parents eat dinner that night, she chatters on and on about her Easter weekend. Liz sits in her usual sideways position, ready to respond if Dan needs something. She doesn't have long to wait.

"A-1 Sauce, Liz. How can I eat this without…"

"Coming. Coming." She's up, in the kitchen and back again, starts to sit when…

"Get me a sharper knife, Liz. This thing is like…"

Up again, Jolene watches with disgust as her mother heads back to the kitchen. Why can't Daddy get his own knife, she wonders? Why does Mommy have to jump up and down during every meal? It's not fair, she thinks. Not fair. They both work. She wonders why her mother doesn't say something. Boy, if I ever get married, I'd sure say something.

Liz returns. "Go on, Jolene. Tell us what happened next."

Continuing her story, Jolene starts to give details of their lunch at the Brown Derby when…

Wiping his mouth, Dan looks with disgust at Jolene's unfinished plate and speaks sharply, "Eat, Jolene! Stop chattering. Gawd! Don't you know when to stop? Lottie this, Lottie that. You're driving me crazy."

Liz intervenes, "She had an exciting weekend, Dan. Let her share it."

"Get me some water, Liz."

Holding down the desire to respond, Liz rises slowly and heads for the kitchen. Jolene musters all her willpower not to look daggers at her father and continues to eat.

"When a person sits down to eat, they should eat. Not talk, talk, talk, and say nothing!"

Dan admonishes her. "Why can't you just say something once and then shut up? I hate hearing your voice going on and on and on."

Jolene cringes. He hates the sound of her voice. Oh, that hurts too much. The lump begins to form. She chokes on her food.

Returning, Liz sees her daughter's distress, pours water into a glass, instructs her to drink. Sitting down, she addresses her husband. "What in hell's the matter with you, Dan? Leave the kid alone. She had a big adventure. It's a lot more interesting than listening to you moan and groan about business all the time."

Dan throws down his napkin and gives Liz a dirty look. "If you'd rather listen to her than me, you can have her." He grabs a puzzle and heads for the bathroom.

Trying to recapture the merriment of the discussion before the uproar, Liz tells Jolene not to mind and urges her to continue. Hesitantly, Jolene begins again. Gradually, her excitement returns as she relives the weekend's events. Delighted, she finds Liz enjoying every incident almost as much as she did.

"And then..."

Liz listens, watches, fascinated. She sees her daughter cut her lamb chop into tiny pieces the way Pola had taught her, crook her baby finger as she lifts her glass of milk the way Lottie had taught her. Teasing, Liz asks Jolene, "Who are you, little lady? I don't recognize this person sitting across the table from me. Hmm! Hmm! Maybe they gave me the wrong baby in the hospital, huh! What do you think?"

Not knowing if her mother is joking or becoming angry with her, Jolene stops eating and asks, "Did I...Did I say...Do something wrong?"

Laughing, Liz tells her, "No! No! It's nice seeing you like this. Nice." She watches as her daughter eats with gusto, enjoying every morsel until her plate is clean. Sighing, Liz thinks, "If only Dan could enjoy..." Her sadness returns as she realizes, "I hardly know this person sitting across the table from me, this young stranger. I've let others teach her the things I should be showing her. She's growing up, and I don't even know her."

Later, as Jolene models her Easter outfit for Liz, she tells her mother about Lottie purchasing the alligator purse.

"$100.00! Lottie paid $100.00 for a purse?" Liz reacts. "My Gawd! That could feed us all year." Fingering Jolene's coat, she says, "I can only imagine how much this cost."

Liz stares at her daughter, dressed in her new outfit, standing so proud, so tall in front of the mirror. "I can't believe it," she tells her. "Friday, when you left, you were still a little girl. Today, you look almost grown-up." With misgivings, she says, "I wish we could afford to buy clothes like that for you, Jolene. I really do."

Hesitant, Jolene looks down, not sure if she's made her mother happy or sad. "If you don't want me to keep them, I won't, Mommy, I..."

"Don't be a ninny, Jolene. Of course, you're not going to give them back." Laughing with bitterness, Liz tells her, "Who am I kidding? Even if we had the money, I don't have Lottie's taste. It would have been a disaster." She tells Jolene to turn around and model the outfit for her.

Relieved, Jolene sighs and turns, so grateful not to have made her mother angry. Above all, she's so thankful she can keep her first Easter outfit, not just the memories.

One day, Keiko asks if Jolene wants to go to her families' temple with her. Thrilled, Jolene asks her parents. With their permission, she joins them, wearing her Easter finery. Keiko's family looks so delicate and refined in their silken, embroidered ensembles, tiny tapestry shoes on the women's feet, engraved ivory combs in their hair, a black silk suit on Mr. Sunaka.

He drives them to the Buddhist temple downtown. Red and golden spires pierce the sky. Distinctive on the outside, the temple is breathtaking inside. Heavy with incense, the inner room houses an enormous, seated golden male figurine with a distended stomach. As people approach the statue, they bow low, paying their homage.

"They bow to Buddha, Jolene," Keiko whispers. "He is our God!"

Jolene bows with the others and looks at the walls. She is surprised to see hundreds of slots lining each wall. Within each slot are tiny ribbon-tied scrolls.

She nods toward a wall, "Keiko! What are those?"

"Prayers!"

"You pray to walls?"

"No, silly. We pray to Buddha."

"To do what?"

"To protect us."

"And…?"

"And," Keiko looks down, embarrassed, "we ask for a secret wish."

"Can I wish…pray, too?"

"Sure!"

Keiko gives Jolene paper and a pen. Both busy themselves, composing prayers.

Jolene writes, "Dear Mr. Buddha. Please keep me safe from harm. And…"—her secret wish—"…may I please have my own piano someday?"

Keiko rolls their prayers into tiny scrolls, ties them with ribbons, places them in slots. They bow, thank Buddha for granting their wishes, and leave.

Exited, Jolene wonders how long it will take Keiko's God to get to her wish, now that she has two Gods working on getting her a piano.

December 7, 1941

"They've bombed Pearl Harbor! The Japs have bombed Pearl Harbor! Thousands are dead! Planes and submarines are on the way here! They're going to kill us all!"

News of the bombing spreads fast—facts and figures terrify all who hear. No one knows the truth. People stop what they are doing and stay glued to the radio. They listen, wait, are fearful. What should they do? Where can they go?

Then, the cold, hard truth hits. They listen solemnly as President Roosevelt tells of the bombing of Pearl Harbor and declares war on Japan.

World War II has begun.

Chapter Seventeen
1942

Jolene doesn't even know where Pearl Harbor is.

But she learns soon enough. At school, other history lessons become secondary. The tiny island of Japan has become a daily discussion. Just like "drop drills" become daily rituals. These are drills to protect them if there is an air raid.

"Drop drills" terrify the children.

If an alarm bell rings, the teacher tells the children to stop whatever they're doing, drop to the floor, crawl under anything nearby; a desk, a bench, a chair, something solid that will protect them from a bomb, falling glass, or shrapnel. As if any of these items could save anyone from anything—if a bomb did fall.

So the children scramble to find some protection, then wait, expecting the worst. Jolene has never known such fear.

However, Jolene's fear is nothing compared to what her friend, Keiko, and her family are experiencing. Unruly crowds break into their store. Merchandise is pillaged and stolen.

At school, former friends shun Keiko, and some call her slant eyes and murderer. Others, more cowardly, surround her, taunt her, yell, "Go home, little Jap! Go back home, where you belong!"

"But I am home," cries Keiko in Jolene's arms. "What do they mean, go home? I was born here. My parents, my grandparents were born here! Where do they want us to go? What do they mean?"

Having no answers, Jolene does her best to comfort Keiko. She's distressed over the pain and unfairness her best friend is experiencing and can't understand what is happening. Her loyalty to Keiko brings nastiness her way, too. Some of the children at school turn on her, taunt, "Jap lover! Jap lover!"

When Jolene asks her mother what is happening, Liz tells her, "Don't worry, Jolene. Keiko and her family haven't done anything wrong. They're Americans. They didn't bomb Pearl Harbor. This unpleasantness will pass, you'll see."

But it doesn't pass.

May 3, 1942

It is a school day. Jolene walks to Keiko's house as she does every morning, every weekday. Calling out, she waits so they can walk to school together. She waits and waits. Keiko doesn't come out. Wondering why her friend doesn't respond, she runs upstairs and is surprised to find the front door ajar. Knocking on the open door, Jolene calls out Keiko's name. Still no answer. Knocking several more times, Jolene calls out for her friend again, then Keiko's parents. No answer. What's happening, she wonders? Where are they? Why is the door open? Tentatively, she pushes the door wider and looks around. What she sees shocks her. Open windows, bamboo shades flapping in the wind unchallenged. Chaos everywhere! Chaos! Items are overturned, some broken. The radio is smashed. Personal items are tossed about here, there, everywhere.

Terrified, Jolene runs down the stairs, away from the house, down the street. Looking up and down, she doesn't know where to go. Who can she talk to? Her parents aren't home. She doesn't know what has happened to Keiko's family. She runs to Rosa's house. Her mother opens the door.

Crying, Jolene blurts out what she saw. "Burglars broke into Keiko's house. Burglars…and they…" She breaks down and begs Rosa's mother to call the police.

With tears in her eyes Rosa's mother folds Jolene into her aproned body and tells her, "Run to school, little one. Run! Go! Go right away." Pushing the weeping child gently from her, she says nothing else. Confused, Jolene stands for a moment, turns, and starts running as fast as possible. Rosa's mother cries as she watches until the child disappears from view.

As Jolene runs, she becomes more alarmed and confused because of the scenes she is seeing. Another house broken into; doors and windows are thrown open, toys or articles of clothing are lying about on porches or lawns. A Caucasian woman, holding a slant-eyed infant, sobs as she sits on her porch steps.

Terrified, Jolene runs as fast as she can to school. Arriving breathless, she hears a loudspeaker blaring instructions. It is the principal's voice. "Everyone is to come to the auditorium. Immediately!"

Jolene joins other students who move as one toward the auditorium. When they enter, they find seats and question each other. Each has a similar story to tell. Some look confused. Some cry. A few laugh, make jokes about "yellow bellies." Some are numbed. Many are terrified. As Jolene looks around the auditorium, she realizes not only is her friend Keiko absent, there is not one other Japanese student in the whole place.

"What on earth has happened?" Jolene wonders as she hunkers down into her seat, an uncontrollable fear permeating her entire being. She looks up as she hears the principal's voice.

"Attention! Attention, please!"

Uncomfortable, the principal stands behind a podium and adjusts the microphone.

"May I have your attention, please?"

Louder, "Attention!"

Almost shouting, "Quiet down! Now!"

Gradually the kids quiet.

"Thank you. Thank you. Uh…"

The principal clears her throat. "Um…this is one of the most…unpleasant duties I've ever had to perform," she says.

Choking up, she removes a handkerchief from her pocket, coughs into it, dabs at an eye, and begins to read from the sheet of paper she holds in her hand.

"We've received word that today… Today, the War Department has evacuated all persons of Japanese ancestry from the West Coast. From where we live. Here."

She chokes up and dabs at her eye again. Coughing, she pauses, then continues. "This means that some of your friends…your classmates…have been taken to…"

"To prisons! That's what!"

One of the boys, who had been joking about yellow bellies and had taunted Keiko, shouts out, "My dad says all Japs are spies. They belong in prison! That's where they are now. In prison!"

Gasping is audible throughout the auditorium.

Are their Japanese friends being put in prison? Is this possible? Pandemonium breaks out.

The principal calls for order. When things quiet down, she admonishes the boy who shouted out. Looking directly at him, she scolds, "Mr. Hemming, you and your father, are incorrect." Speaking with more conviction now, she continues. "All Japanese people are not spies. And they have not been taken away to prison. They have been evacuated for their own safety at this time because our government thinks that…Umm…Seems to think that a few Japanese people are…well, what they call 'a security risk'…a danger to this country. Until this matter is cleared up, the government thinks that it is probably better that…"

Still trying to make reason out of this insanity, she chokes up again and says, "I'm sure your friends will be back soon. Return to your classrooms immediately!"

Losing control, she sobs as she runs from the stage.

"Evacuated," Jolene will learn, was the polite way of saying the Japanese had been taken to relocation camps, places inland, east of the Sierra Nevada mountains, where they resided for the entire war. The camps were old Army barracks with cots and minimal necessities. They offered no freedom or external communication until long after the war. Most of the Japanese lost all of their savings and possessions. Facts which Jolene and everyone else learns about later. Much, much later.

That night, no matter how hard they try, Jolene's parents have no answers to her heartbroken questions, "How can they do this? How can they take Keiko away? She was born here. Her parents, too. How can this happen? We're all Americans. I thought this was a free country. Can this happen to us, too? Can they come and take us away in the middle of the night?"

Questions Dan and Liz wonder about themselves, deep-seated fears, as they try to console her. Can this happen to them, too, they wonder? Will the government come some night, as they did with the Japanese, say we're spies trying to overthrow the country, deport us as other countries have done for centuries? Will history repeat itself here, too? In America? Because we're Jews? Questions! Questions! Questions! Terrifying questions which are never expressed because there are no answers!

"It's the war, Jolene. The war. People become paranoid."

"What's paranoid?"

The explanation...

"That's one reason you must never forget you're a Jew, Jolene," Liz reminds her daughter. "Whether you practice the religion or not. Always remember you're a Jew. When things go bad, people want someone to blame. They'll turn on you. Remind you you're a Jew. They'll never let you forget. So you'd better not forget it, either."

"Keiko isn't Jewish. She's Japanese and..."

"I know. I know," Liz, always rationalizing, reassures her. "They can't do this to American citizens, Jolene. I'm sure it's a misunderstanding. She'll be home soon."

And that unsatisfactory reassurance is all that Jolene ever gets. Nothing more. She will never understand how her best friend can be ripped out of her life—forever.

Because Keiko never comes home again. None of the Japanese do.

Besides the painful loss of friendship and the shock of American citizens placed behind barbed wire, the war also generated excitement and patriotism. Men and women enlist. Women go to work. Rosie the Riveter becomes a symbol for the working woman. A blackout is imposed upon the city, and black shades are purchased and placed in every window.

A blackout is an incredible sight.

On the night Jolene experiences the first blackout, she and Dan stand on their front porch, watching it take effect. Slowly, slowly, the lights of Hollywood shut down. They watch, talk, wait until all is dark. The only light showing now are stars sparkling in the darkened sky. Sharing this experience, Jolene recaptures her closeness with her father when she was younger. The times they'd visit the observatory, sharing her father's dreams and fantasies. He is still the only person with whom she can share her dreams and truly understands her. She can tell him almost everything in her heart except how she feels about boys, especially Harold.

Everyone does their part for the war effort.

Dan tries to enlist. Rejected due to his age and because he's a family man, he volunteers to help monitor the blackout. Doing this job makes him feel important. Walking tall as a peacock, he strides along darkened streets with a partner, a hard hat on his head and a red banner on his arm. His bullhorn poised, he calls out if someone hasn't pulled down a shade at dusk, has forgotten a light, warning them of the consequences. He reminds them that enemy dive bombers or submarines can surface and use their light as a beacon or a target.

Women like Liz stand in long lines to receive rationed food stamps for their families each month; only so much meat and butter. They eat soy burgers for the first time.

Weapons are made out of recycled tin. At the school drive, Jolene and her schoolmates collect so many tin cans that they win an award and have their picture appear in the local newspaper sitting atop the mini-mountain of cans they have collected.

Dan has an idea for a new business venture.

He wants to open a coffee shop; with only stools and homemade food; breakfast, lunch, no dinner. Jolene listens to her parents discuss his idea daily and learns that having stools instead of chairs as seats means a faster turnover. Fast turnover means more profit, more tips. And Dan's smooth-talking does it again.

This time, even Liz thinks it's a good idea because she knows the business inside and out. She's sure they'll be able to pay Reuben back in spades if he's willing to loan them money again.

"Will you never learn?" Marcus bellows when he hears his older brother has agreed to one of Dan's schemes again. "Like throwing money down a well, Reuben. Why don't you piss on it? Burn it? You got so much money, you can throw some my way, too."

Reuben laughs and tries to defend himself. "This is different, Marcus. The café is going to be Liz's place. She knows the business."

"If it were just Liz, I'd say you had a chance, my dumb brother. But with Dan involved, kiss your greenbacks goodbye. The guy's nothing but a loser."

Several months later, LIZ'S CAFE opens its doors. Located on Los Feliz Boulevard, it is a few blocks west of Reuben's store, on the opposite side of the street. Upon entering the café, one sees 16 red-leather stools, a gleaming chrome-lined counter, smells of brewed coffee, freshly-baked cinnamon rolls. There is a warm feeling to the place. Even though the menu is limited, the hearty bargain breakfasts and home-cooked lunches fill one's stomach and aren't hard on the wallet.

This time, Liz is sure they have a winner. A lot of work, sure, but a winner. Dan handles the purchasing and the cash register. Liz will cook and serve the meals, and both will share the clean-up.

Part of Liz's brother's agreement is that he eats his meals daily at the café free. Reuben is pleased with the arrangement because his wife, Anne, hasn't cooked a meal for him in years.

While Reuben eats at the café, Aunt Anne, shows her displeasure some days by running up and down the sidewalk in front of the café, screaming obscenities at him. He's so good-natured, Liz's brother, that he usually shrugs, smiles, and continues to eat. At first, some patrons are annoyed or surprised by her antics. In due time, she becomes a form of entertainment for all.

"If Anne doesn't feed you or sleep with you, what's she good for?" asks Dan. "She's no wife. She's a liability. Why don't you divorce her," Dan often asks his brother-in-law?

"Why don't you have her institutionalized, Reuben?" Liz adds. "She's a fruitcake."

Reuben smiles, says nothing, and enjoys his meals, ignoring their comments and his wife's tirades.

One day, after Reuben leaves, Dan tells Liz, "He should be paying us, Liz. Your brother eats like a horse."

"Can't believe you're saying that, Dan," she admonishes him. "Where would we be without Reuben? It's nice for him to be able to eat decent food. And I like seeing him every day."

"Feel like he's checking up on us."

"So? What if he is? It's his money."

"You don't have to remind me of it every day."

"Sometimes I think I do."

"Drop it!"

"Dropped!"

Liz returns to her back-breaking work in the kitchen. Dan gets back to his schmoozing, the part he likes and does best, shooting the breeze. Dan yaks and yaks and yaks with every customer as he refills their cups of coffee for free, keeping them engrossed in conversation long after they've finished their meal.

Liz complains. "We need a faster turnover, Dan. Stop schmoozing so much."

"It's goodwill."

With all of Dan's "goodwill", they're still in the red at the end of six months. Liz isn't pleased about it.

"Takes time," reminds Dan.

"I know, I know," Liz agrees, then mumbles, "Seems like I've heard that one before."

Liz and Dan are working seven days a week now, long hours. Sometimes, Jolene joins them on the weekend and hangs out at the café until she gets on their nerves. Then they send her over to Uncle Reuben's store to play. Jolene likes it better at Sorkin's Unpainted Furniture store, anyway. It's more exciting.

Reuben's store is a constant source of adventure. A replica of her father's former store, except far more extensive. Reuben's place takes up an entire city block. All types of unpainted and patio furniture are on display. The many salespeople are always busy with customers who wander up and down aisles, make selections, usually pay in cash. Every time a sale is completed, the money is placed in an old cash register, which clangs every time. Clanging, clanging, clanging all day long, the ancient cash register shows the sale amount but never offers a receipt. So no one ever knows how much money has been taken in at the end of the day. And some of the cash is often removed if someone needs petty cash to purchase coffee, hamburgers, French fries, or malts at Bob's Big Boy, which is just around the corner.

Jolene has heard her parents say that every unpainted furniture store opened in Los Angeles by a former employee of Uncle Reuben is money stolen from him. But Jolene wonders if what she hears her parents say is true because everyone who works for Uncle Reuben seems to love him. And he remains friends with them for life.

Jolene's uncle is such a trusting man. Each evening, he empties the register drawers and places all of the money into pockets inside his jacket for deposit the next day. If it's Friday or Saturday, the cash remains in those same pockets until he deposits on Monday.

Friends and family worry about him.

"You're going to get killed one of these days, Reuben, carrying around so much cash," they warn him.

Yet, nothing happens. Uncle Reuben continues to trust, always smiles or laughs, and places his faith in God and the Bible. And so far, God must have been listening because no one ever bumps him on the head or empties his bulging pockets.

The store is his life. He works every day, Monday through Friday, 8 AM to 10 PM. Saturday and Sundays, 10 AM to 5 PM. Even though Uncle Reuben is an Orthodox Jew, he knows God will forgive him if he works on Saturdays.

Behind the store is a small cottage. Reuben and Aunt Anne live there. They moved in when he bought the store in 1935. It has a tiny living room, a smaller bedroom, a kitchenette, and a bathroom. Reuben likes living there because it is so convenient to the store. Why move, he reasons?

Anne has hated the place from the day they were married. "No privacy, Reuben," she had told him. "Feels like I'm living in a fishbowl."

"Draw the curtains," he'd told her.

Ten years later, they are still there, sharing that tiny excuse of a house. Except that now, they no longer share the bed, according to Liz. Reuben sleeps on the couch and has slept there for eight years. "No wonder Anne's meshuganah (crazy)," she says, tapping her head with her finger, "no sex!"

Behind the cottage is an enormous warehouse, where merchandise is stacked clear up to the ceiling. An old red truck, Sorkin Unpainted Furniture painted on both sides, pulls up, and parks in the alley between the buildings.

Raymond, the truck driver, and his helper, Max, both stout and unshaven, climb out of the cab. With cigarettes dangling from their lips, they smell of putrid smoke and damp armpits if one ventures too close.

Loading the truck with today's orders, they drive off, deliver, return, load up, deliver, return. Every day, six days a week.

Jolene's favorite person at the store is Horatio Jones, Reuben's first employee and the only Negro working there. Horatio refinishes furniture and does just about everything in the store except sell. He can't sell because he doesn't know how to read or write.

"Couldn't run this place without Horatio," Reuben often tells Jolene. "He's my right arm."

Everyone knows he's more than that. Horatio is Reuben's best friend.

This Sunday, Jolene converses with Horatio as he repeatedly sands a piece of furniture, rubbing, sanding, and repeating the process, until the wood is as smooth as silk. He takes great pride in his work. Satisfied the surface is ready, he applies coats of stain or clear gloss, careful to preserve the wood grain. After finishing the piece, Horatio leaves to take on another task.

Jolene wanders and ends up in the warehouse, meandering in and out of the stacked furniture. She loves the smell of raw wood and exploring the nooks and crannies. As she continues to wander, she hears a sound and stops. It is a frightening sound, "Uuuugh! Uuuugh!" like an animal in pain.

Clambering onto a desk, Jolene stands on tiptoe to peer out of a window and sees the delivery truck parked in the back of the store. Her Aunt Anne sits on Raymond's lap with her back to him in the passenger seat.

Jolene's eyes widen as she sees her aunt going up and down, up and down, emitting those awful sounds, "Uuuugh! Uuuugh! Uuuugh!" coming from her as she bounces. Salvia dribbles down the side of her mouth.

Seeing the saliva on her aunt's face, she remembers the boy who got sick at school. He had fallen to the floor, saliva foaming at the mouth. It was what the teacher had called an epileptic fit. Sure her aunt is having a fit, too; Jolene jumps down from the desk and runs to get her uncle.

"Uncle Reuben. Uncle Reuben! Come quick!" she screams as she runs, "Auntie Anne's sick!"

A few moments later, Reuben arrives. Opening the truck door, he grabs his wife by the hair and pulls her from the truck onto the pavement. Dragging her to a nearby sink, he turns on the faucet and holds her under it, with her face up.

The gurgling sounds her aunt now makes as she chokes on the water frighten Jolene more than the sounds her aunt had made before. She wonders if this is another way to treat a person when they have an epileptic fit. At school that day, the teacher had put an ice cream stick on the boy's tongue and had held him down so he wouldn't hurt himself. She doesn't understand why Uncle Reuben keeps holding Aunt Anne under the faucet because now, her aunt is gagging and turning purple.

Horatio arrives.

He doesn't take time to wonder. Turning off the faucet, Horatio pulls Reuben away, then rolls Anne onto her stomach and presses on her back, hard. He pushes and pushes and pushes until water begins to spurt from her mouth.

"It's about time he started divorce proceedings. Should have done it years ago," Dan discusses the incident with Liz as they drive home later that day, unmindful of Jolene in the back.

"What's a divorce?"

An explanation follows.

"It's horrible, horrible!" Liz exclaims. "Don't understand why he doesn't put her in the booby hatch."

"What's a booby hatch?"

An irritated explanation.

"That's where she belongs," Liz continues. "In a booby hatch. Gawd knows!" she exclaims, concerned. "Another explosion like that, Reuben could end up in jail."

"Why would Uncle Reuben have to go to…?"

"Oh, shut up, or you'll get it!" Liz threatens.

Ignoring Jolene, Dan explains, "Reuben said if he puts Anne in an institution, he's stuck with her for life, Liz. Said he'd never be free. He couldn't get a divorce and never remarry. What kind of a life would that be?"

"Hmmm! Never thought of it like that," muses Liz.

How strange adults are, thinks Jolene. She pictures her kind, quiet, and usually laughing Uncle Reuben, holding Aunt Anne under the faucet. Holding her so that water gushed down her throat, gushing, gushing, until…!

Then, she wonders why he would have to go to jail?

Images of Aunt Anne fill her mind, too, making those awful sounds, bouncing, bouncing on Raymond. Then, so purple, gagging, and saliva-faced. She wonders what brought her aunt and uncle to such a terrible place. As she continues to think about what happened that day, she wonders who is crazier, Aunt Anne or Uncle Reuben?

A few weeks later, Dan tells Jolene they are moving again.

"Closer to the café," he says.

"I can't believe you're doing this to me again," she wails. Distraught, she knows another move means another school, leaving friends. She doesn't want to go. Oh, how can her parents be so cruel, so selfish, she thinks. Again, she fantasizes about killing herself to get even with them yet takes no action. Then, she asks them the question she most dreads, "Does this mean…I mean…LIKE I DID, OSCAR, do I have to leave Twinkie behind, too?"

Relieved, she hears their answer.

"No! Of course not. No way!" they promise, "Twinkie comes with us."

Their new home on Brunswick Avenue isn't as nice as the house they leave. It isn't even a house. Just half a house, a duplex, her parents call it. The small rooms are attached to a long dark hallway. People live on the other side.

The neighbors' muffled voices often mix with theirs. But at least Jolene still has her own bedroom, a tiny room at the very back. It looks out on a small building that used to be a backyard. The owner of the duplex lives there. A small patch of dirt next to the driveway is the only open land.

"Perfect for a Victory Garden, Jolene," Liz says, trying to ease the discomfort of the move as they look at the tiny strip of dirt.

"What's a Victory Garden?" Jolene asks.

"A vegetable garden. To help the war effort," Liz responds.

Surprised at her mother's response, Jolene wonders if they'll ever plant anything there.

A mile from the café, their new home is three blocks east of railroad tracks which divide their neighborhood from the posh city of Glendale. Not close enough to hear the rush of oncoming trains, they still can hear daily whistle blasts as one slowly chugs by. If the train slows down enough, transients sometimes drop to the ground without getting hurt and are seen wandering through the neighborhood. Liz warns Jolene to stay away from them.

Surprisingly, theirs is the only duplex on the entire block. The rest of the tree-lined street has well-kept single-family homes with tended lawns. Blue and white-collared families live in these houses. Many have a Germanic background.

When Jolene takes Twinkie for their first walk around the block of her new home, she is surprised to see large, rambling ranch houses on the street behind them. These gracious homes have horses and stables on their deep lots and back up to city acreage bordering the Los Angeles River viaduct.

The river, a seemingly never-ending ugly concrete basin that roams throughout the San Fernando Valley and northern part of the city, was built years before to control floods. It is hard to picture this river which is nothing more than a tiny trickle today, destroying lives, crops, and property in 1932.

On the far side of the viaduct, past the constant flow of traffic on Riverside Drive, are the lush greened hills of Griffith Park.

Half a block north of Brunswick, the street Jolene lives on, is Chevy Chase. Her new school has the same name and is located on that street, two blocks away. Chevy Chase also divides her neighborhood from a Mexican barrio called Toonerville.

As Jolene plays with Twinkie on her front porch a few days later, she hears voices and looks up.

A large group of Mexican youths comes into view as they cross Chevy Chase. What is different about these young men is that they not only walk on the sidewalks as most people do, they also form a line in the street, moving forward as one, arms linked, extending from sidewalk to sidewalk, swaggering as though they owned the road—or the world.

Fascinated, Jolene stares, never having seen young men like this before. They resemble each other, each with ebony hair slicked back, wearing black baggy pants and black jackets with such exaggerated shoulder pads that Jolene thinks they'd fall over if a strong wind came up. In a way, they're very attractive, almost theatrical and exciting. Yet, there is something about them, something menacing, too.

An automobile drives down Jolene's street toward the youths. Surprised at what he sees, the driver begins to honk impatiently when he realizes the road is blocked. As one, the line of young men stops. Some shout taunts. Some lift their arms and make fists in defiance. When the driver is close enough to see who blocks the street, he does a fast U-turn and speeds away.

Beginning to feel uneasy, Jolene gathers Twinkie into her arms and rushes into the house. Latching the door, she peeks out of the window and tries to quiet Twinkie. But the dog, sensing danger, barks to protect her when they enter the house until long after the weaving black line passes their place and is out of sight.

Hearing Jolene's story the next day after school, Mrs. Browning, their next-door neighbor, tells her, "Pachucos, Jolene! Those young Mexicans are called Pachucos. You did right getting into the house, young lady, locking the door." She hands Jolene a thick slice of freshly baked bread piled high with dripping butter and raspberry jam. Then she warns, "You don't ever want to mix with them, Jolene. Never! Even the police leave Pachucos alone."

Jolene's new neighborhood is full of interesting people. Not long after they move in, she meets the family on the other side of their duplex, Mrs. Wagner and her son. Jolene, nor her parents, can hardly believe that Malcolm, the strange, semi-giant Mrs. Wagner introduces, is only 14 years old. Yet, that is his age, she insists. "Malcolm," she says, "goes to a special school."

That night, Twinkie's barking awakens Jolene. Hearing a noise at the window, she looks up. Lit by moonlight, she can see Malcolm's giant face looking at her.

He stands there staring at her, staring and breathing heavily, staring and breathing heavily, as he masturbates.

Jolene screams and calls for her parents.

Realizing it's not very neighborly, Liz goes next door the next day and tells Mrs. Wagner to keep her boy at home. Apologetic, Mrs. Wagner agrees.

It is months before Malcolm's face appears at Jolene's window again.

The first school day holds surprises for Jolene, both pleasant and unpleasant.

What pleases her immensely is when she learns that she only has two classmates: Carmen Gomez and Carmen Rios. When she asks her teacher why the class is so small, she is told that the school has been condemned and will close in June. Jolene was accepted because she's in the sixth grade and will graduate in February.

The unpleasant surprise occurs at the day's end.

As Jolene leaves the school grounds, a group of girls awaits her. One girl, obviously the leader, stands in front of the group and challenges her.

"I don't like the way you talk, new girl! And, I'm going to change the shape of your mouth! What do you think about that?"

The threat comes from a squat-bodied girl in the class below her. She shoves her snout-nosed face into Jolene's and says, "My name's Norma, and I don't like how you talk!"

Hoping to avoid a confrontation, Jolene tries to pass. Norma blocks her way and pokes her finger repeatedly into her chest.

"Come on, coward, fight me! Fight! Come on!" Doubling her fists, she pokes at her again and again.

"I...I don't want to fight. Leave me alone," mutters Jolene, trying to get away.

Unbeknownst to her, one of the other girls crouches behind her. Norma shoves. Jolene falls and lands hard on the pavement. All of the girls laugh and snicker, her tormentor the loudest.

Lying there, hurt, frightened, not knowing what to do, Jolene whimpers, "Leave me alone. Go away."

"Aw, get up, you baby, and fight!" commands Norma.

"I don't want to fight you! I don't even know you. What do you have against me?" Jolene asks, bewildered.

"I don't like how you talk," Norma repeats, "with that phony Aaaah in your voice!"

The broad Canadian aah, the way she spoke after staying with Aunt Pola. Many have commented about her speech before. But no one has ever reacted like this. Except maybe her father, who said he didn't like the sound of her voice. What's wrong with her voice, she wonders? Why does this girl want to hurt her? Well, she's going to have to face this Norma person sometime. It might as well be now, she decides. Standing up, bruised, her dress now torn, Jolene faces the bully, fighting back the only way she knows how—with words.

"This is the way I talk, Norma, like it or not! And I'm not going to fight you with fists! Not today. Not ever. Ladies don't fight like that!"

With dignity, Jolene turns her back on Norma and the group and walks away, her head held high, not looking back.

She hears Norma's taunts behind her, "A lady doesn't fight with fists! A lady doesn't…"

As she walks rapidly away, Jolene's heart pounds louder and louder when she hears footsteps behind her. Fearing the worst, she begins to run, expecting to be knocked down again.

Instead, she hears a girl's voice calling out to her, "Wait! Wait!"

It is not the voice of her tormentor.

Breathless, Jolene stops, turns around, and is surprised to see one of the girls from the group running toward her. The girl catches up and extends her hand.

"Hi!" she greets Jolene. "You sure stood up to Norma! My name's Joyce! What's yours?"

To Jolene's surprise, Liz does plant a Victory garden with her. In the tiny, ever-hardened plot of earth next to the driveway, radishes, carrots, and worm-eaten tomatoes try to sustain life.

A new family is moving in down the street.

Jolene and her new friend Joyce sit on the porch steps, watching as a woman directs two teenage boys to unload a pick-up truck.

The heavy-set woman gives instructions as the boys remove boxes. "In my room, Bill, yours, Bobbie, living room, the kitchen."

The sound of a low flying airplane fills the sky.

The woman looks up. Spotting the plane, she becomes distraught and lets out an ear-splitting screech. Running up the street toward them, she begins to sob hysterically, "It's happening again! Again!" Covering her face, she moans, "Oh, my Gawd! They're going to kill us all! Oh, my Gawd!"

Dropping the box he's unloading, the older boy, Bill, runs after his mother. Catching up to her in front of Jolene's house, he tries to calm her.

Holding her in his arms, he tells her, "We're okay, Mom. We're not in Pearl Harbor. We're in California. California, Mom. We're safe here. Safe!"

Gradually, his mother calms down. Her sobs lessen. He leads her back toward their house, where they disappear from view, unloading forgotten.

Oh, the poor woman, thinks Jolene. The poor woman. For the first time, Jolene begins to understand more about the war. President Roosevelt didn't declare war because the Japanese just dropped bombs on naval ships. People had died there during the bombing. People, real flesh and blood folks like this family, were involved. Perhaps the woman's husband was killed. Sadly, Jolene realizes this is probably why some people hated Keiko and were afraid of all yellow-skinned people.

Whenever Jolene visits Aunt Lottie and Uncle Arthur, she runs her fingers over their new grand piano keys. The sounds her fingers create when she places them on the ivory keys fill her with unspeakable joy. Aware of her niece's fascination with the instrument, Lottie makes it her business to speak to Liz.

"The girl needs piano lessons, Liz. If you find a teacher, we'll pay for it."

"We don't have a piano, Lottie."

"We'll get her one."

"We don't have room."

"There must be a way…"

The situation is resolved when Jolene discovers an old upright piano in the school auditorium and asks to practice before school begins. Delighted someone is going to make use of it, the principal agrees.

They find a teacher who lives up the block. Mrs. Schwarnoff is a delightful older woman who refuses to divulge her age and is full of anecdotes of previous concerts and former students who have risen to fame. Liz engages her for $1.00 an hour.

After piano lessons begin, Jolene doesn't have to be reminded to practice. Daily she arrives at school early and warms up her hands before the janitor puts a key in the lock. She lives for this uninterrupted hour of keyboard exploration before the bell rings, drawing her away from the musical world she is learning to love.

After several months, Mrs. Schwarnoff tells Liz, "The child has talent."

Dan, Lottie, and Arthur are pleased with her progress. At first, Liz is non-committal. As time goes by, she realizes how important the piano has become to Jolene. It keeps her happy and occupied. Much as Liz hates to admit it, Lottie's idea seems to have benefited all of them.

But none are more pleased than Jolene. At last! She has found something that gives her unspeakable fulfillment and makes her feel special.

Both of Jolene's new classmates are bright, friendly Latino girls. Carmen Rios is big-boned, plain-featured, and speaks of going to college. Carmen Gomez is gorgeous. Though the same age, she is already exotic, with silky, raven hair, light, toast-colored skin, flashing umbra eyes. Jolene thinks she's the most beautiful person she's ever seen, except for Aunt Lottie.

One day, Carmen Gomez invites her to sleep over, which will be Jolene's first foray into the barrio. On the one hand, she's very excited. On the other, she's apprehensive.

Toonerville!

Houses are much smaller in Toonerville than those on her street. And old, battered cars are parked everywhere, curbside, or on untended front yards. Debris, auto and bicycle parts, toys are strewn on driveways, browned lawns, and porches. Occasionally, there is a well-tended small garden, but not many. Mexicans of all ages are everywhere, too, chattering away, oblivious to the loud, pulsating Latin music which blares from houses and cars. Some people stare at her as she and Carmen pass. Most people ignore them.

In some ways, the barrio reminds Jolene of Boyle Heights, where her Grampa Abe used to live. Everyone there resembled each other too, spoke a different language. Toonerville, like Boyle Heights, was a different world. So different from her world. But in some ways, it was the same.

People in Toonerville resemble each other. Most are dark-skinned, have jet black hair, speak in a foreign tongue. Yet, Toonerville is only one block away from where she lives. That's what is so surprising.

There is also one huge difference between Boyle Heights and Toonerville. In the Heights, Jolene saw only a few young children. In the barrio, children of all ages run, scream, and play everywhere, even in the street. Snot-nosed babies abound. Many are nursing in young girls' arms, looking not much older than Carmen. Some nursing women look old enough to be grandmothers. The Mexican women converse amongst themselves and call out to toddlers. Men and young boys huddle together on porches, lean on battered cars, drink beer, and leer at the females.

Excited over this new adventure, Jolene chats non-stop with her friend. Suddenly, Carmen stiffens and tells Jolene to stop talking, look straight ahead, and walk faster.

At the house they are approaching, Jolene sees a group of young men, "Pachucos," she notes, sitting on the porch's steps. Two teenage Mexican girls sit with them. The young men stare disrespectfully as they near, shouting Spanish words that Jolene doesn't understand. But whatever is said makes Carmen blush. Becoming upset, one of the teenage girls rises from the stoop, screams out a word, starts down the steps as she reaches for the lacquered roll, which is part of her hairdo.

"Run," instructs Carmen. "Run!"

Frightened, Jolene runs as fast as possible, sure she will never get out of this place alive.

But they finally arrive at Carmen's house unscathed and are greeted by scores of family members.

In the kitchen, Jolene meets Carmen's mother, who looks old enough to be her grandmother. When Jolene learns that Carmen's mother is the same age as her mom, she wonders how this can be when she looks so old. When Carmen explains that her mother had her first child at age 15 and had 14 more children, Jolene understands why. Her friend, Carmen, is next to the youngest.

When introduced to her daughter's new friend, Mrs. Gomez speaks no English and shows shyness. But that shyness turns into friendliness as she watches Jolene put away her homemade tacos with much enthusiasm a short time later. By day's end, Jolene has become one of the family.

That night Jolene and Carmen watch as a teenage sister gets ready to go out. Dressed in black, she brushes her ebony hair. Carmen's sister rolls her hair around a strip of material on top of her head.

Jolene asks, "Why do you and the older girls wear your hair like that?"

"The pompadour," she tells Jolene as she slicks grease onto the now tightened roll and then casually slips a thin blade inside, "houses my stiletto."

Rising, she checks herself in the mirror and finishes her explanation with pride to the now gaping young girl, "...and guarantees my position."

Later, as the two young friends lie in bed talking, Jolene asks, "Carmen, you're not...You're not going to become a Pachuco girlfriend, too, are you?"

"No! No! Don't think so. But, in the barrio, one doesn't have too many choices."

"You could become a movie star. You're beautiful enough."

Carmen laughs.

"Or, you could be a teacher, go to college...like Carmen Rios plans to do."

Her friend laughs again, "Carmen's a horse, Jolene. No one will come after her. She has only one brother. There is a chance she will get out of the barrio. Get an education. For me..." sighs. "There is no money. Too many mouths to feed. The boys are already sniffing around."

She sighs again, "I am a good Catholic, Jolene. For me, there aren't too many choices."

Remembering the withered face and body of Mrs. Gomez, Jolene thinks how sad it will be if that is to be the fate of her beautiful friend.

Chapter Eighteen
1943

Before Jolene realizes it, graduation is upon them. To celebrate, their teacher plans a party. Carmen Rios' mom sends frijoles. Mrs. Gomez sends rice. Bagels and cream cheese are Liz's contributions. Nowhere have three young girls graduated with more enthusiasm. After they are given their report cards and told they've all passed with flying colors, they giggle and squeeze each other in a group hug. Then they proceed to eat every last morsel of food. Afterward, they dance the Mexican Hat Dance on a giant sombrero flung on the floor for that purpose. As they dance, they sing, "Sing Chapanacas, Aye Yay, Aye Yay," then clap twice and sing, "Sing Chapana…" at the top of their lungs.

The following Monday, Jolene and the Carmens stand amongst a group of young people waiting at Brunswick and Chevy Chase for a school bus. They are excited and nervous, too. Today is their first day at Washington Irving Junior High. The brothers, who recently moved in, stand away from the others. The older one waits quietly as the younger one fidgets and fidgets. A bespectacled girl stands alone, oblivious to all as she reads. When the bus arrives, the girl with glasses boards sits down then resumes reading. Without inviting Jolene to join them, the Carmens sit together, laugh, joke with other Mexican youths. Feeling left out, Jolene sits next to the girl who reads.

After the brothers board the bus and look for seats, the younger one accidentally steps on someone's foot. A confrontation ensues. Bill, the older brother, intervenes. Jolene watches and tries to make eye contact with him. Unaware of her or anyone else, he guides his protesting brother to the seat behind her. As he clambers in, she feels his hot breath on her neck, causing her to shudder.

Introducing herself to the girl next to her, Jolene receives a mumbled, "I'm Sunny or something."

The girl doesn't even look up from her book.

Oh, thinks Jolene, how I wish my friend Joyce were here.

Washington Irving Junior High is such a large school. So many kids rush, laugh, push, joke around, seeming to know each other. She doesn't know anyone except the Carmens, and they only mingle and eat with the few other Mexicans. Jolene feels lonely, almost invisible.

Seated alphabetically in her homeroom, kids with German and Italian-sounding names fill the seats, and all ignore her.

At recess, as she exits the building, she hears someone shout, "Kike! Kike! Christ killer!"

Stopping to see what is happening, she sees several boys kick, yell, and hit a small boy with a large, Semitic nose. As he crouches on the pavement, trying to protect his head from the blows, children converge on the scene, crowd around, and block her view. Most of the kids watch in silence, not condoning, yet not condemning.

"Why are they hitting him?" she asks the boy standing next to her. "What did he do? What's happening?"

"He's a Jew, that's why I guess. A Jew!" the boy answers.

There is no time for further conversation.

A teacher pushes past them and breaks up the beating. Assisting the bleeding, sobbing boy to his feet, the teacher angrily upbraids the attackers and shepherds them toward the administration building.

When Jolene tells her parents of the incident that evening at dinner, Dan comments, "Even in America, they call you a Christ killer."

"Remember what I told you, Jolene," Liz adds. "You can change your name, your looks, where you live, even your religion. But you can't run away from being born a Jew. The world will never let you forget!"

If that's so, wonders Jolene, how come her parents don't act like Jews? Why don't they do like Uncle Reuben? He's such a good Jew that he doesn't even eat pork or drive on Saturdays.

The school orchestra is having tryouts. Jolene decides to try out for the piano player and is excited over the prospect. But she is humbled when she hears other students perform. True, Jolene plays with great feeling. But many of the other pianists have taken lessons for years, have better technical skills, and read music faster than she does, so she is not chosen for the position. However, the orchestra leader, Miss Darling, suggests she try another instrument, "The string bass, perhaps," she says, "because you're so tall." Wanting desperately to be a member of the orchestra, Jolene agrees.

Within weeks, she and one of the cello players, a gangly girl named Caroline, become fast friends.

"It's nice, Jolene, the way you make friends so easily," Liz tells her one day, as she goes on and on about Caroline this and Caroline that. "Wish I had time for friends."

Friends don't take that much time, Jolene thinks. Her mother could find the time, too. Then, she remembers her parents' nasty fights, the few times her mother has brought a friend home. Ugly fights, where her father accused her mother of liking the person more than him. And each time, her mother told him she wouldn't see the person again. And she didn't.

"Why don't you invite Caroline over so that we can meet her?" Liz asks one day after Jolene mentions her new friend again.

Jolene agrees, and a few days later, she brings Caroline home and introduces her to Liz.

"Hahahahahow dodododo youyouyouyou do, Mimimimimi Mrs. Hartman," Caroline says in response to the introduction.

Liz's displeasure is obvious. She remains cold and rude the entire time Caroline is there. As soon as the door closes, Jolene turns on her mother, "I'm never bringing anyone home again. How can you be so mean to my friends? How can you? You're just as bad as Daddy is about your friends!"

Outraged at her daughter's audacity, Liz slaps her across the face and lashes out, "This has nothing to do with your father or my friends, you little brat," she retorts. "This refers only to this girl. This… this… Caroline. I don't want you associating with her anymore. Do you hear me? Find yourself a new friend! End of discussion." Ignoring her daughter's protestations, Liz storms out of the room.

Her mother ignores anything Jolene says when she brings up the subject. She doesn't respond until the day Jolene is so frustrated and angry over the Caroline incident that she blurts out, "Itititit's not fair, Mommy! Not fair!"

"See! See!" screams Liz as she turns on her. "That's what I mean! It's catching."

Furious at her mother, Jolene runs from the room and slams the door. Unable to express her anger and frustration, she does what she has started doing to release her feelings—she strips her bed, then remakes it. By then, her rage has usually diminished, and the lump in the back of her throat has eased. Only then can she calmly sit on the bed, thinking how unfair it is to stop being Caroline's friend just because she stutters. Then she remembers how often her mother has snapped at her if she's stared at someone disabled or in a wheelchair. Grownups are fakers, she decides. They tell you to do one thing, and then they go ahead and do just the opposite. They're just lousy fakers. When I grow up, she determines, I'll be honest with my kids, honest with everyone.

Thump, thump, thump. That's what Jolene plays on the string bass during orchestra practice. Never melody, never solos. Just thump, thump, thump.

"But you're the orchestra's foundation," Mrs. Darling reminds her if she complains.

Daily, Mrs. Darling, the orchestra teacher, tells them she's going to the bathroom. The kids know she's lying and sneaking down to the janitor's basement, that hidden place where all the teachers go to smoke.

While she's gone, Marilyn, the lead pianist, conducts.

Jolene often starts jazzing up the rhythm during the teacher's absence as they play. Soon, percussion players join in. By the time Mrs. Darling returns, a lively jam session is ongoing. Knowing Jolene is at the bottom of it, Mrs. Darling sends her to the girls' vice principal's office. This happens weekly.

These visits become so frequent that Mrs. Gray, the girls' vice principal, decides to make the time productive for both of them and teaches Jolene how to file.

The smell of freshly baked goodies greets Jolene as she passes her neighbor's house on the way home from school. Delicious odors waft through the open kitchen windows of Mrs. Browning next door. Usually, Jolene can tell what she has baked that day. A chocolate smell means brownies or chocolate cake, her favorite. Cinnamon means cinnamon buns. Vanilla, well, vanilla is more of a mystery. Sometimes vanilla means cookies, sweet rolls, or bread pudding. Sometimes, but never on Mondays, Mrs. Browning invites her in for a sweet or slice of freshly baked bread if she sees her walking Twinkie. Then she serves a slab of homemade creamy butter and spoonfuls of canned jam with the bread. As Jolene snacks, Mrs. Browning questions her about the school, her music, and her friends, showing interest in everything Jolene does.

When Jolene tells her mom about Mrs. Browning, Liz tells her she's probably interested because she has no children.

Such a kind, gentle woman Mrs. Browning is. Everyone likes her—everyone but her husband, and no one likes him. Jolene has often wondered why such a sweet lady married such a mean man.

Mrs. Browning said her husband works in a garage and comes home with his hands, clothes, and face grease-stained. After getting his paycheck on Friday nights, he goes to a bar and comes home drunk. Then he shouts vile obscenities at her.

Mrs. Browning closes all the windows on the weekends. Then there are no more chocolate, cinnamon, or vanilla smells, only the sounds of Mr. Browning yelling, breaking dishes, or Mrs. Browning's moans or soft crying.

"Can't we do something, ask him to stop? What if he's hurting her?" Jolene asks her mother one night when Mrs. Browning's cries seem louder than usual.

Liz replies with the stock answer she has for almost anything unpleasant. "Better not to get involved, Jolene. What you don't know never hurts you!"

One Friday night, the crashing, the noise, Mr. Browning's bellowing, Mrs. Browning's cries of distress became louder. The radio helps to drown out some of it, but not all. The disturbance becomes louder and louder. Her cries become more distinct. Liz and Jolene become upset and don't know what to do, who to turn to since Dan isn't home.

Then, running footsteps are heard. A timid knocking begins at their front door. Jolene looks at her mother and asks if she should open it. At first, Liz nods in the negative. Reconsidering, she wipes her hands on her apron and opens the door herself.

A face they hardly recognize appears. Poor Mrs. Browning. So battered, so bruised, so apologetic, as she leans against the doorframe, saying, "I'm so…so sorry to bother you. But I…" and collapses into Liz's arms.

Liz calls the police.

A few minutes later, Mr. Browning is there, pounding and pounding on their door, shouting out for his wife, cursing them for taking her in. The three huddle, frightened, until the police come, take that cruel alcoholic man away. Shortly after, Mrs. Browning's brother arrives to care for his sister.

"See what happens when you get involved? You can get yourself killed! The luck of a good Samaritan," says Liz, as she shares the event with family members at a Saturday night poker game. "And for what? Things never change!"

As always, Liz is right.

Not more than two days later, there he is again, Mr. Browning, out of jail, living at home, right next door. And there she is, Mrs. Browning, baking delicious loaves of bread and goodies every day, except on weekends. On those days, the kitchen windows were still tightly shut and curtained. But they are not closed tight enough to hide the brutality going on inside.

Now that she's in Junior High, Jolene doesn't have access to a piano. Learning of this, Aunt Lottie offers to give them her upright piano, but Liz rejects the offer, saying she doesn't want a piano crowding her too-small living room. Finally, she gives in when she realizes how important the piano is to her daughter.

Jolene is in heaven, having her own piano. Now, she can practice any time she wishes, except when Liz is home.

"The noise," as Liz calls her practice sessions, is too annoying.

But others in the neighborhood do not have Liz's sensitivity. They await her daily practice times. Memorizing comes easily to Jolene. Now she knows many pieces she can play by heart. Neighbors often stop what they are doing when they hear her warm-up scales. Some open their windows wider, turn off radios, shush older children, rock infants, and settle in to listen. Even some kids on the block sit on the porch or lie on the grass in front, waiting to hear the first tinkling notes.

At first, a few scales to warm up her fingers. Then renditions of "The Butterfly", "Warsaw Concerto", and "Clair de Lune" follow. Few of her neighbors know the titles of the compositions played. Nor can they name the composers. However, some of her neighbors' hum along with the melodies, so familiar have they become with Jolene's mini-recital.

Beethoven's "Moonlight Sonata" floats out of her opened windows. Eyes half-closed, Jolene plays not only with her fingers but from the heart. She loves this piece. It is her father's favorite, too. Often, he will ask her to play it for him. How wonderful, she thinks, to bring such joy to others—and herself at the same time.

As she holds the final chord, her fingers rest on the keys until every vibration of the last note is gone. Sighing, she closes the cover, pleased as she hears quiet applause from outside. Then, play and conversation resume. Jolene smiles, spent. Rising, she places the sheet music back into her bench and pushes it toward the piano. The children disperse as they hear their mothers calling them for dinner. Neighbors close windows and turn on radios. Jolene is left alone with her piano. But others, including Bill Clifford, the older brother down the street, hold onto memories and melodies she has shared with them. They look forward to tomorrow as they resume their tasks when Jolene opens her windows and sits down to practice the piano again.

After she practices, Jolene often takes Twinkie to walk around the block, always passing the Clifford place. Sometimes she sees Bill working around the house or in the yard. He never speaks to her, only nods as she passes. She's heard he's graduating this year. Then she'll probably never see him again. Even now, he doesn't take the bus anymore. He probably has a job or something.

When she mentions the Clifford family to Liz, her mother tells her to leave well enough alone. "That family has been through hell, Jolene. The scars are deep."

They hear Bill is like the father in the family. No one ever sees the mother. She never leaves the house. Sometimes there is an occasional glimpse of her behind a kitchen window, peeking out. Gossip has it that the younger boy is a trouble-maker.

Jolene hears a lawnmower. It's Bill, she knows, doing yard work. Her thoughts jumble when she thinks of him.

How old he is, she wonders, 15? 16? He's so big and beautiful, she thinks. If only he'd say something to her. But... He probably thinks she's just a kid.

As she nears his house, she holds her head high and doesn't look his way. The motor ceases.

"I liked the last song you just played. What is it called?"

"Uh... Uh... It's uh... 'Moonlight Sonata'," she stutters, almost stumbling, as she rushes down the street, her heart beating so loud, she's sure he can hear it.

Rounding the corner, Twinkie barks at a Great Dane. The enormous dog plays in a yard with Sunny, its owner. Sunny is the girl with glasses Jolene had tried to befriend on the bus the first day of school. Once Jolene realized Sunny wasn't unfriendly, just very shy, they'd become good friends.

To Jolene, Sunny lives in the perfect house. It's a rambling, white, ranch-style dwelling trimmed in blue. The home sits on a double lot enclosed by a white picket fence. A wooden swing shares space with ceramic pots overflowing with colorful perennials on the long porch, welcoming one and all. Multi-colored flower beds surround a manicured lawn. The long driveway meanders back to a triple garage. The two horses' stables are behind that, at least 50 feet or more away from their dwelling. One horse belongs to Sunny. The other is to her older sister Darlene.

Everything is also picture-perfect inside the house—bright, warm, and welcoming. Her new friend lives in the perfect home and has the perfect family in Jolene's mind.

Sunny resembles her father, Mr. Schroeder, a tall, lean, quiet, scholarly C.P.A. Not overly effusive, he still greets family members with a quick kiss on the forehead when he arrives home from work each day. No matter how busy he is, Mr. Schroeder always stops whatever he is doing and is ready to listen to someone's tale of the day.

As she insists Jolene call her, Mrs. Schroeder, or Charlotte, is soft and pretty and always smells nice. A frilly apron covers her flowered feminine garments. Shaking her dark, curly-haired head, she scolds them in her definitive Southern drawl and teases them if they don't eat enough of her freshly baked goodies that await them when they arrive home from school.

Four years older than Sunny, Darlene is a shorter, plumper version of Charlotte and has competed as a champion equestrian since she was five years old. Hundreds of ribbons and medals adorn her bedroom walls. Cabinets heave from the weight of shining trophies.

"There was a time when the only thing Darlene talked about was horses," says Sunny. "Now, all she talks about is Randall this, Randall that!"

Randall, Darlene's new boyfriend, is an Army private. They met at the USO, where she volunteers on Friday nights. The USO is where service members come to dance. He is the first man Darlene has ever dated, and she can't believe her luck because Randall is exceptionally handsome. Almost too handsome.

When Jolene meets him, she agrees. Not only is Randall good-looking, but he's also super charming. Within moments, he has every female in the room laughing and blushing, teasing them with his soft Southern twang, evoking near-hysterical trills from Sunny's mom.

The picture-perfect scene continues until the day Jolene is having Sunday brunch at Sunny's house. In one of his story-telling moods, Randall details purchasing a watch from a buddy.

"...and I was able to Jew him down," he says, laughing, rubbing his nose downward with his fingers.

"What does Jew them down mean, Randall?" Jolene asks.

As one, the Schroeder family stops eating and looks uncomfortable.

Randall responds, "You know! Get the best deal, Jolene. Everyone knows Jews are thieves, will steal you blind and—"

"Randall! I'm Jewish. And I'm not a thief," Jolene speaks out defensively, embarrassed that she's making such an issue but flushing at his insinuation.

"I don't think Randall meant anything by..." Mr. Schroeder addresses Jolene. "He had no idea you were Jewish." Turning to Randall, "However, I think an apology is due here, Randall, don't you?"

Trying to make light of it, Randall taps Jolene on the head, jests, "Hey, kiddo, I didn't mean you...mean all Jews. Hey! One of my best buddies on the base is Jewish and..."

Rising from the table, Charlotte announces, "I made the most delicious dessert. Wait 'til you taste it. Darlene, Randall, why don't you help me serve?"

The three of them leave the room as Jolene mumbles her apologies to Sunny and her father, who stops her mid-sentence, saying, "Some people think with their behinds, not their brains, Jolene." Relieved, the three of them break into laughter, easing the tension.

Yet later, Jolene ponders what has happened. Is this what her mother meant? About the world never letting you forget you're a Jew? It's strange. People who don't even know you say and think bad things about you because you're Jewish. That seems so unfair, she thinks. Unfair and rotten.

Her parents are getting along better than Jolene can ever remember, really enjoying being owners of a coffee shop. Business is picking up. Liz was right. Soon, they will have Reuben's loan paid off. School, friends, and music keep Jolene busy. Life is good. Maybe they can become a picture-perfect family, too. Buy the red brick house her father had promised her long ago.

Jolene is rarely alone with her father anymore. Everyone is so busy. But when he is near her and Liz's not around, he still has the power to place his hands and lips in places that instantly arouse her. Whispering to her, he reminds her that she's still his 'Little Mommy,' even though she's as tall as he is now. Her young body, having been caressed so long, still responds to his touches, his commands. Whether she wants to or not, she still desires the ultimate pleasure she knows he will bring to her.

But self-loathing, guilt, and disgust are constant companions to her now. So, she tries to keep away from him as much as possible. Self-pleasure has become a habit, too; rubbing on a pillow in bed when cravings surface and overcome her. Each time she is grateful for the release. Yet, she cannot rid herself of the guilt accompanying the action. Jolene learns that masturbating is a sin from sermons heard in church with friends. Between that and being her father's 'Little Mommy,' she knows she is damned. Punished, punished. And she knows she will probably go to hell.

Summer is here.

Jolene and Sunny want to walk to the Griffith Park Pool. Dan is against it. "No way. Two little girls walking to a public swimming pool? Not a good idea." It is hard for him to admit that Jolene is growing up.

"They're not little girls anymore!" Liz snorts, responding to Dan's comment. "They're 12 years old! It's less than a mile from here. Los Feliz is a busy street. There's no way they can get lost, get into trouble. When I was 10, Barbara and I took the trolley downtown and…"

"Times are different now, Liz."

Losing patience, she tells him, "Okay, then, okay. She's your responsibility! End of discussion."

"Okay! Okay! Let them go."

Given two dimes and a nickel, Jolene ties them in a knotted handkerchief and pins it to her bathing suit under her dress. Fifteen cents is needed to enter the pool. The extra dime. Well! She has it in case of an emergency.

They pay admission and race to the showers. Jolene exits first and becomes chilled as she waits for Sunny. Telling her she'll be in the shallow end, she enters the pool area and is surprised to see many people in bathing suits standing on the deck. They stand there, quietly talking amongst themselves, watching those few swimming in the pool.

Those who stand on the deck are white.

Those who swim, splash, or play in the Olympic-sized swimming pool, are black.

Jolene walks over to the pool, sits on the edge, sticks her toe in to test the water. Determining it is not too cold, she eases herself in.

People on the deck stop talking and watch her. People in the pool stop frolicking, or swimming, eye her with suspicion.

Unaware of what's happening, she approaches the nearest child and greets her, "Hi! I'm Jolene. What's your name?"

Instead of getting a friendly response, hostility greets her.

"Why you in here? Time's not up," the child addresses her accusingly. Then she screams out to a woman who swims in the deep end. "Mama! Mama! Clock don says 1:00. Do we gotta get out now?"

Sunny now stands on the deck, waving frantically at Jolene to come out of the water. But Jolene remains because she is so surprised at what is happening.

The child's mother rushes toward her angry offspring, "Maybe the clock's wrong, Ramy. Don't want trouble." Without another word, she pulls the protesting child out of the pool.

Within moments, all the other blacks follow suit. The pool is now empty except for Jolene, who stands there shocked, still not understanding what is happening.

One of the people waiting on the deck lets out a cheer. There is laughter and more cheers. Then all the white folks jump into the pool. One of them claps Jolene on the back and comments, "Great going, little girl. You got us an extra ten minutes. Thanks."

A teenager splashes her and snaps. "How can you get in the water with niggers? You a nigger lover or something?"

Climbing out of the pool, Jolene takes Sunny's hand as Sunny keeps apologizing, "So sorry. Sorry. I thought you knew…Thought you knew."

"Knew what?"

Not comprehending what has happened, Jolene can't understand the looks of hatred from the Negroes as they leave the pool area.

Almost in tears, Jolene questions her friend.

"Why are people getting so angry? What did I do?"

Instead of answering her friend's tearful queries, she keeps repeating, "Thought you knew the pool's rules, Jolene. So sorry! So sorry!"

Everyone seems to know the rules of the pool—except Jolene.

Negroes and whites know that black folks cannot swim again until the next day. They understand because there is a big sign in front of the Griffith Park Swimming Pool. A sign that Jolene wasn't aware existed.

Negroes allowed 12:00 PM to 1:00 PM.
Monday through Friday only!

When Jolene reads the sign, she is appalled. *How can this be?* she wonders. Everything is beautiful here, with fancy-sounding street names like Griffith Park Boulevard, Riverside Drive, and Los Feliz. Across the street, a fountain shoots water into the air. Smartly dressed people laugh and joke as they ride horses along trails in the nearby rolling hills. Towering shade trees that offer protection from the afternoon sun dot gentle slopes of neatly trimmed lawns as far as the eye can see. This is Griffith Park. A public park where everyone is welcome, she had thought. Everything seemed so serene, almost perfect. Yet, it isn't. This place isn't as lovely as it appeared to be. Jolene can't believe it! People are mean here, too. Worse in some ways than the people who taunted Keiko. Dejected, Jolene realizes that people can be mean anywhere. She wonders, how can a place be so beautiful and yet so ugly?

"This is a first," bandleader Russ Morgan announces a few months later as he stands on the stage in a lavish ballroom called the Cocoanut Grove, located in the bowels of the Ambassador Hotel on Wilshire Boulevard.

"This is the first time I've ever congratulated someone on their…"

A drum roll begins.

Strident bugle notes resound.

Swaying couples on the sleek dance floor pause.

Diners stop eating. All becomes quiet.

This room is one of the city's finest nightclubs, decorated with monkeys peering out of the branches of fake palm trees. A wine steward with a golden chain presides over tables like royalty, luring unsuspecting customers into purchasing wines more expensive than their meals.

As the room quiets, the band leader continues.

"Believe this, if you will. One of our guests, Mr. Reuben Sorkin, is here tonight with his family members to celebrate a memorable occasion. Now listen carefully, folks. It's not often you hear this kind of announcement. Mr. Sorkin is here tonight to celebrate his deeeeeevorce!"

A howl of laughter fills the room. The band plays The *Anniversary Waltz* off-key and ends on an extended sour note. More laughter, much applause.

A spotlight finds the Sorkin table, then focuses on Rueben, who flushes with embarrassment. He rises and bows. Roars of laughter fill the room, accompanied by cheers, applause, then more laughter. The spotlight travels the rest of the table, highlighting each family member dressed in their finest—Jolene, her parents, aunts, uncles, and cousins. All the Sorkins are there, and all are uncomfortable with the attention. Tonight, they are here as Reuben's guests to share in the celebration.

The wine steward arrives at the table with complimentary champagne and opens bottles with a flourish, followed by whooshing pops: more laughter and cheers.

Jolene tastes "bubbly" for the first time.

"To Reuben's freedom!" they toast.

Throughout the room, the toast is repeated, "To Reuben's freedom!"

More cheers. More applause.

After dinner, they dance. Jolene, held stiffly by Uncle Reuben, dipped by Red, bounced around the floor with Marcus, leading Alisa because she's the tallest.

As they eat their dessert, a waiter leans into Reuben and tells him he's wanted on the phone by a "Mr. Jones."

"Horatio?" Reuben shows surprise.

"Probably wants to congratulate you," says Liz.

"He did at the store and closed up for me tonight."

"Thought he didn't work nights," Liz says.

"Doesn't usually," Reuben admits. "But tonight was special, so he said he'd stay. Wonder why he's calling?"

"Only way you'll find out is to go to the damned phone," bellows Marcus.

Laughter accompanies Rueben as he rushes from the ballroom. People clap him on the back and congratulate him as he exits.

It is almost midnight as they sit, Red and Marcus, waiting at the Glendale Police Station. Quiet, scared, they watch Rueben as he stands at the desk filling out papers, handing over cash. They wonder why Horatio is here. Why did he call Reuben to bail him out? What did he do? Reuben joins them, sits down, doesn't say a word. They don't question him.

In time, two policemen appear with Horatio between them. Unable to walk, he is held upright by the stone-faced uniformed men. Reuben, Dan and Marcus rush forward, showing dismay at the sight of his swollen face.

When Horatio sees Reuben, he cries out, "Mr. Reuben, suh. I tried to tell 'em. Tried to tell 'em what you told me. Didn't believe me. Didn't believe a single word."

It is more than a month before Horatio is back at work. But there are many things he can't do now. One arm is still in a sling. He can't lift either because it takes months for ribs to heal.

But it didn't take months for Jolene to find out what happened to Horatio that night. On the night of the divorce celebration.

That night Horatio closed up the store as he'd promised Rueben he would do. He removed all the cash and placed it in his pockets as Reuben had instructed him to do. Then, he'd walked to the bus stop as he always did every day when he finished work.

Except, this time, it wasn't daytime. Horatio had been very nervous because it was nighttime and dark, and he'd hoped the bus would come soon. And he'd waited and waited.

The bus didn't arrive, but a police car did.

The two policemen questioned him. "Didn't he know the law? Didn't he know…?" And they'd hit him, hit him, hit him.

"Yes, yes," Horatio had cried out, "I know the law, suh, I know, but…"

Reuben knew the law, too, but with all the excitement of the celebration, he'd forgotten the Glendale law that said Negroes weren't allowed on the streets after dark. It was because of that law that Horatio never worked nights.

As Horatio had laid on the ground that night during the beating, the police officers found the money in his pocket and asked him whom he'd robbed. When he told them why he had the money, they'd laughed and laughed at him and hit him repeatedly, not stopping until he'd passed out.

Uncle Reuben made sure that Horatio never worked after sundown again.

They wait. Jolene and her parents stand waiting in anticipation at Union Station for Paul, her father's younger brother, and his family to arrive. They are coming from Vancouver, Canada, and plan to live here.

"There he is!" shouts Red. He runs and embraces his brother as he emerges from the crowd. Balder, darker, taller, and fleshier, Paul resembles the Hartman clan.

His wife, Rachel, appears. She is dark-haired and slim, with alabaster skin, and seems apprehensive as she pulls along two small boys. Paul greets everyone with bear hugs. Jolene is pleased by her new aunt's tender greeting, gentle kiss on her cheek, and an immediate bond forms.

Then she eyes her two pale new cousins. The boys resemble their father but are opposites. The older one is tall and slim. The younger is short, plump, sullen, clings to his mother, and is ever demanding. They stand there, staring back at her, looking out of place in their stiff white shirts and dark and tailored jackets. Jolene almost giggles when she sees that they are wearing shorts. Yes, shorts. Not the kind of shorts people wear to the beach or play in. Her cousins' dark shorts are made from trouser fabric and hit them just above their knobby pale knees. Heavy black shoes and long black stockings complete their outfits. They are the funniest-looking boys she has ever seen, and she has a tough time keeping from laughing out loud. Containing herself, she greets them. "Hi! I'm Jolene!"

The tall, skinny five-year-old responds, almost with relief, as he extends his hand and tells her, "Hi! I'm Soloman. This is Simon."

Soloman's grip is firm for one so young. Jolene takes an instant liking to him as her hand grips his.

Three-year-old Simon wraps himself around Aunt Rachel's leg at the sound of his name and whines until she lifts him.

Much as she doesn't want to admit it, Jolene forms an instant dislike for this younger cousin, and it is years before they become friends.

Gathering their luggage, they leave the station in great spirits. Except for Simon's constant whining or crying, Jolene feels excited and loving toward this new addition to her family.

Dan is animated as he drives them to his brother's newly rented home in Boyle Heights. Their place isn't too far from where Grampa Abraham used to live. The Heights is the same. Acrid smells are still pungent as they cross the bridge. Orthodox Jews still live here, speaking a language Jolene does not understand. She wonders why her mother keeps telling her, "They may speak a different language than you, Jolene. But these are your people. Your people!"

Jolene's first Jewish holiday dinner occurs because Uncle Paul has invited them to his house for Passover.

Liz doesn't want to go. She grumbles about how boring and depressing these things are. How much work it is. Dan insists they must attend out of respect for his brother.

Rachel did all of the cooking. They bring matzo, macaroon cookies, and kosher wine.

They are only seven, Paul's family and the three of them. Uncle Arthur and Aunt Lottie had declined.

The formal table, set with fine china and engraved silverware, has delicate crystal goblets filled and re-filled with sweet kosher wine. A little wine is given, even to the children.

Paul begins the reading and drones on and on in Hebrew, sometimes in English. As he tells the story of the liberation of the Jews from slavery in Egypt, he asks questions of his sons and instructs Rachel to serve this, do that, get this. She is up and down, up and down. At one point, she brings in a basin of water and a towel to carry around so that each male may wash and dry his hands, even young Simon.

"This," whispers Liz to her daughter, "is why I don't enjoy Jewish holidays!"

Jolene has difficulty staying awake between the wine and the long unfamiliar rituals and readings.

When the service ends, the females serve the food. So much food. Seven courses in all. The male members of the family remain seated. Aunt Rachel, Liz, and Jolene wait and serve, wait and serve, even do all of the clean-up later. Everyone overeats. Simon whines and cries during the service and meal and manages to spill two glasses of wine on the table cloth and hot soup on himself. The only one who seems to enjoy the entire evening is cousin Soloman, who receives a reward from his father after finding a hidden piece of matzo.

It is one of the few times Jolene and her mother agree. Jewish holiday dinners are dull, dull, and too much work.

In addition to playing string bass in the orchestra, Jolene's soprano voice has found a home in the school chorus. Mr. Ballinger, the choral director, chooses her as a Soloist for the upcoming noon-day Christmas concert.

Thrilled, Jolene tells her parents about it and asks them to come to the concert.

"Probably can't make it, Jolene," they tell her. "Work, you know. Sorry!"

Disgusted, Jolene wonders why, just once, her parents can't put her first, close the coffee shop, hear her sing, or see her play the bass. Just once! Why is it, she wonders, when things are going really great, her parents always manage to pop her balloon?

The day of the performance arrives.

It is no surprise to Jolene when her parents do not show up. Her disappointment is sharp but momentarily because it doesn't cut into the satisfaction of the day. She feels proud when she stands in front of that solidly-packed auditorium and sings "Away in the Manger."

Her voice is authentic and lyrical. She feels, in her heart, every word that she sings about the baby Jesus. She feels so strongly that her cheeks are wet with tears when she finishes and takes her bows. She sees several women dabbing at their eyes as she looks out at the audience. That day, she doesn't care if her parents share this moment with her or not. The applause, appreciation, and sweet success of her special moment with the baby Jesus was hers to keep forever.

It is a week before Christmas and such a happy time for Jolene. She loves everything about this holiday: the decorations, how people act nicer, the presents, good food, the Christmas carols, and especially the Christmas tree. It is the best time of the year, as far as she is concerned.

"When are we getting our tree?" Jolene asks her father. Christmas is almost here, and they still haven't bought a tree. Busy with a crossword puzzle, he doesn't respond. She repeats the question. He doesn't look up and mumbles something about not having a tree this year.

"We're what?"

"You heard me. No tree!"

"Mommy!" Not believing, she turns to Liz.

"You heard right, Jolene!" Her mother's words drip with sarcasm. "Out of respect for your dad's religious little brother, we can't have a Christmas tree."

"Liz!"

"Well! It's true, isn't it? Why can't you stand up to him, Dan, the way Arthur does and…"

"So, they're not speaking now."

"It's not because of a lousy Christmas tree, Dan. It's because your little brother called Lottie, another non-religious shiksa, who couldn't give him children," Liz retorts.

"He only referred to Lottie as 'a gentile wife,' Liz."

"Everyone knows all of Arthur's wives haven't been Jewish," Liz responds. "He didn't have to imply that if Arthur had married a Jewish woman, he'd probably be a father today and—"

"I don't want to discuss it any further, Liz."

"Daddy, we've got to have a tree," Jolene laments.

They ignore her outburst.

"Dan!" Liz persists. "Paul insulted Lottie. I'd be hurt and angry if I were Lottie, too. I'm just saying the problem between your brothers isn't about a tree."

"It won't be Christmas without a tree," Jolene shouts, now crying.

They still ignore her.

"Paul's my baby brother, Liz. I haven't seen him in years. He feels strongly about his religion, and I don't want to hurt his feelings. Let's just drop the subject, okay?" Dan returns to his crossword.

Jolene intervenes and begs, "Please, Daddy. Please. Can't we have a Christmas tree?"

Dan ignores his daughter's pleas.

"What about our feelings?" Liz persists. "You don't have to get into a hassle with Paul, Dan. Just let him know how we feel. We've been enjoying Christmas lately, with the tree and all. It has nothing to do with Christianity. He should respect how we feel, too."

Not looking up from his crossword, Dan responds, "It's not a big deal if we don't have a tree this year, Liz. Maybe, by next year, he'll be more flexible. We can still exchange presents and…"

Jolene can't believe she's hearing this conversation. It's as though she doesn't exist, is invisible. No one even asks her how she feels, what she wants, or if this hurts her? This isn't right.

"Daddy, how can you be so unfair?" she blurts out.

"Don't get involved in this, Jolene!" Becoming angry, Dan holds up his hand to stop her. "This has nothing to do with you. We're not getting a tree. And that's it!" Uncomfortable with the entire subject, he goes back to his puzzle.

Mocking him, Liz says softly, "And that's it. End of discussion?"

"Yes! And as you so often say, end of discussion."

Sobbing, Jolene runs to her room, strips, and remakes her bed three times that day.

It is the day before Christmas.

Jolene's parents have been gone all day. They told her they would be late because they had some errands to run after closing the café. Last-minute Christmas shopping, she guesses.

Deciding she will have a Christmas tree, even if she has to buy it herself, Jolene checks her drawers and pockets, searching for lost coins she may not have used to purchase gifts for her parents. Not much luck. Hardly anything. Just one nickel. Not enough.

Jolene enters her parent's bedroom and opens a dresser drawer like a conspirator. There, in tin cans, is her father's coin collection. With deliberation, Jolene counts out two dimes and puts everything else back in its place. She thinks twenty-five cents should be enough to buy a left-over tree on Christmas eve. Taking the coins, she leaves the house.

Even on Christmas eve, Jolene finds twenty-five cents doesn't buy much. Most trees cost at least 50 cents. After looking through scores of trees, she finally finds one, and it's almost three feet tall. Jolene can't believe her luck. Soon, she finds out why the tree is so cheap. The tree can barely stand up because it is so lop-sided. It is very green on one side, with hardly a branch on the other.

"It will be just fine," Jolene tells the vendor. "I'll place the bare side against the wall. No one will see it."

When she brings the tree home, she cannot get it to stand upright. No matter what she does, the tree keeps toppling to the floor. Finally, she props it so that even though it is still awry, it does remain standing. Then she searches for the few Christmas ornaments they had accumulated over the last few years. Not finding them, she knows her father lied to her. He must have thrown them out, too, knowing they would not have a Christmas tree again.

Enraged, this makes Jolene even more determined to make her tree beautiful. She'll string popcorn as they'd done with their first Christmas tree. That wasn't too hard. Yet, try as she will this time; many kernels don't open. And those that do are not so easy to string. The task takes hours and hours. When she has strung the last piece of popcorn, she loops the uneven ropes back and forth, back and forth on the side facing the room. Finished, she sits back and contemplates her effort. Not bad, she thinks. She's seen better, true. But at least she has a tree. Proud of her accomplishment, she checks it from every angle and decides packages would make it look more festive. Rising, she goes to her bedroom.

All year Jolene has been saving pennies and nickels, even her birthday money, to buy presents for her parents. Removing two boxes from under the bed, she handles each one as though it contains the royal jewels. Jolene hopes they will like her gifts; her father, a monogrammed handkerchief; and her mother, a bra. She has no idea it is three sizes too large.

Placing the gift boxes wrapped in last year's paper under the tree, Jolene stands back and is delighted. "That's better," she thinks, "much better."

Pleased with her accomplishment, Jolene can't wait to see her parents' reaction. She doesn't have long to wait. Within the hour, she hears their key in the lock.

As they enter, she yells, "Surprise! Surprise!"

But it isn't her parents who get the big surprise. It is Jolene. As the door opens, a strong gust of wind rushes into the room and engulfs the precariously perched tree. Down, down, down it crashes, landing on top of the presents, spewing branches and popcorn everywhere.

Caught off guard, Dan and Liz don't know whether to laugh, scold, or comfort.

Jolene's Christmas tree is never upright again. Dan removes it from the room and throws it into the trash. Sent to her room, Jolene tears her bed apart but is so upset that she doesn't remake it; she just plops down and sobs her disappointment.

Hearing her daughter's wails of distress, Liz sweeps up the mess in the living room. Bending down, she picks up a poorly stitched strand of popcorn. Looking at it, she knows how difficult this must have been for Jolene and wonders if they will ever be able to make it up to her.

They can't, and they don't.

Jolene's parents never find out the truth about how she got the money to buy the tree. She lies whenever the subject comes up and says she got it for free because it was so lopsided.

And somehow, the warm spirit of Christmas never re-enters the Hartman household again.

Chapter Nineteen
1944

Once a week, there is a dancing class at school.

Lining up by size, the girls stand on one side of the room, and the boys stand on the other. Jolene is second in line because Perry Beth is taller, almost six feet, Jolene thinks. But no one knows because she stands stooped way over.

There are two boys as tall or taller than Jolene; James Franklin and Helmut Gruen. Both prove to be a challenge.

James is almost as tall as Perry Beth, easily two heads taller than most boys his age. Whenever they stand in a dance position, he tries to press Jolene close to his body.

"To lead better," he tells her.

Usually, she wouldn't mind because James is becoming a good dancer. And, she has found dancing is something she loves to do. When she and James dance, what annoys her every week is the piston that rises between his legs.

Embarrassed to say something to the instructor or James, Jolene doesn't want to cause a class incident. She resolves the situation by placing her right elbow smack into his chest as they dance. Her elbow keeps a distance between their bodies. Most of the time, it works. But not always, as he tries, repeatedly, to pull her close to him. So, every dance with James Franklin turns into a contest of strength and willpower between them.

Sometimes, it's easier to dance with Helmut.

He's A Nice Boy, Helmut Is. Sweet, Polite, Much Better Looking Than James, even though he doesn't dance as well. She likes him a lot. Yet, there's something about him that is difficult to handle. Helmut wears a bag of garlic around his neck, under his shirt. The garlic, his father, has told him, is to protect him from germs and evil spirits. Jolene wonders if his father is also trying to keep girls away from his son.

It's a difficult choice, Tuesday afternoons at the dance class. Is it to be a wrestling match with James and his piston, or trying to enjoy the rhythm while inhaling Helmut's garlic bag?

"I took the liberty of having Jolene play for a friend," Mrs. Schwarnoff, the piano teacher, tells Liz one day.

"Why?"

"Because I think Jolene is very gifted."

"Umm!"

"My friend, who was visiting, agrees. She teaches at the Conservatory of Music in Chicago and thinks Jolene would qualify for a year's scholarship at the conservatory. I wonder, would you and your husband consider allowing her to attend?"

"Attend what?"

"The Chicago Conservatory!"

"You're kidding! Chicago? A conservatory? Jolene plays well, but..." Then she snorts, "She was so disappointed when she didn't even make the pianist in the school orchestra. There were lots of kids who played better than she did. Why let her in for more disappointment?"

"She needs instruction, discipline. At the conservatory, she would learn what she needed to know. I've taught her all I can. What she needs, they can teach her."

"Wow! A year's scholarship!" exclaims Dan when Liz tells him the news. "Can you believe it! They want my kid! Course they do! And why not? She's got my talent! It runs in the family. Imagine! My kid, a concert pianist!" Dan's enthusiasm is boundless.

"Do you realize it means she'd be living in Chicago? Alone in a big city? A couple of thousand miles away from us? She's only 13, for Gawd's sake!"

"She wouldn't be alone. There are other students and teachers. What an opportunity! I wish someone had offered me something like that. Life would be so different."

Liz's concern is evident as she paces the floor and snaps, "No, she's not going! I'm not in favor of it. No! There's no way I'm letting her go to Chicago. She's not going anywhere. It's out of the question. The whole idea is ridiculous! She's not good enough. There's no chance she'd become professional, no chance in Hell even if she were. Name me, one female concert pianist! Go ahead! Just one!"

He looks blank.

"Right! You can't! Because there aren't any. End of discussion." And she walks out of the room.

But the discussion doesn't end there.

Instead, puffed up with pride, Dan speaks of the scholarship to everyone. All are impressed.

Jolene chatters on about it non-stop. She is so excited at the prospect. A whole year. A year in the world of music. What could be more glorious, she thinks? And maybe, just maybe, if I'm good enough.

She begs, pleads. Sometimes her reward for bringing up the subject results in a slap across the face. But it stops one day when Jolene blocks the blow and grabs her mother's wrist. Holding onto it tightly, she looks Liz squarely in the face and says, "Don't you ever hit me again, Mommy. I don't deserve it."

The intensity in Jolene's eyes stops Liz. And the honesty of her words strikes home. Liz never raises her hand against her daughter again.

But the question of whether Jolene should go to Chicago continues.

Nightly, Jolene prays to God for an answer. "Oh, please God, tell me! Should I go to the Conservatory or not?"

In the end, it is not God who gives her the answer—it is her mother.

"Are you sure you want to go to Chicago, Jolene? Live in a strange city?" Liz asks her. "Think how lonely you'd be. No family. No friends. No Twinkie! All you'd have is your music. Do you think that would be enough? Do you want to practice eight hours a day, every day, when we both know it will be for nothing? There are no female concert pianists in this country, only men. You'd just be wasting your life practicing, practicing, practicing. And for what? There's nothing in the future for you. After all that work, maybe you could teach, like Mrs. Schwarnoff. You want to be like her? Alone with a piano and memories? Why not be practical, Jolene? Play piano if you want, but play for fun, for pleasure. Don't take it so seriously. You'd better enjoy yourself while you're young because the fun ends once you become an adult."

Her mother's logic makes sense. Jolene decides she doesn't want to go, and Liz breathes a sigh of relief. Dan treats it as another of life's disappointments, and the subject of the Chicago Conservatory scholarship doesn't come up again.

Liz proves right on another point as well.

The most disappointed person about Jolene not going to Chicago is Ms. Schwarnoff, her piano teacher. She will have one less famous student and one less special memory.

Chapter Twenty
September 1986 Therapy

Finishing the story about the piano scholarship at the therapy session has drained me, both physically and emotionally. And somehow, I feel angry.

"How selfish! How selfish she was," I say to Ramona. "Mom shouldn't have talked me out of going. She shouldn't have stopped me from doing something I loved? From possibly having the career of a lifetime? Maybe even a chance to become famous or something. Damn! Don't tell me she didn't want me to go to Chicago just to…just to…"

"… Save her marriage?" Ramona finishes my troubling statement. "Perhaps, Jolene. It's probably true. If you'd gone away, there's a good chance your father would have left her for good."

"What a bummer!" one of the women says.

"Why are women so weak?" another interjects.

"I don't know if I'd call it weakness, Gwynn," Ramona interrupts the woman. "Jolene's mother was not necessarily weak. She was a survivor, trying to hold onto the only world she knew. Even if it was a very, very sick, twisted world, it was her comfort zone. The known. Her cocoon, if you will."

"I wonder how different my life would have been if I'd gone to the Conservatory?"

"Probably not too different, Jolene," Ramona responds. "Perhaps worse. Because in her way, your mother was telling the truth, as she knew it. You probably wouldn't have gotten much farther than being able to teach. Not in those days. Do we know how much talent you had? And with the history of your neediness. Being away from home alone, without loved ones nearby, you might have been one miserable young girl. Instead of taking the chance of a lifetime away from you, Jolene, your mother, without realizing it, may have saved you from a lot of unhappiness."

Snorting in disgust, I attack the therapist. "Or, I might have made many new friends and become the first woman whatever..."

Several of the women laugh as Ramona smiles.

But I don't feel like laughing. I'm angry with Mom and mad at Ramona for taking her side.

"Well, Ramona," I spit out sarcastically, "you're certainly a master at turning things around, aren't you? Nothing like putting a positive twist on something so rotten."

Bristling, Ramona responds, "I'm only showing you options, Jolene. What she did, she did! You can't change her action. The only thing you can change is how you react to what she did. It's up to you to condemn, try to understand, forgive, forget or just move on. It's your choice."

"I know! I know! I still have a right to wonder what my life would have been like, don't I, if...?"

"If? We all wonder 'what if'...don't we?" Ramona directs the question to the entire group. "If! If! If!...What if the things that caused you to be here—had never happened? What if...?"

"Alright! Alright!"

Smiling, I make a checkpoint in the air with my finger, "Point well made, Ramona! Well made!"

Ramona looks at the woman to my right, "Ready, Gwynn?"

Settling back into my chair, I pay attention to the new speaker.

Chapter Twenty-One
1944 Continued

Heeding her mother's advice, Jolene decides to have fun with the piano. She quits Mrs. Schwarnoff and begins jazz lessons with another teacher. Soon, she can play boogie-woogie and popular songs. Popular music brings new friends and invitations to parties. She starts to socialize with Jean, Arliss, Beverly, and Joan, the class leaders. They are a gang, a group, not world beauties, these as yet undeveloped young girls, but with much potential, very bright, and always together. Jolene is the joker in the group. School is Jolene's favorite place now. So busy with orchestra, chorus, and piano, enjoying her classes, and she loves being part of an "in" group.

Class leaders are to be selected. Telling no one, Jolene decides to run for class secretary and fills out the application. When the big day arrives, her friends are surprised to see her name on the ballot. Votes are tallied. She corners a friend who had helped count the votes and asks, "Did I lose by much?"

Her friend laughs, "You're kidding, aren't you? You didn't even come close. You weren't expecting to win, were you?"

Surprised at her friend's answer, Jolene presses for more details, is shocked to learn she received only two votes, and one was her own. Devastated, she chokes up and starts crying.

Shocked at her reaction, her friend tries to console her. "Everyone thought you were fooling around, Jolene, joking. Honestly! You know how you kid around all the time," she said. "We had no idea you wanted us to vote for you, that you wanted the office. Why didn't you say something? Why? Everyone would have voted for you if…"

Without hearing the end of her friend's response, Jolene runs away, thoughts running rampant in her mind. She should have known better. Why did she run for office thinking she could become a class officer? Things don't change. She knows God punished her again because she's a sinner. She wonders how many of her friends have guessed her dirty secret? Wondering if that is the real reason they didn't vote for her, Jolene promises herself never, never to run for anything in school again. And she doesn't.

Sunny's sister, Darlene, hasn't been riding her horse anymore. Lately, she's always throwing up.

"Something I ate," she'll groan as she runs for the bathroom again.

"Guess what?" Sunny whispers to Jolene confidentially as they watch Darlene retreat.

"What?"

"Darlene is getting married. In two weeks! Right here, in the living room. And I'm the maid of honor!"

"How exciting!"

"Isn't it?"

"Yeah!"

The two girls seem to be the only ones who are excited. During the next few weeks, Darlene stays in her room most of the time, except when she runs for the bathroom. Charlotte is so busy cleaning, cooking, making floral arrangements. Instead of being happy about the upcoming event, sometimes she'll start to cry. If Randall enters the room, Mr. Schroeder walks out. There is ongoing tension within the family. Jolene and Sunny have no idea what is happening.

Sunny's picture-perfect family doesn't seem so perfect now. Jolene can't figure out why. She always thought weddings were supposed to be happy events. Maybe the Schroeders didn't want Darlene to get married so young. Maybe they wanted her to wait and go to college. That's it. They probably think she is too young to marry. There are so many maybes. She wonders if her parents will be happy when she gets married. But she doesn't ponder the question too long. Marriage seems so far off.

A few days later, an office attendant rushes into Jolene's homeroom, hands a note to the teacher, and leaves. After reading the message, the teacher looks up and motions Jolene to approach the desk.

"Your uncle is here, Jolene. There's been an accident. Your mother was injured and is in the hospital and…"

They never found out what went wrong when Liz lit the stove that morning at the café. All they did know was that the damn thing blew up in her face.

Liz's face is hairless for the second time in her life. She has no eyelashes or eyebrows and singed fuzz on her head. Her arms are badly burned because she had thrown them in front of her face to protect herself, a reaction that had saved her eyesight. Considering everything that happened, she was lucky to be alive.

The café was a shambles. There was no insurance and no way to rebuild. Liz's cCafé never reopens.

When Liz recovers, she has to look for work because Dan can't seem to get over another loss.

Soon, she gets a waitress job at the Tam O'Shanter Inn, one of L.A.'s best-known restaurants down the street from Reuben's furniture store. The Tam is where Walt Disney and many celebrities often dine.

Jolene loves the uniform her mother has to wear at her new job; a short plaid skirt, a white starched blouse with a red vest. A perky tam with a bright red knit ball sits on her head, where some hair has grown back. And Jolene's favorite item, the colorful red stockings reaching just below her knees.

Dan hates the outfit and says it's too revealing, showing her legs.

"It gets me great tips!"

"They should be paying for service, not to cop a feel."

"It's a different clientele, not like the Deli customers," retorts Liz.

"Says you. I see what I see."

"You want me to quit? What do we do for money? Aren't things tough enough without you complaining, grumbling, lying around, doing nothing but grousing? Why don't you get a job? Do something!"

Disgusted, she leaves for work, leaving him poring over his stamps.

A few weeks later, Dan shows up in uniform.

"I've joined the Merchant Marine. I'll be shipping out Monday!"

Sobbing, Liz scolds him, "I didn't mean for you to do something like this, you idiot. I didn't mean something like this."

Dan leaves.

It may not be combat, but at least he feels he's doing something important for the war effort, being on board a non-military ship, carrying supplies to foreign shores.

As Jolene walks her dog Twinkie a few weeks later, she wonders what has happened to Bill, the boy down the block who makes her heart flutter whenever she thinks of him. She hasn't seen him in months. Wonders if he's gotten a job? Hearing the sound of a lawnmower before she reaches his house makes her heart pound in earnest. Maybe it's him, she thinks. Maybe... As she approaches, she glances discreetly in his direction. Yes! Yes! He's there, working in the yard. Taking a deep breath, she looks directly at him and nods a greeting.

Nodding in response, he smiles, turns off the mower, addresses her, "So...you're playing boogie-woogie now! What happened to the serious stuff?"

Caught off-guard, she stops and can't answer.

He continues, "I liked listening to those songs you used to play."

Finding her voice, she mumbles, "Well, um, I'll, I'll play them for you if you want. Whenever..."

"Great! How about tomorrow? I'm finally getting a day off. Ten okay?"

Beet red, she finds it impossible to respond.

Seeing her distress, he asks, "Too early? Doesn't work? Hey! We can make it another time..."

"No! No!" hardly audible, "Ten is fine. Just fine!" And she's off in a run, eager to share her fantastic news with Sunny.

The next day, Bill is at her front door at ten sharp. She doesn't invite him into the house. Rules are rules, no boys in the house when her parents aren't home. Leaving the door open, she asks him to sit outside on the porch steps. Then, she plays everything she knows, occasionally stopping to peek out the window to see if he's still there. He's not only still there but seems to be thoroughly enjoying his private concert. After finishing with *Moonlight Sonata*, Jolene puts away her sheet music and joins him outside.

After thanking her, he asks, "Do you want to go for a walk?"

"Sure!"

Strolling toward Los Feliz Boulevard, they hardly exchange a word. But their shyness soon melts away, like the mile-high banana split they share at the local ice cream parlor. They ate so much and laughed so hard that both had a stomach ache.

Walking home later hand-in-hand, Jolene chatters a mile a minute to cover her nervousness as they talk about everything other than his family or Pearl Harbor. And, for the first time in her life, she doesn't question him about things that he doesn't offer, so overwhelmed is she by the touch of his hand.

They return to sit on her porch stairs, so young yet sensitive to each other's needs. Laying her head against his shoulder, she feels comforted as he strokes her hair, gently touching her cheek, running his fingers along her chin and across her lips.

There are many long walks and picnics in the park during the upcoming weeks; lovely, long hours together. Often, she plays the piano for him. He is so admiring, so attentive. At the movies, they sit close, always, always holding hands. She feels so protected when her hand is in his, so safe. So very safe.

And it is Bill who teaches her how loving a kiss can be, how lips can be pressed ever so lightly upon lips, gently, ever so gently, never demanding anything, yet bringing exquisite joy.

Her father's kisses have always been to entice, ensnare. His warnings were damaging, with lies that kissing a boy would bring a baby and that he was the only one who should kiss her. Lies, lies, all lies! Yet, some of the fear he instilled in her about kissing boys remains, even though she knows they are lies. Those fears lingered within her until she met Bill. When Bill kisses her, she feels no fear, only flaming ecstasy. At the same time, she knows she is safe in his arms and protected—from her father's lies and all the world's falsehoods.

Since her father joined the Merchant Marine, Jolene and her mother have had a closer relationship. Liz is thrilled that Jolene has a boyfriend now and wants to know all about him, giving her advice about what to do and not to do. It's terrific not worrying about her father's jealousy, being able to invite Bill to her house when Liz is home.

Jolene hangs out at the Tam O'Shanter a lot now and eats dinner almost every night, getting to know her mother's co-workers and watching her waitress. She never knew how much Liz enjoyed what she did, joking around, laughing a lot. Liz has made friends there, too. Sometimes, one of the waitresses invites them over for dinner when they're not working. Sometimes, they all go to the movies together. Jolene can't remember seeing her mother so happy, relaxed, and able to have friends. They hardly ever have a skirmish now. It's almost like they have become friends or sisters.

Several months later, as Jolene takes Twinkie for a walk, she approaches Bill's house and sees his mother standing next to a half-filled pickup truck. She calls out a greeting to her. Startled, Bill's mother doesn't respond. Instead, she hurries back toward the house. In her rush, she bumps into Bill, knocking the box of household items he carries to the ground. Cursing, he begins picking things up, unaware of Jolene, who watches, apprehensive. His mother enters the house, slams the door, peers out from behind a kitchen curtain.

Not understanding what she is seeing, Jolene calls out, "Bill! Bill! What's happening here? Where are you going?"

Hearing her voice, Bill looks up and flushes. Glancing toward the house, he sees his mother watching. Then the curtain drops. Looking uncomfortable, he approaches Jolene, leans down, pets Twinkie, still says nothing.

Stunned at his silence, Jolene repeats her question. "Bill! Bill! What's going on? Are you...? Where are you going?"

Nodding in the affirmative, he still can't face her.

Angry, she tries to get him to look at her as she cries out, "I don't believe you! What were you going to do? Sneak away? Say nothing?" Placing her hands on both sides of his face, she forces him to rise and look at her. Sobs now punctuate her words. "Bill! What's happening? I thought you, thought we..."

At last, he looks directly at her and speaks. "It's not us, Jolene. It's...It's my brother. He's in a lot of trouble. We've got to get him out of the state right away! We're going to some relatives in Texas. I was going to tell you, soon's we loaded. I was going to come over, tell you everything. Honest."

Emotion overcomes him, and he pulls her toward him.

As Bill embraces her, Jolene says nothing, her knees buckling like her world. Holding her tightly in his embrace, he tries to comfort her in much the same way he had done for his mother on the first day she saw him. So compassionate to his mother he had been on that day, as he tries to be now. In his boy-man voice, trying to reassure her, "It's alright, Jolene, alright."

Except for this time, it is not just the comforted one in distress. The one who comforts is also choking up as he kisses away her tears, saying anything that will ease this awful pain, this wrenching agony of being torn apart.

"But how...when will we see each other again?" she asks.

Not having an answer, he takes her hand and covers it with his large hands. "I'll call, Jolene. Let you know where we'll be. Promise!"

She nods, unable to speak, wondering if they will ever see each other again.

Bill keeps his word.

He calls the following week, from somewhere near Houston, Texas, he says. She'll be getting his new address in a few days. They'll write to each other every day. The operator cuts in and tells them, "Time is up."

"I love you," quickly choked out. Then no more change, nothing. Just the buzzing of a line that had gone dead.

A few days pass, three, four. Then a week.

Jolene hears and receives nothing from him, just silence.

A blurb on the radio says something about flash floods in parts of Texas; people died, no names, though.

It can't be Bill and his family, Jolene thinks. They have names. It can't be Bill...

Time passes. Still silence. Did something terrible happen, she wonders? Were they hurt, killed? Or did he just forget her, meet someone else?

Her questions never receive answers. Never. And they haunt her for years.

Dan comes home on leave.

Grateful he is back, he and Liz are like lovers again.

Dan is surprised at Jolene's sadness and asks what's wrong? She wishes she could share her feelings with him. It's always been so easy to talk to him. But she has no idea how he would react if he knew about Bill, so she says nothing. And Liz has enough sense to do the same.

Her friend, Sunny, doesn't understand her pain either because she's never had a date or a crush. Nor have any of her other friends begun dating yet. How can they relate to what she is feeling? She tries to talk to her mother.

Liz wants to help her, hates to see how she's hurting. "We can't discuss it right now," she tells Jolene. "Not when your father is home. When he leaves, we'll talk, Jolene. When he leaves..."

There is no one for Jolene to share her loss, no one at all. Melancholy sets in. Endless crying, endless.

Later that night, as Dan sleeps, Jolene cries. Liz hears her and goes to her. Rocking her in her arms, she tries to ease her daughter's pain and tells her that no matter how awful things seem at night, they always look brighter in the morning.

And sure enough, when Jolene wakes up the following day, life doesn't seem so tragic.

Even though Jolene doesn't tell Dan about Bill, he knows something is wrong, so she tries to avoid him. She tries with all her heart to keep him at a distance. But he knows her so well, physically and emotionally.

Without getting answers to his questions, he consoles her and empathizes. In short order, his comfort turns to caresses. Even though she is repulsed and tries to resist, a lifetime of his manipulation activates her bodily needs.

While Liz works at the restaurant, Jolene becomes her father's 'Little Mommy' once again, even though she is now taller than he is. She hates her body for this need and hates herself for being so weak. She also loathes the physical desire he arouses in her. And her self-hatred remains long after the physical pleasure has passed.

When her father asks her to play "Moonlight Sonata" for him, she tries but can't finish. Bursting into tears, she says she can no longer play piano and runs from the room.

Dan confronts Liz and wants to know what's going on with Jolene.

"What's going on," Liz repeats. "I told you the piano was just a phase."

Knowing why Jolene doesn't want to play, she doesn't want him questioning her further and acknowledges, "Everything in life is just a phase, isn't it?"

For once, Dan has to agree. Soon after, he leaves.

Time passes. Jolene continues to mope, stays in her room, doesn't socialize, doesn't show interest in anything. Even Twinkie's persistent licking and affection don't ease her pain. She keeps moping until the day Sunny tells her she is taking junior lifeguard lessons and asks Jolene if she wants to come along?

Indecisive, Liz decides for Jolene and pays for the lessons. The girls' test to see if they are strong enough swimmers, and both pass, so they begin.

Jolene and her gang go swimming at the Pickwick swim complex in Burbank a few weeks later. One of the largest pools in the city, the enormous circular body of water goes from three feet around the perimeter to 12 feet in the middle, where the diving platform is.

The five girls enter the pool. Challenging them to meet her on the platform, Jolene swims toward the deep water. The others follow. All of them reach the platform except Beverly. Frightened at being in deep water, she flounders and begins to sink. Jolene swims back to assist her since she's been taking lifeguard lessons and thinks she can help. Planning to place her hand across her friend's chest and swim her to the surface, as she's learned, Jolene reaches out, but things don't work out as planned.

Terrified, Beverly grabs Jolene's hand and drags her down until she can stand on her shoulders. Then she wraps her feet around Jolene's throat so that her head is now above water.

But no one can see Jolene on the bottom.

Choking, choking, Jolene swallows water as she gasps for air and knows she will drown if she doesn't do something drastic. Grabbing Beverly's toe, Jolene bites it with all her might. Beverly's hold loosens. Jolene breaks away, shoots to the surface as Beverly flounders, and then sinks again.

Shouting for lifeguards to rescue her friend, Jolene clambers onto the platform, gasping, spitting up water.

Three results come from this near-drowning episode: Jolene decides lifeguarding isn't for her. Sunny decides to become a junior lifeguard, and Jolene develops a crush on the lifeguard who saves Beverly.

A few months later, Jolene and Sunny are dropped off one Saturday afternoon after seeing a movie. Someone's mother had driven them home, so they arrived much earlier than usual.

Sunny hadn't expected anyone to be home because her father works on Saturdays, her sister was taking a baby-care class, and her mother had a lunch date, so she was surprised when she saw Randall's car parked in the driveway.

"Guess he got a weekend pass or something," Sunny comments trying to open the front door, which is usually unlocked, but it doesn't open, so she knocks. There is no answer. She rings the bell. Still no answer.

"Hmmm. Strange. Wonder where Randy is," Sunny comments. "Oh, well. There's a key on the back porch. Let's get that."

The girls' chatter as they walk around the house, find the key and enter.

Sunny calls out, "Randy! Randy! You here?"

There is no response.

"Maybe a friend picked him up. That's why he left his car. Who cares!" she says, then asks, "You hungry?"

"When have I ever not been hungry?" Jolene responds.

The two friends laugh and jostle each other as they scrounge around for food until they hear a strange sound coming from the inner bowels of the house.

Freezing with fright, they grab each other, faces white, eyes wide.

The muffled mixture of a woman's rising groans, blending into a man's guttural grunts, can be heard again. Filtering, filtering, filtering into the kitchen. Into the ears of these unsuspecting, playful young girls.

It is a sound Sunny has never heard yet familiar to Jolene. The unwelcome sound of sexual activities behind a closed bedroom door.

Alarmed, Sunny asks, "Did you hear it, Jolene? Did you? Oh my gosh! My gosh! It sounds like Mom is hurt! She's hurting."

Breaking away, she rushes out of the kitchen.

Knowing how naïve Sunny is, Jolene wants to protect her, runs after her, grabs her arm, and tries to stop her.

"No! No, Sunny! Don't go! Please! Your Mom isn't hurt, hurting. Please don't! You don't want to see… Please…"

Shrugging off Jolene's arm, Sunny continues to run down the long hallway toward her parents' bedroom. As she approaches the closed French doors, the sounds become louder and louder. Bursting into the room, Sunny calls out, "Momma! Momma! Are you alright?"

Then she stands there, staring, frozen, not believing.

As Jolene enters the hallway, she hears her friend gasp, then the sugary voice of Charlotte, trying to make it okay for her daughter.

"Sweetheart, sweetheart, it's not what you think…It's not…"

Then the sound of Sunny wheezing, wheezing, gasping, trying to draw in air, trying to breathe but not succeeding. Unable to get to her friend in time, Jolene watches in dismay as Sunny collapses and falls to the floor, unconscious.

Jolene's dear friend, Sunny, is not the only one who suffers from Charlotte's indiscretion.

When she hears of the incident, Darlene goes into early labor and gives birth to a four-pound premature boy. Her son is not only tiny; he is deaf and deformed because Randall, that lousy rascal of a husband, was not only a philanderer. He had also forgotten to tell his wife that he had contracted syphilis.

In time Randall was court-martialed and imprisoned for his misdeeds.

Sunny's only salvation is her father, who tries, with quiet dignity, to maintain a state of calm.

Jolene's picture-perfect family and home now have an air of somberness. No laughter, joy or freshly baked cookies greet Jolene anymore when she visits Sunny. Only the incessant squalling of a sickly, unhappy baby and the quiet tears and distress of the three females who tend to him.

Chapter Twenty-Two
1945

1945 is a year of memorable events; for Jolene, the country, and the world.

Around midnight, Jolene and Liz hear screeching, a terrible crash, and then sirens. The next day they learn that Sunny's father, having had too much to drink, had miscalculated the driveway, wrapped his car around a tree in his yard, and was taken to the hospital, pretty banged up.

After the accident, Sunny doesn't return to school. Jolene becomes worried and inquires. They tell her Sunny is sick.

While walking Twinkie a few weeks later, Jolene sees Schroeder's car driven by Darlene, pull up in the driveway. Excited to see her friends, she runs across the street to greet them.

Darlene and Charlotte nod as they assist Mr. Schroeder into a wheelchair. He gives her the warmest welcome of the three. Sunny is in the back seat but doesn't open the door.

Jolene taps on the window and shouts, "Sunny, hi! Hi!"

Her friend doesn't react or respond and sits like a robot.

Upset, Jolene calls out, "Sunny! Are you mad at me? Did I do something wrong? Why won't you talk to me?"

"We're all tired, Jolene, tired. Why don't you come around another day?" drawls Charlotte as she removes baby Patrick from the car and walks toward the house.

Darlene addresses Sunny, "Be right back, Sis," as she pushes her father's wheelchair up the driveway.

Uncomfortable, Jolene looks at Sunny, who sits immobile in the backseat, saying nothing, just staring into space. Opening the car door, Jolene asks, "Sunny, why won't you speak to me? Aren't we still friends?"

Shock and horror engulf her as she looks into her friend's face. Sunny isn't acknowledging her even though her eyes are wide open. Her friend has no idea Jolene is there. Choking back tears, Jolene pulls Twinkie away and runs home.

After telling Liz what happened, Jolene tries to make sense of her mother's explanation: "Sunny had withdrawn into her safe world, just like Gramma Bubbe had done after the earthquake. Sunny's father's accident probably was the last straw she could take," explained Liz. "So now, she was in a safe world."

Not long after, a "For Sale" sign appears on the front lawn of the Schroeder house. Then a "Sold" sign. Sunny's family moves away with no goodbyes. Shortly after, a new family moves in.

And another good friend disappears from Jolene's life.

The world learns of the Holocaust!

When Jolene hears that millions of Jews have died in gas chambers, she and everyone else can't believe it. Never understanding or wanting to be Jewish before, Jolene now feels she should somehow honor being a Jew and have many children to help replace the ones who had been killed. But how? She's almost 14 years old and hasn't had her first menstrual period yet. So, how can she bear children?

Every night she asks God to forgive her for being a sinner and let her get her period so she can have lots and lots of Jewish children. But God doesn't answer.

Each month the gym teacher asks for a show of hands of the girls who haven't menstruated. Then they are not excused from physical activity. Last semester, many girls raised their hands whenever she asked. In December, a few girls raised their hands. This month, to Jolene's mortification, she was the only one in the entire gym class who raised her hand.

Now, everyone in the gym, and probably the whole world, knows that she is being punished and will never have a period.

Punishment! Punishment! Punishment!

Jolene is sure everyone condemns her and knows her dirty secret, so she will never have children.

Yet, shortly before her 14th birthday, Jolene feels moisture between her legs as she walks down the school hallway. A friend's teasing about the stain on her dress doesn't diminish the relief she experiences at the sight of fresh, bright red blood. Her head hurts, and her stomach cramps. She goes to the infirmary, is told to lie down, and is given a tablespoon of molasses. Even as she groans and holds tightly to her belly, her period seems not a curse but a miracle.

At last, she now knows that she is not cursed and thanks God for forgiving her. She is so grateful that she even promises to be a good Jew.

April 12, 1945

While attending her sewing class, a teacher rushes into the room. In her arms, she carries a radio. Plugging it into the wall, she tells Jolene's teacher and the class to stop what they are doing and listen.

As one, they listen as an announcer says, "President Franklin Delano Roosevelt has died today of…"

Bewildered, Jolene can't imagine that President Roosevelt is dead. He is the only president she has ever known. She'd just assumed he'd always be president.

The rest of the announcer's words are drowned out as two girls, sitting across the table from Jolene, begin to cheer and yell, "Yeah! Yeah! Hooray! Hooray! The ole cripple is dead!" almost falling over themselves, laughing, so happy are they, at the news.

Everyone in the room, many of whom are crying, is surprised by the girls' untimely behavior. Bewildered, Jolene asks, "Why are you laughing? How can you be happy when someone dies, especially our president?"

"Well, I guess we know how your parents vote, dirty Democrat, dirty Democrat!" one girl spits out, jabbing a finger toward Jolene's tearful face.

The other retorts, "It's about time the lying, old cripple hit the dirt," which sets off another spasm of laughter for the two.

It's too much.

Usually a nonviolent person, Jolene cannot believe what she hears and lunges across the table, grabbing the speaker's hair. The girl cries out.

"Girls! Girls!"

The teacher intervenes and sends Jolene to the girls' vice principal's office. So familiar with this place, Jolene sits quietly, waiting to be reprimanded, and wonders how much filing she'll have to do today as she cries silently into her balled-up hankie.

Instead of requiring her to work, the girls' vice principal offers her a clean handkerchief and a carton of chocolate milk as they share stories of the unique man they've just lost.

Jolene and Liz swim at Long Beach, not far from the pier a few months later, on a hot July afternoon. They are close enough to view the roller coaster and hear screams of pleasure from riders on this bright and beautiful day. Today is different from their first attempt years before. Jolene is the stronger swimmer now. They frolic in the ocean's deep waters for hours, coming out only to eat. Liz still swims with her head above water, always facing the shore. Jolene swims the Australian Crawl, looking both ways when she lifts her head to breathe. Now and then, she dives underneath the waves to tease Liz and pull at her legs.

As Jolene surfaces and looks toward the shore, she sees a strange scene. Sunbathers scurry toward the boardwalk as lifeguards motion swimmers to exit the water.

Wondering what could be causing this frenzy, Jolene turns her head but cannot see the sky, seeing only a wall of water as it comes crashing down on her. She is slammed down, down, down, into the sea, floundering deep within the bowels of the ocean. Even though she is at risk of drowning, she can only think of her mother. Is she alright? Where is she? What is happening to her?

Fighting her way upward and upward, she surfaces, her lungs bursting. Coughing and trying to gulp fresh air, she is crushed again by tons of seawater. Instead of thrusting her downward, the second wave pitches her toward the pier and into a piling. Grabbing onto a timber, she wraps around it, ignoring the multiple cuts the barnacles are causing to her hands, arms, and body. As the surf recedes, she sees her mother clinging to another piling a few feet away. Fighting to hold onto the piling as the force of water almost drags her out, she breathes a sigh of relief and thanks God that her mother is safe.

Lifeguards swim out when the sea calms and tows them to shore. Jolene and Liz look like someone has taken a razor blade and made hundreds of tiny incisions. Not deep cuts, most of them, but they all hurt.

They marvel at their near brush with death as they tend to each other's cuts and bruises that night.

"I was so worried about you, Mom, that I didn't even fight the water to save myself. I just kept hoping you were okay."

"God works in mysterious ways, Jolene," Liz tells her. "I wasn't thinking about what was happening to me either. I just kept praying that you were okay."

Embracing her daughter, Liz says the words Jolene has been waiting to hear all her life.

"I love you so much, Jolene. So much. It would have broken my heart if something had happened to you."

And at that moment, both knew they would always be there for each other.

The next day, an article in the *Los Angeles Times* explained what had happened at the beach. Excessively high winds and groundswells in Northern California had caused 30-foot waves to hit the shores from Malibu to the Long Beach coastline. Unexpected, of course. Unusual, the article stated. Fortunately, there was no loss of life.

When Jolene ventures back into the ocean after her cuts heal, everyone is amazed. But Liz never enters the briny deep again.

The War Ends!

The following month, the new president, Harry Truman, approved releasing atomic bombs over the cities of Hiroshima and Nagasaki: "To save lives and help end the war," everyone said. Yet, hundreds of thousands of Japanese citizens die. Untold numbers are injured. Jolene tries but cannot comprehend how this inhuman act can be good. Yet, a treaty was signed a few weeks later, ending the war. Things begin to go back to normal. Loved ones can return home, and Dan is one of them.

Dan arrives and expects a hero's welcome. Dressed in his merchant marine uniform, cap tilted jauntily on his head. Liz, of course, doesn't disappoint him. Jolene's greeting is less cordial. Giving him a cool kiss on the cheek, she pulls away when he tries to embrace her. Surprised, he is distracted by others who have come to welcome him home.

Days go by before Dan gets Jolene alone.

Expecting to resume their relationship, he is surprised by her cool detachment and open hostility when he approaches her.

Reverting to being charming, he asks, "Hey! 'Little Mommy,' hey! Is this the way you greet your hero? Thought you'd be hungry for a little loving." He tries to caress, kiss her.

Rigid, she resists and pulls away.

Then, she starts saying the most important words of her young life, "Don't touch me, Daddy. Don't ever touch me again! God has forgiven me for being your 'Little Mommy.' I know he has Daddy because I finally got my period."

Amused, he looks at her and says, "Well, congratulations, little girl. Congratulations! That doesn't have to change anything between us. You know I never entered you and…" Again, he reaches out for her.

"No," she replies in a raised voice as she pulls away.

The sharpness in her voice surprises him.

"No!" she repeats. "I'm almost a woman now, Daddy. I can have babies of my own, despite your lies. And I never want you coming near me again, you hear?" She spits out the last word. "Never!"

Not amused now, Dan becomes resentful, grabs both of her arms, and begins to shake her.

"Who do you think you are, talking to me like that, little girl. I can do whatever I want with you, you understand? I'm your father. You're my daughter, my property. You do what I say!"

Her teeth chatter, hardly allowing her to speak.

"No! no, I won't! You can't make me do anything anymore, you hear? No more. Never! You have no right!"

"Have a right? Have a right?"

Stunned, he stops shaking her, but his grip remains so tight she winces.

"Who do you think you are, telling me what I can or cannot do? A woman?" He laughs with sarcasm. "You're no woman. You're my little girl, you hear? Just because you're taller than me doesn't give you the right not to obey me."

Recognizing he's hurting her, he changes tactics, eases his grip, asks, "Are you trying to tell me you don't love me anymore, baby?"

"No! No!" Jolene's cries of pain turn to sobs of anguish. "I'm not saying that, Daddy. I do love you. I'll always love you. But…But I won't be your 'Little Mommy' anymore, that's all. I can't be. Can't! Not now. Not ever!"

"Jolene, honey. You'll always be my…"

"No! No!" She tries to pull away.

Releasing his hold on her arms, he tries to embrace her. "You just missed me, I know. You're just upset and…"

Again she recoils from his embrace, and he is surprised at the hatred he sees in her determined, now-slitted eyes, so he resists a further attempt. These are not the eyes of a little girl. He is looking into the world-worn eyes of a girl who has experienced more than she should have at this tender age approaching womanhood.

Words rush from her in a torrent, unstoppable.

"You disgust me, Daddy! With all your women! Your lies. Hurting Mommy and me, repeatedly, and making me feel so, so, dirty, so sinful."

He reaches out again, "But I love you, baby. All I want is to give you pleasure. You know that. Don't I make you feel good?"

She backs away and sobs, "Yes! No! I hate myself for the way you make me feel. I hate myself, not you, Daddy. But it has to end. End, Daddy! Do you understand? I don't want your kisses. I want other boys to kiss me!"

Dan looks like he's been slapped in the face. "You're letting others—"

"Yes! Yes! And I promise…"

"If you ever touch me again, I'll leave. I'll go live with Uncle Arthur and Aunt Lottie. They love me."

"What would your mother think, Jolene? Think how'll you'll be hurting her. She'd die if…"

Jolene whitens, pauses, shakes her head, takes a deep breath, and regains courage. "I'll never tell Mommy. Never! And I know she loves me, Daddy. She told me so."

"So, she'd still be unhappy and question…?"

Jolene sighs, "She's thrilled you're home again, Daddy, and I'm sure you'd be able to make up some story."

He threatens, "You'll be sorry! And I'm not sure we'd let you come back when you realize how foolish…"

Determined, she says in almost a whisper, "I'll never come back if you touch me again. I don't ever want to be your 'Little Mommy' again. Never!"

Running from the room, she goes into her bedroom, slams the door, and throws herself on the bed. This time though, she doesn't need to strip it. No! She feels no anger, no frustration, no sadness, no guilt. She only feels relief, such enormous relief. She feels proud, too. It took a lot of courage to stand up to her daddy. And she knows she has just won one of the biggest battles of her life.

Chapter Twenty-Three
December 1986 Therapy

I'm exhausted as I tell the group about my encounter with my dad. How I finally stood up to him and ended my 'Little Mommy' days. And, as I finish saying, "He never laid a hand on me again!"

"Are you telling me he never even tried?" one of the women asks, somewhat skeptical.

"Oh sure, he'd sidle up to me now and then. But a look from me and he'd back off. Dad knew I meant what I'd said that day, and he knew I kept promises. Of course, he knew. Dad banked on that from the time I was a small child. But he did make my life miserable at times. I had the strictest rules about curfew. If I were two minutes late when I came home from a date, he'd rant and rave about knowing what I must be doing and chase the date away with a broom."

"Like a jealous lover, perhaps?" Ramona queries.

"Yes! Perhaps. I never thought about it like that. But some of my boyfriends thought he was nuts. I was determined to keep him at bay or leave. He knew I meant it. And I did!"

Laughing with cynicism, I added, "How well he knew. I promised him I'd never tell Mommy, Mom. And I never did."

Murmurs from some of the women acknowledge my victory. Gwynn gives me a 'right on' hand slap.

I look around the room a little sadly, knowing that this will be my last therapy session because I've decided to quit and probably won't see these women again.

Some of them had never dropped their armor. Some I had warmed up to, like Holly, dear Holly. She will remain in my heart, though probably not in my life.

And Ramona. Well, Ramona never allowed any of us to enter her world. Perhaps that is the way with therapists. I don't know. Maybe it's just her. Once, when I'd asked Ramona if she'd ever been molested, she'd pointedly told me to mind my own business and said whether she had been or not had nothing to do with her ability to assist us. She's probably right. So, to this day, I still don't know anything about this lady. Absolutely nothing. And I feel nothing toward her either, except gratitude for a job well done.

Turning, I address myself to her. "Ramona, I think, after today…I'm ready to move on, and I—"

"Are you sure?" Ramona interrupts me, "It hasn't even been a year yet, Jolene. Are you sure you want to quit? Do you think you're strong enough? You still haven't gotten in touch with your anger."

"Perhaps some of us are unable to hold onto anger, Ramona. It only hurts you. Not the other person."

Ramona, "I agree. Yet, are you completely free of the past?"

"Will we ever be completely free of the past, Ramona?" I respond. "No! No! Of course not. I may not be completely free. But I'm more comfortable with myself now. I want to move on. Yes! Comfortable is the right word. I'm thankful for the life I've had, the life I have. And I'm grateful for all the insight and support you've given me here, Ramona."

My eyes fill as I look around the room. "From all of you, in your way. Thank you so much. Thanks for sharing your pain, for everything."

Tears sparkle and appear in the eyes of a few. Gwynn gives me another thumbs up. There are a few smiles, a shrug, and a nod. Holly turns away, unable to acknowledge my farewell. That was the toughest part of leaving. I'll miss Holly. Always wonder how she did.

Later, at the end of the session, I felt buoyant and confident, knowing that I could reach out into the world now without my father's shadow or guilt blocking me from loving myself as much as I love life. And I'm more appreciative of the love Charlie gives me.

I feel relief from carrying the burden, knowing that I never hurt my mother and have no resentment anymore. Life is strange in many ways. Even though she sacrificed me to save her marriage, in the long run, she lost Dad anyway. I tried to help during her final five years, yet I could not ease her ultimate pain, illness, or death.

Therapy also helped me determine that I no longer needed to hear my dad say, "I'm sorry" to find closure. I don't need anything from him anymore. Therapy helped me understand this, too. And I realized how important it is to have the proper therapist who understands your world.

Feeling a surge of relief after the group's closing ritual, I almost skip down the hall, eager to share the news with my husband.

That night, as Charlie holds me in his arms, I hear him utter the words he's said to me so often before.

"I love you, Jolene. You're so beautiful."

Pressing into him, I say, "Thank you, sweetheart," and for the first time in my life, I can honestly say, "I finally feel beautiful and cleansed, inside and out."

Epilogue

In 1960, I was shopping for a chest of drawers at my uncle's furniture store while pregnant with my third child, one in a stroller, and the oldest hanging on, verbally exclaiming his delight at the stacks of the chest of drawers piled high on each side of them. It reminded me of the many happy times I'd played in my uncle's store as a young girl. The outdoorsy smell of the unfinished wood filled our nostrils as I tried to decide on a chest when I overheard two women nearby in an animated conversation that ended in loud laughter.

Turning towards them because their voices sounded vaguely familiar, I was shocked to see the mother and sister of my long-ago friend Sunny (who became comatose after the trauma in their family).

Surprised, I called out, "Darlene? Charlotte?"

They looked up and didn't seem to recognize me. Not surprising because I'd been a young girl the last time they'd seen me.

"I'm Sunny's friend from Brunswick Avenue. Remember?"

Both women still looked blank for a moment, then showed recognition.

"Of course! Of course! How are you?"

"Oh, my, dearie! What a beauty you turned out to be. And look at your little ones. How darling!"

"Thanks. How's Sunny?"

"Oh, she's fine. Still happy in her make-believe world."

"What do you mean make-believe? Is she okay?"

"Yes. Yes. Sunny's fine. They take excellent care of her at the 'facility.'"

Charlotte seemed uncomfortable using the word 'facility'.

Trying not to show discomfort, I took a deep breath, then asked, "And Mr. Schroeder?"

"Oh, Daddy never fully recovered from that crash," Darlene responded softly. "He died a couple of years after we moved."

"I'm so sorry!"

"It was for the best," Charlotte responded, in that lilting Southern voice I remembered so clearly. "For the best."

"And Randall, your husband? Is he still in prison?"

Darlene laughed without animosity. "Nope! Remember how charming he was?"

I nodded.

"They gave him five years. With his sweet talk, he was out in three. But prison changed him. Today he's got a nice family and kids, and we see him now and then."

"You're kidding!"

"Nope!"

"That boy sure could sweet talk, that's for sure."

Then I asked, "Have either of you married again?"

"Are you kidding?"

"No way!"

Both women responded at the same time, then laughed.

I showed surprise and wondered how Darlene could be so forgiving and close to her mother after what she did – seducing her husband – which caused her to go into early labor. And then it was a double whammy because the baby boy was not only small but was born deaf and blind because Randall had also forgotten to tell her he had syphilis. That's why he'd gotten prison time.

"My Gawd! And your son? He's what, how old? How is he?"

"He's in our school and doing very well."

"Your school?"

"Yes! We run a school for children with challenges."

My face must have shown amazement as I blurted out, "But how can you be partners, forgive… after…?"

Made uncomfortable by my reaction, they prepared to leave with Charlotte smiling as she chirped, "Good seeing you, dearie. Take care now." and they left.

I stood there in shock, thinking how unfair life was. How Sunny and her father – two innocent people – had been victimized and destroyed by Charlotte's actions. And Darlene and her son, too. And yet, Darlene is now partnered with her mother and is so loving and close. I was amazed at how forgiving some people could be. And I also wondered if Charlotte ever felt any guilt.

***

Years later, my husband and I were attending a motion picture premiere. Some big stars were in the film, and a flock of paparazzi was vying for positions to get good photos.

I noticed a familiar young woman with a camera in the front but could not place her until I realized it was Holly from my therapy group. Pulling my husband aside, I called out her name, rushed over and hugged her. Caught by surprise, she laughed and, with tears in her eyes, said, "I never thought I'd see you again."

Overcome, I told my husband I'd meet him inside as I needed a few minutes alone with Holly. He agreed and entered the theater.

Holly and I moved away from the crowd and chatted. I learned that her father had done prison time, had treatment, and was paying for the upkeep and therapy for her brother.

She told me, "My brother's much better, is in school now, and…" as tears rolled down her cheeks unchecked.

She also told me she was now working with her father as a photographer, and they were getting along great.

Talk about healing and forgiveness. How beautiful!

We promised to get together but never got around to exchanging cards or numbers in the evening rush.

***

Not everyone forgives, nor do they get the chance. And often, the damage remains.

When a young person experiences abuse, be it verbal, physical, sexual, emotional or because they are different physically or mentally, they are robbed of their innocence and self-love.

As an adult, many are often unable to have healthy relationships, or they develop an addiction – be it drugs, sex, alcohol, or food.

I hope that, beyond enjoying Jolene's roller-coaster young life and her constant optimism, readers may also gain insight through the therapy sessions and the importance of seeking appropriate professional help if they have unresolved issues – or secrets.

If you are interested in my later life, "My Love Affair with Hollywood, a memoir," was published in 2020 and is available on Amazon.com for $14.95 in paperback and $4.95 in Kindle.

To contact me, please email jeloveaffair@gmail.com

***

Printed in the USA
CPSIA information can be obtained
at www.ICGtesting.com
LVHW020815051023
760085LV00055B/1155